# In a Forest, a Deer

Breaking traditional modes of expression in terms of language
and content, *In a Forest, a Deer* recounts, among others, the saga
of Tangam Athai, whose husband remarried because she could not
bear him a child and Chinthiru's journey to the forest alongside the
mythological tale of Sita's exile to underscore Chinthiru's unique
search for self-identity.

This collection is an enduring testimony of the ideology and belief
that Ambai's writings affirm—the need to know and be in touch
with a stable or 'grounded' self that allows fluidity and change in
modern times of travel, dislocation, and exile.

**Ambai** is widely regarded as one of the most original modern Indian
writers. Her stories are about contemporary lives and relationships,
and have women who are conscious of their identity, challenge
patriarchal authority, and break social conventions as
their main protagonists.

'Ambai brings to bear upon her tales the weight of her knowledge
of the mythic, literary and Puranic ... A felicity of language and the
easy flow of words make the translation a pleasure to read.'
— *The Hindu*

'Ambai excels in making physical movements parallel the progression
in her stories which are often no more than the stringing together of
a few soliloquies ... Lakshmi Holmström has been able to settle down
so comfortably within the psyche of Ambai, that her translations of
the latter's Tamil writings have the easy flow of the original.'
— *Deccan Herald*

# In a Forest, a Deer
## Stories by Ambai

Ambai

*Translated from Tamil by Lakshmi Holmström*

**OXFORD**
UNIVERSITY PRESS

# OXFORD
UNIVERSITY PRESS

Oxford University Press is a department of the University of Oxford.
It furthers the University's objective of excellence in research, scholarship,
and education by publishing worldwide. Oxford is a registered trademark of
Oxford University Press in the UK and in certain other countries

Published in India by
Oxford University Press
22 Workspace, 2nd Floor, 1/22 Asaf Ali Road, New Delhi 110 002

First Edition published in 2006
Oxford India Paperbacks 2012
21st impression 2025

ISBN-13: 978-0-19-808001-5
ISBN-10: 0-19-808001-8

Typeset in Minion 10.5/12.5
by Sai Graphic Design, New Delhi 110 055
Printed in India by Replika Press Pvt. Ltd.

MR. Omayal Achi MR. Arunachalam Trust was set up in 1976 to further education
and health care particularly in rural areas. The MR. AR Educational Society was
later established by the Trust. One of the Society's activities is to sponsor Indian
literature. This translation is entirely funded by the MR. AR Educational Society as
part of it aims.

for Radhika and Savitri

# Contents

# Author's Note

The stories in this collection were written over the last ten years, for many different journals in Tamil. They were not written in a hurry for there was no deadline to meet. Had they not been written, no one would have missed them except, perhaps, for a group of friends. One writes because the act of writing has become as close to one as breathing. It is difficult to stop.

It is a strange feeling confronting a translation of one's stories. The characters seem different; the images are sketched differently; the colours are not what one imagined and the words sound different. And then as one slowly gets into the mood of the translated language, one sees one's stories bound in a certain way and take wings, traversing the distance between the two languages. This magic of a story taking shape in another language can happen only if, like pushing a fishing boat into the sea, a translation gently nudges a story into the vast ocean of another language. My friend Lakshmi Holmström has that gentle touch. After my stories come back to me from her, there is a moment of non-recognition, but that is soon transformed into the magical experience of my stories becoming my own. For letting me experience this magic time and again I thank Lakshmi. And for making this translated version appear in print I thank Mini Krishnan and Oxford University Press.

AMBAI

# Translator's Note

*A Purple Sea*, the first collection of short stories by Ambai in English translation, came out in 1992. Those stories were collated from her two Tamil anthologies, *Siragugal Muriyum* (1976) and *Veettin Muulaiyil Oru Samayalarai* (1988). Since then, Ambai has written many more short stories, some of which are already well known, and most of which are presented here.

To translate Ambai is a privilege and a pleasure, but her work also presents many challenges. One such challenge is the complex form of some of her short stories—or novellas, rather—which use different perspectives and voices, and interweave different sorts of texts. 'Forest', for example, juxtaposes two life-stories: that of Chenthiru, who is seen as a contemporary Sita, living in the modern world; the other, of the epic Sita, who, however, rewrites her story. 'A Movement, a Folder, some Tears' is even more subtly crafted, moving between memory, reflection, emailed letters—the last of which has an attachment—and a folder full of memos, notes, and papers. The different strands of the novella need to be distinct in the translation, the multiple voices clear, yet without jeopardizing the unity of the whole.

Another challenge is the range of references and quotations from many different languages that Ambai has used in this collection of stories. I have tried to retain the music of this code-switching by indicating, wherever possible, when a language other than Tamil is being used—for example, Kannada in 'First Poems', or Marathi in 'Forest'. Often I have transliterated the first line of a poem and followed it with the translation, for example: Dikku theriyaada kaattil, In the forest, where I cannot find my way…' ('Parasakti and others in a Plastic Box'). The references and quotes are important keys in the book. The song by Subramanya Bharathi, quoted in this particular story, is repeated in another, 'Forest'. Song and music stitch the collection together, as do certain tropes and images—for example, that of the forest, a place of quest and discovery.

Ambai is one of the finest of contemporary short-story writers in Tamil. Perhaps the greatest challenge to the translator is to capture in English the various textures and tones of her writing which can be full of wit and humour ('Journey 3', 'Vaaganam'), effortlessly lyrical ('Forest', 'In a Forest'), or gravely elegiac ('A Folder').

Ambai is also a meticulous reader. I am grateful to her for her comments on the translations. Mini Krishnan has been equally acute and perceptive. My thanks to all the others who have read this book at various stages.

LAKSHMI HOLMSTRÖM

# Introduction[1]

Ambai is one of the finest of modern Tamil short-story writers, much read, much discussed and written about, and much loved for her wit, her inventiveness, the lyrical grace of her writing, and the manner in which she challenges received notions. This book is a translation of her third collection of stories, *Kaattil oru maan* (*Kalachuvadu*, 2000), with the addition of 'A Movement, a File, Some Tears' (*Kalachuvadu*, July–August, 2002).

Ambai follows in the tradition of the great short-story writers in Tamil such as Pudumaippittan and Mauni. Like them, she stretches and reinvents the short-story form, always making it new. Many stories in this collection are intricate both in their content and in the manner of the telling. Often, they are about interwoven or parallel lives, juxtapositions of the past and the present, the mythical and the contemporary. Equally, she employs a variety of narrative forms and mixed texts: letters, dispatches, journals, emails, and attachments, and in one story, a folder of notes, memos, articles.

Ambai's search for new forms and a new language is linked fundamentally with her beliefs and practice as a woman and a writer. As a critic researching the images of women in Tamil fiction, she ended her book *The Face behind the Mask*[2] with a strong plea to other writers to stop reinforcing popular and conventional images of women, and 'to write the truth'. The agenda she sets for the modern Tamil woman writer, and therefore for herself, is to seek and develop a newer and freer form of expression in Tamil which articulates more truly the real experience of women. But such a 'new language', she has indicated, must also find a way of communicating women's silences, and sharing it, in words and images.

As a writer, Ambai starts from a firmly feminist base. But always her work has moved outward into a larger concern. There has always been in her work a thrust towards freedom from bondage, the letting go of identities that we are forced into, one way or another. In this introductory essay I focus on these central themes which run through all her work and are particularly distinctive in this anthology; and I trace them through Ambai's favourite tropes of food and music.

Ambai spent much of her childhood in her grandparents' house in Coimbatore, Tamil Nadu. She draws abundantly from this fund of childhood memories for many of her stories. Her adult life, on the other hand, has been spent outside Tamil Nadu, in Delhi and in particular, Mumbai. The arrangement of the stories in *Kaattil oru maan* tells its own tale: Tamil Nadu and Mumbai-based stories are juxtaposed, and interspersed with others which are placed elsewhere—Spain, America, or imaginary and mythological places like the Milk-ocean or the Ramayana's Asokavanam. Through memories, through the experience of exile (as a Tamil speaker in Mumbai) and through the experience of travel (as an Indian abroad, reflecting on Indian diasporas in America and how they construct themselves), she is constantly exploring the ways in which people describe themselves and the communities to which they could be said to belong.

'A Rat, a Sparrow', a story told from the perspective of a Tamil woman living in Mumbai, is one of her finest stories about the experience of movement and exile within the country, and of life in a sprawling, modern, commercial city: a life which, in the end, is seen to be both dehumanizing and liberating. The story is structured around two sets of images which bring out this paradox: rats living in rat-holes, and sparrows living precariously or in perilous flight. Mumbai has always been the foremost cosmopolitan city of India, in spite of its xenophobic moments; it is home to many groups of exiles within the country, a perfect locale for Ambai to examine how communities and individuals identify each other and themselves. The theme is worked on different levels. At the simplest, food and food-habits become a way for outsiders to stereotype communities other than their own. To some northerners, all Tamils are 'Madrasis', easily caricatured by the way they slurp their *sambar* or *rasam* and rice. Ambai sets off other peoples' facile stereotyping against the protagonist's own nostalgia for Tamil Nadu and its tastes, sounds, and smells. But this too is exposed as an idealization, when it is contrasted with the reality of the Tamil diaspora in Matunga (a Bombay suburb where Tamils congregate). She describes this diaspora ironically, almost satirizing it as a community that clings together, chauvinistically quoting Tiruvalluvar,[3] and bringing with it its own preconceptions and assumptions about Tamil women.

Ambai asks these questions: What groups do we choose to identify with, and when? Do these group identities help us to understand our individual selves? The definition of the self as part of a community is always troubling to Ambai, always ironically treated; the categories and groups change and shift. Many themes found in 'A Rat, a Sparrow' are taken up in different ways in some of her other stories. In 'Journey 2', Dinakaran, far from identifying himself as a 'Madrasi', defines himself narrowly as a person from Tirunelveli, who can only face the day after his bath in the river Tambaraparni (unlike someone from Thanjavur or Madurai, for example). People from this more narrowly-defined geographical area claim to have their own specialized palate and particular foods. Dinakaran's grandfather could distinguish between sixty-four different types of *pacchadi*, he proudly states. But threatened by the unknown, Dinakaran finds comfort in a larger category: when he turns up in Delhi, he cannot feel comfortable until he has sought out 'South Indian' lodgings, and eaten generically Tamil food, never mind the sixty-four varieties of pacchadi exclusive to Tirunelveli.

Ambai is also interested in the way that Indians outside India, while holding on to the category Tamil (or Gujarati, Punjabi, Bengali), construct a larger Indian diaspora: 'South Indian' will do within India, but not outside it. In 'A Rose-coloured Sari Woven with Birds and Swans', Ambai gives an example of this larger diaspora in her description of a 'Festival of India' held near Boston and arranged particularly for Indian children in the US. It turns out to be a hotch-potch of music and dance events—classical, folk, and pop—from different parts of India. The children who dance to '*Thiiraada vilayaattu pillai*' ('Endlessly playful child'), do not fully comprehend the Tamil words, and certainly cannot fully enter into the Krishna myth, its images, and symbols. The food is eclectic: *kachori*, *samosa*, *dhokla*, *idli*, *vadai*, *dosai*. 'Ethnic' cuisine matches 'ethnic' music. The narrator realizes with a pang that many of the children there are

Indian children adopted into American families. Could they be girl babies abandoned in rubbish bins or baskets? Denied an identity by their Indian parents, will they inherit only a notional 'Indianness'?

We identify with different categories at different times and for different reasons. The larger the category, the more eclectic and vague its markers and boundaries, Ambai seems to say. A narrow category is more tightly defined, but it tells you no more about the person who belongs to it than the broader one does. But what is the self that is independent of the community? In contrast to the vague, eclectic, and artificial construct of 'Indianness' which she sees in the Festival of India, the narrator of 'A Rose-coloured Sari' wonders just what makes up her individual 'self'. What is it that sustains and supports it? What she finds by way of an answer is a rag-bag of memories, intense sense-impressions, tastes and smells of food, and, most particularly, the sounds of music and poetry. Such sensations are an important part of a fluid and changing sense of self, but they are randomly remembered. The rag-bag has no particular order or chronology and the sensations, memories, and experiences can be called up at will at moments of need:

The smell of cooking when a properly soured batter is just spreading on a dosai griddle. The smell of sesame in the chilli powder. The smell of *gingili* oil, unstrained, fresh from the press. The tenderness of Bhimsen Joshi's Lalit *raagam*. The deep resonance of Gangubai Hangal's voice. Girija Devi's lilting tones. The kisses she and her lover had exchanged as they stood under a chestnut tree in a small village in Himachal Pradesh. The journey past her house, everyday, of bodies going to the cremation ground. Funeral fires burning at a distance. The voice of her Tamil teacher who had loved and read Tirumular, 'I nurtured my body; indeed I nurtured my life-source'. The poet Ghalib pleading, 'Lord, they have not understood me; they will not understand me. Give them different hearts, or at least give me a new language.' Which of these would her mind seek, and at what moment?

When the narrator wants to bequeath a sense of stability to Rachel, the Indian baby girl adopted by American parents, she gives her the *pallu* of her mother's sari—a sari which had been worn at every important family occasion, which had travelled all over India, and which every girl in the family had borrowed and worn at her 'coming-of-age' ceremony. A sari, Ambai writes, which contained a whole history within itself (made up of random, lived moments, she implies) 'just as the whole of the Mahabharata lies buried in Draupadi's unbound hair'. The sari is a symbol of a personal history, made up of impressionistic moments. Significantly, the narrator tears the sari in order to share it, putting an end to one history, beginning another in a diaspora. There is a severance, but also a continuity.

Both these notions of the loosely-defined self and a personal history of valued moments are explored, once again in a diaspora setting, in 'Parasakti and Others in a Plastic Box'. In the first half of the story, which consists of a long letter from Bharati to her younger sister Dhanam, Bharati writes about her mother's visit to her in America. Bharati's first marriage—we assume it was a conventional arranged marriage—ended in divorce; she is devastated and her mother comes to stay with her. Amma arrives with her jars of pickles, her favourite spices, and her most important gods—Parasakti and a few others, packed in a plastic box. She is an Annapurna, a maker and dispenser of food, a nurturer and carer. Through gifts of food, she easily makes contact with her neighbours. And primarily through her cooking she heals her daughter, and reconnects her, as Ambai writes, 'to the minutiae of her neighbours' lives, to food tasting of salt and tamarind and chilli, to the Tamil songs she had forgotten'—that is, to the world around her and her own history. This done, Amma's purpose is accomplished and she can go home. Ambai suggests this sense of the self, fluid and changing, is not defined by geographic location alone, nor by the conventions and rules of a community. A personal history, with which you are at ease, is what you take with you wherever you go, and wherever you come from. Losing touch with it because of a humiliating divorce, Bharati panics and is overcome with fear and shame. She feels no firm ground beneath her. The metaphor is important. To be able to feel firm ground wherever you tread, rather than to be rooted in one place—that seems to be Ambai's goal. The narrator of 'A Rose-coloured Sari' gives her mother's sari-pallu to the adopted child with the blessing, 'May it ground her'—the Tamil word Ambai uses is *irutthattum*, from *irutthu*, to hold firm, to stabilize, to ground.

In all her stories Ambai questions roles, rules, and identities that are 'given'. For example, there are women in Ambai's stories who cook compulsively, the Annapurnas; but there are also those who cook by choice. Are these Ambas, women–men?[4] In 'Unpublished Manuscript', Tirumagal infuriates her husband by ordering food from a restaurant when she is hard pressed, and cooking only the rice. He sees her as someone who has broken the most fundamental of rules: 'Are you a woman?', 'Call yourself a woman?' he asks repeatedly. Years later, when she has left her violent husband and is living alone, she will live on tea and biscuits when she is working at her writing. Cooking with her daughter is then a means of returning to the ordinary world, when it becomes a pleasurable and even aesthetic activity.

Women who will not cook, or who do not like to cook, overturn rules and roles: they are seen as women turned men. But in Ambai's stories there are also men who enjoy cooking and choose to cook. In 'Unpublished Manuscript', Ramaswami cooks for his daughter and his family: he is a nurturer, creating his role through the making and serving of food. Ambai has always refused to essentialize men and women, insisting that both sexes possess the ability to nurture, and equally. Men such as Ramaswami are capable of 'melting' prescribed roles, dissolving them away. The point is made by the protagonist of this story, Tirumagal, who quotes from a bhakti lyric, '*Nekku nekkul urugi urugi*'—melting, melting to the heart's core.

The reversal of roles (for example, who cooks) and changing the rules (questioning mealtimes, snacking instead of eating a meal, or not eating at all) are all ways, in these stories, of questioning the order within the family, or the bounds of the self. Eating forbidden foods threatens the boundaries of a tightly bound community like a caste. In a more general sense, it threatens the boundaries which define social order, and the right order of the universe—which are symbolized and reinforced by proper behaviour in each situation, (for example, what can or should be eaten, and when).

In a wonderful light-hearted story, 'Journey 3', Ambai describes a Brahmin woman's attempt to negotiate with a lower-caste deity and the disorder that follows, forcing her to abandon her plan. A mother arranges for a yearly food-offering to Mariamman, in order to gain protection for her family and herself against small-pox since the

Sanskritic god Kannika Parameswari, whom she worships usually, does not have that power. But Amma cannot go to the Mariamman temple herself, so the lower-caste woman Marudayi, who works for them, is called in to intercede on her behalf. Mariamman's protection is sought, but Amma has as little contact with her as possible: the offering is made on her own terms.

But she cannot remain in control when she allows her daughter Mythili to join the expedition with Marudayi and Marudayi's daughter, Minakshi. Amma's strict instructions are that Mythili is not to be allowed 'that side', literally across the boundary: the place where chicken and goats are sacrificed to Mariamman, cooked, and eaten. Once outside Amma's control, the children break her rule, crossing both caste and class boundaries, relishing chicken *pulau* (forbidden and polluted food for the upper-caste child), and talking about 'pain, blood, and death'.

Once the main food rule is breached, a classic misrule and disorder follows, if only for a single day. Amma needs Marudayi as a go-between in order to keep her negotiation with Mariamman within limits. Thus Marudayi acquires the power of the gate-keeper who can allow—and even help—Mythili to cross the boundaries. It is true that in the end Amma must give up her attempt at negotiating with the boundaries. She has no other recourse but to put her trust in Kannika Parameswari. Yet Mythili's world has been changed forever.

This story can be read as a light-hearted illustration of Victor Turner's argument in *The Ritual Process*, where he writes of two contrasted models of society: one highly structured, in which the individual is only ambiguously grasped behind the social persona, the other a 'communitas' of idiosyncratic individuals, who, though differing in physical and mental endowment, are nevertheless equal in terms of shared community:

All human societies implicitly or explicitly refer to two contrasting social models. One…is of society as a structure of jural, political, and economic positions, offices, statuses, and roles, in which the individual is only ambiguously grasped behind the social persona. The other is of society as a communitas of concrete idiosyncratic individuals, who, though differing in physical and mental endowment, are nevertheless regarded as equal in terms of shared humanity. The first model is of a differentiated, culturally structured, segmented, and often hierarchical system of institutionalized positions. The second presents society as an undifferentiated, homogeneous whole, in which individuals confront one another integrally, and not as 'segmentalized' into statuses and roles.[5]

Role and status reversals are part of the dialectic between structure and moments of anti-structure. Structure is reasserted in the end, but subtly altered.

Sharing food, particularly between women, is a trope that appears very often in Ambai's work. Cooking and serving food may be a means of controlling and maintaining boundaries or negotiating across them but sharing food can also be a means of breaking down traditional boundaries between generations, communities, and cultures, and creating new groups on the model of Turner's 'communitas'. In 'Gifts',[6] the village women around Tirunelveli share their food with the narrator, an urban woman and researcher who lives outside Tamil Nadu. In 'Age',[7] the Chilean refugee shares white wine with the narrator, who is briefly in England. In 'Camel Ride', the Tamil *hijra* or eunuch, Yamuna, invites the narrator to pull in her scooter by a Mumbai roadside and to share roasted corn-on-the-cob with her. In each case, it is not only food that is shared, but dreams, aspirations, personal histories, and everyday pain. Often more than one food rule is broken. In the last case where street food is eaten by a busy Mumbai main road, it is the hijra who turns hostess, having formed a spontaneous maverick Tamil community in exile, along with the *bhutta*-seller and the narrator.

In Ambai's fiction, sharing the cooking is another aspect of food-sharing, where the dividing line between host and guest, giver and taker, is completely blurred. Sometimes, this happens out of necessity, as in one of Ambai's most recent stories 'A Movement, a Folder, Some Tears'. In this case, although the three women activists come from different parts of India and different communities, much of their working and personal lives have already been shared. Coming to one of their homes late one evening, they can knock up a piping hot meal, cooking together at 2 a.m. But the ideal celebratory feast, planned and yet spontaneous, cutting across boundaries of caste and class, blurring the distinctions between hosts and guests, where the food and drink is both familiar and strange, is described in one of her best stories, 'Forest'.

The feast takes place in the house of Savitabai. She and her fellow-labourers, Rukminibai and Minabai, live in the forests covering the mountains above Mumbai. These three invite Chenthiru, a middle-class professional woman, who for reasons of her own is staying in the government guest house, away from her family. There is no special reason for the celebration: it just happens that the women's husbands are away. In this sense it is a spontaneous occasion. Each of the three women, Savitabai, Rukminibai, and Minabai, contributes some of the materials or ingredients, but the cooking is equally and spontaneously shared between them and Chenthiru. They work to the rhythm of a Bhakti lyric by Bahinibai which Rukminibai sings. When the first part of the cooking is done, they all four pat out the *puranpolis* together 'as if they were well rehearsed at the task'. When the cooking is done, everyone eats together, no one 'serves' another. This is the very opposite of the hierarchy, the food-wars and the jostling for the kitchen keys described so vividly in 'A Kitchen in the Corner of the House'.[8]

The feast asserts the possibility of dissolving boundaries (if only for its duration), but it also asserts the right to pleasure, which sometimes has to be earned through pain. This is specifically referred to in the Bahinibai lyric which Rukminibai sings to the others:

Arré, *sansara*, sansara,[9]
Life is like a griddle on which you bake your *baakris*
It is only when you have burnt your hand
That you get your baakris.

This reference to the bhakti poem is important for several reasons. One of the chief characteristics of the bhakti movement, wherever it arose in India, is its blurring of boundaries and roles. A.K. Ramanujan develops Turner's ideas of 'structure' and 'anti-structure' and applies them to the Indian bhakti movements, particularly that of the Virasaiva saints of Karnataka:

The saints are drawn from every social class, caste and trade, untouchable and untouchable—from kings and ministers to manual workers. ... Furthermore, in the new community, instead of multiple networks of normal social relationships, we have face-to-face dyadic relationships with each other...[10]

Ramanujan also points to the gender shifts and reversals in the bhakti saints:

The male saints wish to become women; they wish to drop their very maleness, their machismo. Saints then become a kind of third gender. The lines between male and female are crossed and re-crossed in their lives.[11]

Equally, he points out, in bhakti movements, women take on qualities that traditionally belong to men. They break the rules of Manu that forbid them to do so.[12]

Neither Ambai nor many of her protagonists are believers in the traditional sense. Women such as Tirumagal or Dhanam never go to a temple or perform a puja. But there are some themes from the bhakti movement which Ambai adopts, in a secularized form, particularly the possibility of an escape from rigidly defined roles and identities. I referred earlier to a passage in 'Unpublished Manuscript' where Tirumagal quotes from a lyric of the *Tiruvasagam* of the eighth-century Saivite saint Manikkavachagar: '*Nekku nekkul urigi urigi*', 'melting, melting to the heart's core'. The notion of melting or dissolving away given roles and categories is central to *Tiruvasagam*, as it is to many bhakti poets. Such a notion is particularly attractive to her, Tirumagal says. Her daughter Senthaamarai, learning from her mother, asks herself:

'If men can soften and dissolve and melt through bhakti (devotion to god), why can't they do so out of (human) love?' She made up her mind about the sort of man she would respect. He must know how to melt. 'Melting, melting to the heart's core'.

Bahinibai's lyric is important for other reasons too. 'I like Bahinibai for her simple similes and metaphors which are so close to everyday life,' Ambai wrote to me. The bhakti movement levelled caste and class as well as gender, but Bahinibai's lyric makes metaphysics part of everyday life. She finds in bhakti a set of precepts which allow her not merely to endure daily life as a woman, but to celebrate it. The next two stanzas of the lyric (which Ambai sent me) are:

Arré sansara, sansara
What is the point of crying about it?
It is only a silly garland about the neck,[13]
Don't call it a harness.

Arré sansara, sansara
Is like a cucumber on the vine
It may be bitter at one end
But the rest of it is sweet.

But the stanza that Ambai uses in her story, and which Rukminibai sings while the women work to its rhythm, is particularly apt in its assertion that food you have cooked and worked for is rightly eaten, shared, and enjoyed. The feast needs no other justification.

And what of the palm toddy? It is the crowning point of the feast, and allows Chenthiru, a middle-class woman, to break another taboo. It allows a 'good high', like a reaching out of the imagination. It makes possible a visionary moment. Immediately after the feast, aware of her own near-intoxication, Chenthiru hears the music of a *rudravina* from the ashrama across the waterfall. The music gives her the insights she needs to make crucial decisions about her life.

The ideal feast is not an orgy. It is not like the day of misrule, when Mariamman takes over from Kannika Parameswari, when excess and indulgence are allowed, even necessary, and every rule is breached for a moment. The ideal feast has its own order and harmony, newly and spontaneously established. It has the immediacy of what Turner calls 'existential or spontaneous communitas' where 'individuals are not segmented into roles and statuses but confront one another rather in the manner of Martin Buber's "I" and "Thou"'.[14] But Ambai is also suggesting that this could be a model for an imagined ideal society.

I return to the notions of self and community I began with, and the tropes that Ambai uses to explore them. There are rules and boundaries, she suggests, which represent different ways in which we identify ourselves with the communities to which we belong. But it is impossible to define the fluid, changing, historical, and individual self by such rules or by the communities with which we associate ourselves at different times. Particularly in modern times of travel, dislocation, exile, and diaspora, we need to know and to be in touch with a stable or 'grounded' self, which allows fluidity and change. This quest is at the core of all Ambai's work. In 'Forest', a musical metaphor comes closest to describing it. Chenthiru meets an *ustad*, or music master, who explains that it is the right pitch, the *sur* that holds one in tune, enabling the singer to engage with the tune as the perfectly-tuned rudravina does. But the pitch cannot be held captive, it can be easily lost; it must be constantly sought after, kept in mind with vigilance. The ustad gives the example of his mother who, at the age of eighty could hear the perfect execution of the Bilaval raga in the cooing of a dove in a crowded Mumbai lane and hold it in mind, above the roaring of a bus or train.

Ambai's own position as a Tamil speaker living in Mumbai gives point to her enquiry into the relation between the individual and the community. But this takes on a special urgency in the current political climate in India. In her recent story, 'A Movement, a Folder, Some Tears', published in the aftermath of the Hindu–Muslim riots in Gujarat, she counters the demand that people identify themselves by the most rigid of identities, and the narrowest of tests: 'Are you a Hindu? Answer yes or no.' 'Are you a Muslim? Do you read the Koran? Do you say your prayers?' Such identities are meaningless, she implies. The story recalls a time, particularly in the 1980s, when activists in the women's movement were prepared to defy and outface all hostility with an energy that said, 'You can't define us. We will break your definitions, your grammars, your rules.' The story mourns the loss of this energy, and its replacement now, very often, with the darkest despair. There is a sharp political edge here as Ambai continues to explore the possibility of a more fluid notion of the self, and to seek an open-ended society where—as in the ideal feast—we encounter each other not through given roles and identities, but as individuals and as equals.

LAKSHMI HOLMSTRÖM

## NOTES

1. This is a version of paper presented at a seminar at SOAS, London, on 27 October 2003.
2. C.S. Lakshmi, *The Face behind the Mask: Women in Tamil Literature*, New Delhi: Vikas, 1984.
3. The fifth-century Tamil poet who wrote the *Tirukkural*, one of the best-known and loved texts in Tamil, a collection of couplets under the heads Virtue, Wealth, and Love.
4. In the Mahabharata, Amba, rejected by Bhishma, retires to the forest

and swears vengeance. With the aid of Shiva she is born again as a man,
Sikhandin, and eventually slays Bhishma.

5. Victor Turner, *The Ritual Process: Structure and Anti-structure*, London:
   Routledge, 1969, p. 177.
6. From *A Purple Sea*, Madras: Affiliated East-West Press, 1992.
7. Ibid.
8. Ibid.
9. Sansara, samsara: the cycle of mundane existence; worldly life.
10. A.K. Ramanujan, *Speaking of Siva*, Harmondsworth: Penguin, 1973,
    p. 35.
11. A.K. Ramanujan, 'Talking to God in the Mother Tongue', *Manushi*, Nos.
    50–52, January–June, Tenth Anniversary issue, 1989, p. 10.
12. Ibid., p. 11.
13. The reference is to the wedding garland.
14. Turner, *The Ritual Process*, pp. 131–2.

# Journey 1

The bus stood there as if it were a heaven-sent vehicle, meant just for her. A brand new one. It had a single seat next to the driver. It was parked some distance away from the other buses. They said it would leave in about fifteen minutes, but as yet there were no passengers. Making sure she had her ticket with her, she climbed in and sat down in the single seat. She had let several buses go by for the sake of that particular seat. At least on her return journey she wanted to travel without anyone bothering her. She wanted to sit well away from the other passengers. These were people who expected her, if she only opened her mouth, to lay out her entire life before them. This single seat was going to be her line of defence. Nobody was going to get past it. Any stripling Abhimanyu[1] attempting such a thing would be felled immediately. She sat there, making her plans as if they were strategies in preparation for war. Because she had taken no such precautions during her forward journey she had suffered inordinately. And so her lap had been drenched by a child's urine, the shoulder of her *choli* had been dribbled upon by a sleeping and exhausted woman, her sari-*pallav* stained by tobacco-juice borne across from the front seat by the wind. She had not set out prepared for all this. She had been exposed to torment because she had no safeguards; no protective armour at all.

The morning had begun well enough. Because she slept against a window opening eastward, she had been touched by the sun's very first needles of light. As she opened her eyes slowly, the rays of light were like long threads, extending from the ball of red cotton behind the distant *neem* tree. When she shut her eyes again and faced the light, her eyes were flooded with red. Then when she turned away from the light, closing them with her hands, they filled with peacock-green. By the time she had done this four times, her body had accepted the world. And prepared itself to move about in it.

She could hear the water pump being worked downstairs. Must be Valli. She had asked Valli to come quite early and pump up some water. She had to go to Tiruchi that day. She had already sent word to the person whom she was to meet there. After Valli had pumped the water and cleaned the house, she bought some idli and dosai from the *aappam*-stall woman at the corner of the street, ate her share, and then left.

When asked, 'What do you want from Tiruchi, Valli?' Valli had retorted, 'Are you likely to bring me the *prasadam* from the hill-top Pillayaar? '[2]

Valli knew well enough she would not go to the temple. So she too had just smiled, and said nothing.

She had her bath and put on her mango-coloured tie-dyed sari with a black border, and a choli of black handloomed cotton with fine yellow checks. The sari was stiff with starch. She did not care for starch in her clothes. Valli, however, did. 'It only looks good that way,' she would say emphatically. In all these matters, it was Valli who organized her life. Valli had taken over the burden of these day-to-day decisions and left her the neem tree, the *koel* which nested there, the street, the sky. Gifts made over to her by Valli.

That morning, because she aimed to reach Tiruchi in good time, she climbed into the first bus that was ready to go, and went and sat by the window, on a seat meant for two. Just as the bus was about to depart, a couple climbed in, with their baby. The husband wore a stiffly starched shirt. A crackling new silk *veshti*. The wife wore a blue silk sari, blindingly bright at that early hour, with a red border. Golden motifs covered the entire body of the sari. Her wet hair was heavy with flowers. Her neck was over-crowded with jewellery. Her gold-worked choli, stretched tightly across her body, was wet in large patches under her arms. The baby was in her arms, of course. Soon after they boarded the bus, when it was clear that there was no possibility of their sitting together, the wife came and sat next to her. The woman then placed the child on the thigh nearest her, so that he faced her directly. For some reason, perhaps to announce to the whole world that he was a male child, he had been dressed only in a chocolate-coloured shirt covering his upper half. Now, in rhythm with the speed of the bus, the baby began to stretch his ankleted feet towards her waist and lap.

The woman petted him and said, 'Don't make trouble, Kannan.'

Perhaps he melted when she called him 'Kannan' so fondly; at any rate, the little darling braced his feet comfortably against her waist and began to pee. Startled as she felt the dampness over her waist and hands and sari, she said sharply, 'See to your child, will you?'

The woman said casually, 'Oh, you've gone and wetted her sari, you naughty boy!'

She spoke in anger, 'What is this, *amma*? Can't you hold the baby properly in your own lap? I'm on my way to Tiruchi on business. Can I turn up like this, in a wet sari?'

'What's happened, amma?' asked the old woman seated behind them.

The mother answered, 'She's shouting because the baby made her wet.'

'What?' asked the woman in surprise. 'If people are so refined as all that they should go about in a pleasure car. Who is asking them to travel by bus?'

She rounded on the old lady, 'Is there some sort of law that if I come by bus I should let all the babies here urinate on my sari?'

'Why, *thayi*, don't you have any children yourself? Or, have you borne babies who never pee?'

Someone else glanced at her neck and put in, 'Looks as if she isn't even married, anyway.'

She argued loudly, 'Why sir, where's the connection between this business and whether I am married or not? Why couldn't she bring the baby with a piece of cloth wrapped around him? Why should he wet other people's clothes? The baby's father is managing to travel with his shirt and veshti uncrushed, I see. But I have to suffer instead!'

The child's father who had been swaying, half-asleep, now woke up, startled.

'What's the matter?'

An elderly person said to him, 'It's nothing. You carry on sleeping.

An unmarried girl here is getting cross. What does she know about the joy of children?'

'Amma,' said the old lady, touching her shoulder lovingly, 'I tell you this. May the moment dawn when you too are touched by your child's urine. You'll have a baby in your own arms by next year, just see if you don't.'

'You tell her out of your own mouth, *paatti*. Let good times come to her.'

She turned away and gazed out of the window, afraid that were she to say anything more, they would find her a bridegroom and tie the knot between them there and then. She could not explain to them that she was indeed married, that her husband worked in a different town, and that she didn't believe in such outward symbols like a *tali*. In any case, all sorts of questions would be sure to follow, like 'Why don't you have children?' It was while she was deep in such thoughts, that she suddenly became aware of a certain weight and dampness at the shoulder of her choli. The woman had fallen asleep against her shoulder, the boy Kannan held firmly in her lap and facing forward. Kannan's head too was drooping. Perhaps he had not allowed her to sleep all night. Or, she might have woken up very early that morning to wash her hair. By the time she had massaged in the oil and the *shiyakai*, her arm would have pretty nearly broken. Time would have passed swiftly while she bathed, then bathed, dressed, and suckled the child before donning her gold-worked choli. Perhaps she had set off after just a cup of coffee, as they were on their way to a temple or a wedding. As soon as there was a convenient shoulder —a shoulder wearing handloomed cotton, from which her head was not likely to slip off—the woman must have dropped off. When that shoulder was jerked, the woman sat up, wiping the dribble from the corner of her mouth. She glanced at the shoulder she was sleeping against, pulled out a handkerchief, and tried to wipe it.

'Forgive me, *akka*,' she said.

By this time, Kannan too opened his eyes, and as if he had already determined upon his next ploy, thrust the strap of her handbag into his mouth, and began chewing on it forcefully, with all four of his existing teeth. She freed her handbag from his grasp. Immediately he bent forward and fastened his mouth upon her watch strap. If this went on any longer, she might find herself singing 'Thaye, Yasoda', she thought. It was while she was preventing Kannan's further attacks that the consecration by tobacco-juice happened. The old lady seated behind her noticed this and called out, 'Who's spitting?' and patted her. As if she were saying, 'Just you get married and you won't ever be bothered like this again.'

As soon as they reached the Tiruchi terminus, she went into the changing rooms and re-tied her sari, turning it around and wearing the outer edge inside, hiding all traces of the journey. Seeking out a single seat now was by way of ridding herself of all the distress of the morning.

Other passengers began to board the bus. The driver took his seat. The vehicle had filled up. When there were just a few seconds before departure, someone came up to her and called out to her most compassionately, 'Amma.' She turned towards him as if about to ask, in her turn, 'What is it, my son?'

'Won't you move over to the Ladies' side?' he asked, pointing to the corner of a seat which already held three people. He was making a grave mistake. He was attempting to pierce through her line of defence. But this time she was ready.

'No, I will not,' she replied with determination. He was somewhat taken aback, but went on, 'Ladies shouldn't sit here, amma.'

'Why, is there some rule to that effect?' she asked.

'There isn't a rule as such. But I usually sit here and go on chatting with the driver-*annacchi.*'

'Well, I too intend to sit here and go on chatting to the driver-annacchi,' she told him.

The driver looked at her in surprise. The man who had called out to her asked, 'Are you travelling on your own?'

She nodded and turned away. 'Leave it out, *ya,*' said the driver, starting up the bus. His friend gazed all round the bus, as if he wanted to inform all the passengers about some scandalous happening.

Two stops later, an old woman boarded the bus, along with a ten-year-old boy. The woman sat down at the extreme edge of a seat meant for three people. The boy stood nearby, holding on to the back of her seat. She turned slightly and looked at him. He was wearing khaki shorts. His much-washed T-shirt was unironed and carried the name of an American university on the chest. Perhaps, he had liked the symbol and bought it just for that. He stood there, watching the reflection of the street in the mirror in front of him. His hair was combed down smoothly. Piercing dark eyes, fringed with long lashes. She moved along her seat a little, turned around and asked, 'Thambi, would you like to sit down?'

He hesitated a moment, then came and sat down. The bus went on its way. A tiny bird with a black tail, yellow breast, and sharp beak seated on a telegraph wire grazed the eye and then disappeared. She and the boy saw it together. Then he turned and smiled at her. She smiled back.

'What's its name?' he asked.

She told him she didn't know its name, but that there was a book which told you all about the birds in India. She said that it explained about birds in each region. She told him about Salim Ali. She explained that it was his favourite pastime to watch birds through a telescope.

'Can I find that book?'

'Mm. It must be in your school library. Look out for it.'

'Our school took us to Vedathangal. There were birds there which had come even from Russia. I wondered how they come from such a distance.'

'Is that so?'

'Sometimes, I go with my father when he is guarding the fields; we sleep overnight there. Say, you suddenly wake up at two, two-thirty. If you look up you can see a crowd of seven or eight birds, white as white, flying quietly past. Sometimes, I even think I'm dreaming.'

'Really?'

After a moment's silence, he said, as if he were sharing a secret with her, 'I reared a squirrel, once.'

'When?'

'When I was in the fourth. It had fallen under a papaya tree. I took it and put it in the cardboard box in which *Appa*'s clock was packed, and I put a cloth underneath it. Amma fed it with a piece of cotton-wool dipped in milk. Later I fed it with an ink-filler. It drank up the milk and ran all over my arms.'

'Mm.'

'It died,' he said, his throat choking.

'How?'

'I don't know.'

'Did you make holes in the box?'

'Of course I did. How would it breathe otherwise?'

'Then how did it die?'

'I don't know.'

As they were talking, they heard an uproar outside, 'Stop the bus! Stop the bus!' There was a crowd of villagers out there. Some had stones in their hands. A cry was raised, 'Chuck the stones at it, *da!*' The hands holding the stones went up.

Instantly she hugged the boy to herself, and leant down.

The driver stopped the bus in a panic, and climbed out.

'How dare you drive past, ya? You knocked over one of our people this morning and coolly drove off; now you think you can escape, do you? Are we likely to let you off?'

'Set the bus on fire, da!'

When the shouting and the outcry died down a little, the driver explained that his was not the bus they meant. And after a few others intervened to make peace, the bus was finally on its way again.

The boy was still trembling slightly, all over. He leaned back against the arm she had placed on his shoulder. A little while later he fell asleep, his head laid back. There were still traces of fear on his face.

When she glanced at him, and then turned away to the right, the sun was sinking, floating in an orange sky. Cool circle of fire.

'Thambi,' she said, waking him.

When he woke up with a start, she pointed to the sunset. 'Look there.'

He opened his eyes wide to see. She told him about an extraordinary sunset she had seen as a child in Karnataka, at a place called Agumbe. She told him how the sun seemed to take all sorts of forms as it sank, appearing to the eye as square, or oblong, or wine-cup shaped.

'Truly?' asked the boy, in wonder.

The bus entered the terminus and came to a stop. The old woman who had boarded the bus with the boy caught hold of his hand again and climbed down. She too got off the bus. The boy took the old lady's hand and began to walk towards the exit of the bus station.

When he reached the gate, he turned around and looked at her. In the gathering dusk, his eyes gleamed.

*Nigazh*, October 1995

### NOTES

1. The son of Arjuna by his wife Subhadra. On the thirteenth day of the battle of Kurukshetra, he managed to penetrate the 'lotus formation' of the Kaurava troops, but fell fighting heroically.
2. The Tamil name for Ganapati.

# Journey 2

Sivapragasam had told her that unless she set off before break of day, she would never be able to return by nightfall. She got herself ready, made sure that her pen, her notes, and paper were all in place in her bag, locked her room; and when she came out of the hotel, found Dinakaran standing there. For a moment she didn't recognize him. As usual he wore his veshti doubled up. And a half-sleeved shirt.

'How are you?' he asked.

'How did you know I was here?'

'Sivapragasam told me. I came by, thinking we could talk during the journey.'

'You've had to wake up terribly early! You are going to be tired out.'

'It's nothing. I'm quite used to it,' he said.

In a few moments the sun would rise. As soon as they reached the bus station, he set off towards the tea-stall. He hadn't forgotten her usual ways. The tea-stall owner took one look at her and reached for the ginger from its basket on the top shelf. He broke off a piece, peeled it, crushed it, and threw it into boiling water.

Dinakaran glanced at her and smiled.

'It looks as if you will never give up your Delhi habits.'

They sat down on the wooden bench outside the tea-stall.

'Give me just coffee, *Annacchi*. I can't stomach ginger and all that first thing in the morning.'

'See, it's this mulishness that I object to,' she said to him.

He laughed.

He got his coffee, and she her tea. There wasn't much going on at the bus station at that early hour. The sun had not yet risen completely. In the pale light of dawn, the buses were like tortoises, hidden in their shells.

She was quiet, drinking her ginger-flavoured tea.

'Lizzy too can make *masala* tea. Just the way Gujaratis drink it. Her father was in Baroda for a year.'

'Which Lizzy?'

'A distant relative.'

'Oh.'

As soon as the first bus which was going to her destination arrived, they climbed in. Dinakaran was clearly tired. Within a few moments after the bus started, he leaned his head on the metal bar behind the seat and fell asleep, his mouth slightly open.

Dinakaran had accompanied her on many of the journeys she had made in connection with her work. As soon as she asked him whether he could go with her, he'd set off with soap and towel, to bathe in the river. It was only after his special bath in the Tambaraparni river that he was able to take delight in the world around him. Until such a moment, he would toss upon his bed, or lean against a wall without any show of interest. Usually, he opened his small bookshop only after mid-day. If he actually managed to sell a couple of books in a day, his joy was unbounded. 'The reading habit hasn't died out yet,' he'd rejoice.

Several times he had stood with her outside some small town, by the side of a long and silent road, waiting for a bus. They had talked about several things as they stood waiting for a bus, at a long road edged with trees and unlit by lamps. Taking courage because there was no one about, they had sung aloud the songs of Pattukottai Kalyanasundaram. 'White goat, you become the prey of the very same men who feed you', they had sung out loudly, their voices piercing through the darkness. There had been times when cyclists or bullock-cart men had glowered at them, hearing the racket. He used to profess amazement that she from Delhi, and he from the shores of the Tambaraparni could be thinking together about Pattukottaiyaar, at such a godforsaken place.

'How did you get to be like this?' he would ask her.

'What do you mean, like this? You sound as if I've got a contagious disease or something.'

'No, not like that...'

'Then how? I know someone who says that unless you are born on the soil of Thanjavur, you will never be able to appreciate the beauty in anything. As for you, you speak as if it is only by dipping into the Tambaraparni that one can learn to appreciate things. If you divide up the earth like this, each one staking a claim to their own piece, then people like me who wander around in many places must go and stand on wastelands, or what?'

'*Appa*, how furious you are!'

Dinakaran had come to stay with her once, when he came to Delhi on business. She and another young woman shared the rooms in the back of a large house. She had to rush off at 6.30 to take the first lessons of the morning, at her college. She had laid in plenty of bread and butter and fruit; and so she said to him, 'Dinakaran, I'll be back only in the evening. But there's lots of bread and fruit and everything.'

'Bread?' he had asked, shocked. Thoughts of idli, dosai, and *pongal* were apparently tormenting him.

'And the mid-day meal?'

'I've just drained the rice. Please help yourself, and eat it with curd.'

'What, by myself?'

'No, no. As soon as it strikes one, an angel will appear through this window, mix the rice and curd and serve it on your plate. She'll open the jar and help you to the pickles. She'll pour out the water so that you can wash your hands. Then she'll wash your plate and put it away. She'll tidy up the place after you have finished eating.'

'Are you teasing me?'

'What then?'

He went around for a couple of days, looking as if he had been hit by a thunderbolt. After that he found lodgings in Karol Bagh, where South Indians usually stayed. After eight to ten idlis, dosai and vadai had all disappeared down his throat, and after he had eaten his fill of rice, *rasam*, fried vegetables, eggs, chicken, fish, and sambar, at last he began to glow with life again, like a man who has died and been resurrected.

At that time, a famous author was writing a travelogue for a weekly journal. Whatever corner of the world he went to, Tamil families would seek him out and entertain him at their home, placing a pile of jasmine-soft idlis in front of him. Showered by their love, he was thrilled, ecstatic. She teased Dinakaran, asking him whether he was related to this writer.

He claimed that people born of the Tambaraparni soil had extremely subtle palates. He put the entire responsibility for his own love of food on to his grandfather, who could distinguish between sixty-four different types of pacchadi.

'If his food lacked a tiny crystal of salt, he'd be aware of it. Such a fine palate he had. If he brought you vegetables, he'd tell you exactly how each one should be cooked. He knew how to appreciate good things. After he visited his brother in Pondicherry, he acquired a taste for fish. One day he fried some fish, rubbing the pieces with ginger and garlic, turmeric and chilli powder, and turning them over and over slowly until they were done. When he had eaten, he washed his hands and sighed, "*Appané*, Muruga!" That was all. His life was gone. My grandmother just shrivelled away after that, saying, "Who is there for me to cook for, any more..."'

'I suppose you, her grandson, have turned up now at last, to appreciate her cooking?'

'Look here,' he said, frowning, 'You shouldn't joke about matters related to food.'

In spite of all this, she was not sure whether she knew who Dinakaran the individual actually was. It was only those bus journeys, the long walks, and the Pattukottaiyaar songs that she really knew.

Dinakaran did not open his eyes until they reached Tiruvanantapuram.

It was evening by the time her work was done. When she wanted to look for a pay-toilet, he said, 'Lizzy's house is just nearby. Why don't you come there?'

'Without giving her any warning or anything? How am I to turn up...? Didn't you say she was a distant relative?'

'No, no, don't worry. Let's go there. She won't mind.'

They stopped an autorickshaw and went to Lizzy's house. Lizzy's face broke into a wide smile as soon as she saw them.

'Come in, come in; I've heard about you,' she said, welcoming them warmly.

There was a picture of Jesus hanging on a wall in the small living room. On the opposite wall, on a small wooden shelf, there were two candle-shaped lights, electrically lit. A wedding photograph of her husband and herself, standing together, was placed on a small stool. Two or three photographs of a small child. The boy's face seemed vaguely familiar.

Lizzy brought them two glasses of water.

'Lizzy, first I must use your bathroom,' she said, and was shown the way.

As soon as she returned, Lizzy asked, 'What shall I cook for you?'

'Lizzy, we must start back soon. Otherwise it will get really late.'

'*Ayyo*, Jesus! How can you go away without eating anything, after coming all this way?'

Dinakaran put in, 'I have to admit, my stomach feels empty.'

'I won't be a minute,' Lizzy said, hurrying inside. She followed her in, asking, 'Isn't it time for your husband to be coming home from work, Lizzy?'

'No, *Akka*, he's not in town. He's a medical sales rep. He's out of town for nearly twenty days in the month.'

'Can I help you in any way?'

'No thanks, Akka. The batter is all ground and ready for dosais. I'll just cook them.'

There was a big brass *andaa* in the corner of the kitchen, with ornamental handles. She touched those handles with some curiosity.

Lizzy looked up from the dosai she was making and said, 'It belonged to Dinakaran's mother. I've known everyone in that family since I was a small girl.'

When they had eaten their dosais, Lizzy brought them masala tea.

'Shall we go then, Dinakaran?'

'Wait just a moment, Akka. Let the little boy come.'

In ten minutes, a four-year-old boy came in, pushing a little tricycle. He saw her and stood still, hesitant.

'Come here,' Dinakaran called out to him.

The little one went up to Dinakaran and buried his head in his lap. Dinakaran stroked his head and said, 'Tell this aunty your name.'

The little boy lifted up his head and said, 'Ravikumar.'

Then, clasping both arms around Dinakaran's waist and hugging him, he looked up into his face and smiled.

Dinakaran gave a smile, immensely full of love. He stroked the boy's face. The boy reached up, climbed on to Dinakaran's lap and laid his face against Dinakaran's.

A little while later, when they attempted to leave yet again, Lizzy went in and brought a round tin with a cake in it, whose smell declared that it was freshly baked. She cut two small pieces, gave them to the little boy and asked him to put one piece into each of her guests' mouths. She closed the tin after that, and gave it to Dinakaran.

In the bus, on their way back, Dinakaran sat with his eyes closed. Outside it had darkened completely. Through the windows of the speeding bus, the trees were dark shadows. All of a sudden, at times, the glowing eyes of an owl flashed past. At other times, the white veshti of someone walking along the road, or their turban, or the glimmer of a gold-bordered sari darted across and disappeared.

Dinakaran's eyes stayed shut. He held on to the tin tightly, so that it would not slide off his lap.

He opened his eyes at last when the bus stopped. Just as he was about to leave, having accompanied her to the entrance of her hotel, he looked directly at her and smiled shyly.

*Manjari*, January 1997

# One and Another

The little bus went rattling along the mountain's narrow, winding road. Bundles of vegetables, carried up the mountain from the plains beneath, lay about everywhere. A mingled smell of cabbage, coriander leaf, bottle-gourd, tomato, carrot, onion, and ginger wafted throughout the vehicle. It would be sunset in a very short while. In the pale light mixed with red that pervaded the bus, its passengers could be seen, interspersed among the vegetable bundles. An infant slept, white-faced, hair bleached brown, just behind a bundle from which scarlet tomatoes protruded. A white-turbaned figure clasped a bag of onions high against its chest. A woman wearing a dark green veil and bangles of green, red, and yellow rested her arms against a bundle of bottle-gourd. Each one of the passengers in that bus looked as if they were paintings, done with extreme care by someone unknown.

How many of them had appeared in Matthew Nathan's paintings as streaks of colour, or floating eyes, or as outspread veil, or as nude forms without adornment, Arulan thought, as he observed the passengers. The young boy, Viru, who sat by his side holding his wrinkled hand, gazed up at him, as if he understood the flow of his thoughts. Arulan's long white beard brushed against Viru's forehead. Viru's eyes ran along Arulan's hair, now completely white, and tied back with a jute string. Normally, his white hair tumbled against his shoulders. Tossed by the wind. But this was a special day. A day when his tumbling hair needed to be tied back. It was the day that Matthew Nathan's body was buried under a *deodar* tree that soared skywards. He smiled slightly at the boy who gazed up at him. Viru leaned up against him more closely.

Viru worked in one of the potato fields nearby. At other times, he went about in Arulan's and Matthew's house, as if he were their

child, or trusted relation. They had set off that day, as they did every
Friday, to go down to the plains for the tubes of colours that they
needed for their painting. They continued this Friday ritual even
though Nathan was no longer there. Besides, there were two small
canvasses and some paper for Viru to practise his painting. These sat
carefully on Viru's lap.

Seated together in just such a bus, Nathan and he had come to live
in this mountain village forty years ago. They had met at a party,
only a week before that. Arulan's father, who had been a soldier
many years ago, came to live in the lap of this mountain. He
remembered, as if in a dream, his father looking up at the mountain
in the morning sometimes, and singing in almost a roaring voice:
'The Himalaya mountain in the north, *Paappaa*; Kumari's tip where
she dwells in the south, Paappaa.' When he sang 'Kumari's tip', his
voice would break discordantly, as if it had caught on a hook. That
was as much as Arulan knew of his father's relationship with his
town. After his parents died, Arulan lived for many years in the town
beneath the mountain, preoccupied with his writing and his music.
Among his friends were many who came to holiday in the mountain.
The party had been given by some of these people.

Matthew sat there, laughing and talking, surrounded by many
men and women. Quite recently there had been an article in a
newspaper, describing him as an artist, born of an Indian father and
a mother from abroad. 'Have you come here in search of your roots?'
a journalist had asked him.

To this he replied, 'That would limit my search. For people like
me, our roots are everywhere in the world. All airports where we
have to spend hours before changing planes are like travellers' inns
to us. When my father first left India and went abroad, it was in the
early years of the twentieth century. After the First World War. When
he left, he took with him, in a packet, a couple of handfuls of earth
from the garden of his home in Pondicherry. It seems that when he
arrived in Paris, he put that earth in a small pot, and grew a plant
there. And there are a couple of handfuls of earth from that pot in all
the places where he lived in this world. Even though other soil had
mingled with it, he believed that the earth from his own land was
contained there. In Paris, the plants which grew out of that soil have

put down deep and strong roots in our garden. No, my quest is not in connection with roots.'

It was a time when the search for roots was not yet considered an absolute necessity for one's emotional fulfilment. There were still many more years to go before Alex Haley would write about his African roots. It was still a time when people were not as yet broken apart, fractured, utterly shattered; the second decade after the Second World War, when Jews rose again from the horrors they had suffered, and were attempting to put down their roots worldwide. A time when people were prepared to renounce their own countries for the sake of their principles, and for humanity as a whole. Those were the days when some believed that it was possible to live as world citizens, unrestricted by geographical maps. So, what Matthew said about roots disturbed no one. But what he next said certainly raised shock waves among the intelligentsia.

'Perhaps, you have come to India in search of a wife?' someone asked.

'No,' he answered quite casually, 'I am not in search of a wife. I don't desire women.'

Arulan judged that in fact Matthew Nathan had been invited to that party only to be stared at as if he were some strange animal. It was not something to be declared openly. In those days, people who held opinions such as his were like owls hiding in their holes.

At that party on that day, the conversation stretched out in different directions and ended in thoughts about death. They talked of many things such as sudden death, death by disease, and death by accident.

'I don't wish to die alone. I would want someone to be with me,' said Matthew Nathan.

'Whoever is by your side, it is you alone who must die,' Arulan replied.

Sitting where he was, Nathan gazed up towards Arulan who stood at one side. Soft glance of blue eyes.

'How do you wish to die?'

'Like a bird. With no one observing me. Without being nursed. Suddenly. Without any plan. With no one to remember me.'

'Do birds die like that?'

'It must be so. I don't know how else it would be.'

When the party was over, Arulan invited Matthew to his home. They talked for a long time about painting and about poetry. Arulan was lost in Matthew's blue eyes, his long slender fingers, his gentle features. Later, Matthew was to say many times that Arulan's dark skin, his bright sharp eyes, and his long curly hair had all served to captivate and bind him. Very soon, they decided they would live together. They went by bus over wild and rugged mountain roads; they walked; they travelled by motorbike. And so they found a small mountain village where they chose to live. Some people criticized them obliquely, calling their village 'a place where they lived hidden lives'; but Matthew took no notice of this. And Arulan too, would say to Matthew's friends, 'This is our den.'

Many years passed by in painting, writing, leading a movement opposing the cutting down of trees in their mountain district, and teaching young boys and girls like Viru to write and to paint. Before the years could be counted, Matthew fell ill.

The paintings of his last few months had changed greatly. They were such that it seemed they would fly away like fine cotton strands, if hung on a wall. 'No weight. No need for weight,' Matthew said once, looking at them. Then, he drew Viru. Everyday Viru would come and pose for him, in whatever way he wanted. In the picture, Viru lay on his side. Nude. Smiling. An innocent smile. He was totally relaxed; not the least tension anywhere about him. His male member at rest, like a bud slanted. It seemed as if that body was weightless, as if it could rise up into the air from the ground below, like a *gandharva*.

There were only a few days when Matthew was bedridden. The memory of washing his body everyday remained in Arulan's mind, like a well-known poem.

His body was white, much wrinkled because of his mixed European blood. Thin arms with swelling green veins. A narrow neck like a fledgling, fleshless. Cheeks with protruding bones. Blue eyes. Withered lips like dry coconut palm fronds. Falling away from his domed forehead to his shoulders, his soft grey hair, with tints of gold from his youth. A hairless, narrow chest. A waist totally without lines or scars, because he had always worn loose clothes. Thighs and legs like waterfalls which had gone dry. Lying weightless, like withered fruit, his pale pink genitals. Once when he was swabbing him down, little by little, with a towel wrung out in hot water, Matthew caught his hands and said, 'Arul, death is very strange, isn't it?' Then he placed the palm of Arulan's hand against his own withered lips. 'Forgive me, Arul, I have to do this on my own,' he said.

His eyes filling with tears, Arulan patted him. When he woke suddenly from his sleep that night, Matthew was sitting up, looking at him.

'It's a sensation, Arul, as if the ground is moving gently, beneath my feet. As if a paint-brush were drawn to the very edge at the top of a canvas, over its side, beyond its square boundaries, and the paint was allowed to drip down in its own way...,' he said. Then, after a while, 'Will you bury me under a deodar tree?'

'Yes, Matthew.'

After that, for a long time they were silent, without words.

The bus went on its way.

Matthew died, bringing to mind a painting covered in the light of earliest dawn. When Arulan awoke, Matthew lay with his hair spread out over the pillow, his eyes closed as if in sleep. Only his head was slightly more aslant. There was an extraordinary peace about his face.

Arulan went up and stroked his hair with slow hands.

'Saheb, Saheb,' wept Viru, in rising sobs, gasping for breath.

The paintings had already been sent, fifteen days ago, to an art gallery. Only the drawing of Viru was left in front of them, very large. Like both their dreams.

Viru dug a hole under a deodar tree which stood as tall as if it would touch the sky, and whose branches swung about and swished as if they were flying away in the wind. The body was covered in a white cloth and lowered into it. In the background somewhere, some women wept. The body was laid within, covered with earth, and the earth made even above. And then, from somewhere a baby girl came crawling up and tumbled there.

Outside the window, it was sunset time.

The snow-covered peaks of the Himalaya mountains shone like sheets of metal in a forge. The smoke rising from the chimneys of houses in the valley were brush-strokes of grey.

The bus stopped to drop off a few passengers. With a sudden move, Arulan rose to his feet. Startled a little by that abrupt movement, Viru too stood up. It was not the place where they usually got off the bus. Arulan climbed down. Viru climbed down after him and stood next to him, holding on to his canvases and the bag full of tubes of paint. Arulan stood at the verge of the mountain path, gazing at the mountains. He was wearing a veshti and *kurta*, all in white. His white hair shone like a crown. He stroked Viru's hair just once, and then began to slip and slide from the mountain edge. He spread his hands as if he wished to grasp hold of something. His veshti and kurta rose in the wind, like a wave. In the light of the sunset, like a giant bird flying without haste towards its goal, slowly he fell down the steep valley. And then he collided against a rock. As Viru, dumbstruck, tried to call out, 'Saheb,' the red colour began to spread across his white clothes, as if it were painted on with rough random brush-strokes.

*Sadangai*, July–September 1997

# Camel Ride

When her eyes fell upon it for the first time, she saw only a shadowy form. At what is known as the Link Road, joining Juhu–Ville Parle and Versova. Late one night. At a road in a state of disrepair, bordered by huge uninhabited buildings which had been raised as investments. A few huts huddled against empty plots, makeshift houses, motor-repair garages, and wild undergrowth which had been turned into free toilets. Dimly lit street-lights. Late at night and before first light, if you weren't careful, you could easily run into someone squatting beside the road to relieve himself, water-vessel at hand. It had happened often. A Maruti car making a quick swerve once knocked a small boy over. The boy, who fell flat to the ground, held a new kind of plastic mug in his hand as if in token of India's liberalized market; a picture of America's Statue of Liberty holding her torch aloft was emblazoned on his T-shirt. The shit still stuck to his backside.

She would remember all this as soon as she entered the Link Road. And her vehicle would lose speed automatically. On that night too, although it was already very late, she slowed the Kinetic Honda. Then, as she gazed along the street with the lamp-posts running along it, there it was in the distance, walking along from one side of the street to the other. With its excessively long legs and neck, moving in a disjointed and ungainly manner, and looking like a line drawing that has been erased and blurred, it came out suddenly from the empty house-site beside the beach, and began to cross the road. As the vehicle approached it, it stopped at a place where the light from a street lamp fell upon it. When it slowly turned its head from the top of its long neck, she could see its nose, torn on both sides, darkened with clotted blood. It would be one of the camels that gave children and adults pleasure rides along the beach. Camels which were allowed to run along the beach. Camels which were driven along, thick ropes through their nostrils. Camels which headed the processions during Vinayakar Chaturti, at the festival of Visarjan when images of Ganesha were immersed in the sea. At that time they were draped in silk cloths, their faces masked in gilt-covered plates, and bhaktas carrying orange flags rode them. They were led out to the sound of wailing cinema songs and the hooting of lorries, cars, and buses, Ganeshas in many forms and shapes following behind.

These were camels which had once stood ready to make long journeys across boundless, spreading deserts where the sand-dunes rose like waves; journeys during which they would tread the sand slowly, or kick it up at high speed. Camels that had once leaned on the sand, and knelt down, ready to be mounted by their owners who wore deep green or blue or yellow turbans. Camels which might have carried, occasionally, the owner's new bride in her long skirt of *arakku*-red, maroon, or rose-pink sewn with spangles, her choli which only covered her breasts and left her back bare, and her gold-embellished head-piece. Or on certain evenings, walking at a leisurely pace, their feet buried in the sand, they might have carried their owners' children whose hair was bleached red by the sun and who grew up on camel's milk. Camels which had then been brought to Bombay by a Ram Singh or a Lakhan Singh who was struggling to make a living there. Which were driven off in three or four years, when they were exhausted. Which would then begin to walk the tarred roads aimlessly. They would walk constantly, as if they had embarked upon a long journey. And would die at last of hunger, or when they were run over by a lorry.

In the street light, it looked as if it were standing there with its dry, wide eyes, and torn nose with clotted blood underneath, gazing back at her. Could this be a rogue camel which had obstinately refused to walk along the sea-beach? It stood there like a Surpanaka, whose nose had been broken by an epic hero because she had dared to reveal her love.

How convenient a nostril is, for piercing and for threading a rope through! Like that folk tale from oral tradition. In a forest there lived a woman who was independent, under no one's control, and who wandered about at her own will and pleasure. Later on, a man— when they tell this tale, they describe him as a great warrior and a

man of great prowess—put a ring through her nose, subdued her,
and dragged her home. Sometime later, she began to wear the same
ring as an ornament.

Once she had gone past the road, carefully negotiating its
undulations and potholes, her hand rose and touched her own nose.
Just for an instant. She too wore a nose-stud. A jewel embossed with
eight diamonds. It had been made in a hurry, after her father had
decided upon a bridegroom from Tamil Nadu for her, a girl born
and brought up in Singapore. A week before the wedding, the demand
had come from her prospective in-laws, couched as a request, for a
nose-jewel of some kind. Her father had frowned at her when she
said, 'They only said *a nose-jewel*, Appa. Just have something made
for *his* nose.' The first piercing of a needle she received in Tamil
Nadu, was to her nose. How the diamonds sparkle against her
beautiful, dark nose, everyone had said.

After she saw the camel, she informed the Society for the Prevention
of Cruelty to Animals many times, and asked them to look after it.
After that, it was not to be seen for some time. And then one day she
came upon it again. As soon as she entered the street, she saw the
crowds gathered there. When she stopped her scooter and looked
about her, she saw it sitting there amidst the wild plants and bushes.
Its entire hide was wrinkled and had gone dark; as if it could be
peeled away, it hung loose, not touching its bones. Heaven knew
what pain it felt within, for once every few seconds it shuddered and
raised a terrible grunt. Some people said they had informed both the
SPCA and the fire-brigade. It refused to drink, although a bucket of
water was put before it. When they brought some dates to its mouth,
it called out feebly. As she was trying to make out whether there were
any familiar faces in the crowd, she caught sight of Yamuna
approaching.

Yamuna was one of those eunuchs who rush forward towards the
crossroads, clap-clapping their hands loudly, when cars stop at traffic
lights, waiting for them to turn green. Eunuchs put their hands right
inside the cars and bless children. They pinch the cheeks of men who
are travelling on their own, and wink at them. If you don't give them
money they will curse you, threatening that a eunuch's curse never
fails. They can also bless you saying you will marry and have children,

and that your family will flourish. Once, when the lights turned red
and she stopped her scooter, she heard that loud hand-clap. Without
turning around, she had spoken in the Bombay fashion, in Marathi,
asking to be forgiven for her inability to give alms.

'What *yakka*, how can you say that,' she heard a voice say, and
turned swiftly around.

'You are Tamil, are you?'

'Yes, yakka. My name is Yamuna. Why don't you give me some
money, Princess?'

'Where's your hometown?'

'Somewhere or the other, yakka. I've landed up here, anyhow,
struggling to survive. Why can't you give me eight annas?'

'Can't you work?'

'Of course we work, yakka. We weave mats. We make chairs and
baskets out of bamboo. But it doesn't bring in enough, you see.'

When she gave her five rupees, Yamuna leaned across, touched her
on the sides of her temples, and then withdrew and cracked her
knuckles against her own temples.

One evening, Yamuna made her stop her scooter and park it along
the kerb. She tapped the cheek of a boy who was roasting heads of
corn and said, 'Here ayya, Arumugam, take a couple of good heads of
corn and roast them for my akka and myself.'

She remonstrated, 'Yamuna, what's this, let me give you the money.'
But the boy stopped her, saying, 'Please don't. She is from my
hometown. We know her and all her family really well. They are a
family of weavers.'

'Yes, 'Ka. I've worked the loom myself, as a child. Along with my
father. Once we had a special order to weave a sari, and the material
for a long skirt. It was I who wove the *paavaadai*. I remember it well,
even now. It was parrot-green with a dark blue border. Usually, with
parrot green there will only be a *kumkumam*-red border. But my
Appa had a special flair in his weaving. When I suggested we should
give it a gold thread motif of mangos, he said, no, make them stars.
He said that stars would look best against that dark blue background.'

Arumugam roasted the heads of corn, smeared them with lime-
juice, and brought them, sprinkled with salt and chilli powder. As
soon as they had finished, Yamuna sent her on her way, saying, 'Make

a start now, yakka. It will get late for you otherwise.' And as soon as she started the scooter, Yamuna slipped away, clap-clapping her hands.

After that, they met occasionally, for a few moments. As her scooter sped along, she would hear a call from the side of the street, 'Yakka, Tamil-speaking yakka!' And if she turned round, she would see Yamuna, waving to her enthusiastically.

Now Yamuna approached, striding along with her legs apart. She stopped when she saw the crowds, and gazed at the camel. '*Yamma,*' she exclaimed. When she saw her scooter, she searched for her and said, 'Just look at this terrible thing, yakka!'

At that moment, drops of rain began to fall. The camel shivered all over, as the raindrops fell upon its body. A large drop fell on its nose and slid along its mouth. It made a sound like a sob and fell over on to its side, with a thud. Once, with its legs, it kicked the ground covered with rubbish and faeces. It opened its eyes wide, looked up at the sky, and then closed them again, slowly. Its body gave a great shudder, and then became still.

The crowd began to melt away, saying, 'It's gone', and 'Poor thing'.

In that hoarse voice, special to the eunuchs, Yamuna raised a lament like a traditional funeral *oppari*, lengthening the words and calling them out, 'You brought it here from somewhere far away, and murdered it, you bastards...' That lament rose, piercing its way above the noise of the beating rain which was coming down in large drops now; above the sounds of masala being ground in the small plastic-covered hutments on the pavement while the air filled with a mingled smell of garlic, onion, coriander, and chilli; above the roar of the waves, only a short distance away, as they surged up and then dashed against the rocks at great speed. It rose very slowly, higher and higher, as if entreating the black clouds which had assembled there, 'Proclaim this news, wherever you go. ' And then it merged with the wind.

*Sadangai,* July–September 1995

# Direction

At a street corner in their suburb a gigantic cardboard figure of Rama towered, bending his bow, arrow primed at its target. Along with slogans that said, 'We vow in the name of Rama! We will build his temple in that very place!'

In that particular suburb, there was quite a lot of coming and going of the gods. You might have gone to sleep having looked out over a bare pavement. But by daybreak, a small shrine to Sai Baba might well have come up there, made of marble or mosaic tiles of the kind you usually see in a bathroom. And very likely, an orange flag streaming out from its top. Within two days, there could be a bell there too, and a box for receiving money offerings. Soon after that, a *pujari* may turn up there. Stories might begin to spread, about the miracles wrought by the god of the shrine. The very instant that the shrine is completed, people hurrying to their offices will begin to stop there for half a second, to step out of their *chappals* and touch their cheeks in salutation to the god. Passengers in buses that flash past will touch their cheeks as soon as they glimpse the orange flag, in the certainty that there is a shrine nearby. Just next to some of these new shrines there might well be a rubbish bin, overflowing on to the street, stinking of rotten food and perhaps even carrying the stench of a dead animal. You might well have to hold your nose immediately after touching your cheek. The people who accept the shrine accept the rubbish bin equally. There are some who cite examples from the Gita, and the Puranas in praise of this attitude. Others wonder at God's miracle in creating a nose and a cheek so close beside each other.

Nobody raised any objection to the figure of Rama which appeared at the street corner, forcing everyone to look up. She wasn't all that well acquainted with Rama, though. If ever she had a nightmare as a child, her mother used to tell her to repeat to herself 'Rama–Rama' and go back to sleep. In their home, in the puja room, they had a Ravi Varma print of the coronation of Rama. But as she grew up, there were some aspects of Rama that she began to dislike. She was stung to anger at the notion of Rama, in his original form of Vishnu, lying on the serpent Adisesha, with Lakshmi relegated firmly to his feet. She preferred Shiva. She liked the indifferent and defiant nature of Shiva as he went about smoking *ganja*, wandering as he chose, and dancing his immortal *taandavam*. Then, after she saw the film *Sampurna Ramayanam*, as far as she was concerned, Rama became the actor M.T. Rama Rao. What's more, when she heard T.K. Bhagavati singing as Ravana, '*Ga gamagagari rigaririsa rigaririsarisa nidapadasa*' in Kambodhi Raga, her heart inclined more and more towards the *rakshasa*. She had wept when T.K. Bhagavati sang so sorrowfully in Tilang Raga, 'How can any man say to me:  Leave the battlefield now and come back tomorrow!'

It was by way of mirroring all the thoughts in her mind concerning these matters, that she wrote a story at that time and submitted it to her college magazine. The title of the story was, 'For Lakshmi too, an Adisesha'. It went like this:

The Milk Ocean lay outspread. It was interlaced throughout with blue. Perhaps, before Shiva drank the poison, a few drops had fallen into the sea. It was now the colour of that softer blue which results from mixing white with fierce blue. Lakshmi loved that soft blue. She often mentioned this to Vishnu. He would laugh in reply, and say, 'And I too am known as the Blue One, after all!' Just because others gave him that name, he too called himself Nilavannan, the Blue One. To tell the truth, he was Kannan, the Dark One. If those who liked to play with words chose to describe him as blue, in a poetic mode, should he go and believe it literally? How beautiful his dark skin was, anyway! Like shining black ivory, polished with oil! Dark-coloured one. But this blue that she imagined was different. This was the blue of one's dreams. An unattainable blue. An enigmatic blue.

When she looked around, Vishnu lay stretched out on his right side. She was overcome with weariness. She could not renounce certain memories. In a corner of her mind the Kambodhi sounded on a *vinai*. A melting Kambodhi. A Kambodhi which had put a little life into her as she sat amidst the rakshasis in Asokavana, utterly disheartened. A Kambodhi which a certain person had played to her, when the soles of her feet were cracked, her hands roughened, her skin parched and dried out after her many years in the forest.

They called him a rakshasa. Were those who abandoned a pregnant woman on the shores of the Jamuna to be described as human, then? Her eyes filled with tears.

'Lakshmi...'

She turned around to see. Adisesha was calling her.

'Mm,' she said.

'What has happened to you?'

'Nothing. But just look at the way he is sleeping! Adi, do you remember? I stood there alone, Adi. In front of me the river flowed silently. There was no boatman Guhan to ferry me across. No Hanuman to build me a bridge. Not even a squirrel there. Adi, why did I have to be so alone? I too have swum the waters in the form of a fish. I have been a tortoise, walking about with a heavy shell. I have wandered about as a wild boar. But who knows about my incarnations? They are merely stuck on to his *avatars*. Like appendages. To add colour. To exhilarate. To titillate.'

'You don't talk like a goddess, do you?'

'Goddess! Nonsense! Adi, what has ever happened according to my wish? I wanted to walk through deserts, chatting to Fatima. I wished to take the infant Jesus from Mary's arms, to carry him on my hip, and wander around Bethlehem and its surroundings. What good does it do me to sit here like this, at his feet? Do I at least have a serpent bed to rest upon, stretched out at my ease?'

Adi's heart melted when he heard all this. He created another serpent bed. When Vishnu opened his eyes, Lakshmi lay asleep beside him, on her own serpent bed, her entire body comfortably stretched out.

The editor responsible for the college magazine rejected her story. And it was lost finally, buried under a pile of papers. Her story of Lakshmi sleeping on a serpent bed having been lost, she had a notion that she herself surveyed the world while floating on some sort of serpent bed. Because of this, she didn't take any account of the activities of the gods on the pavement. But when the gods began to interfere in her everyday life, she realized she had to climb down from her serpent bed.

When she decided that she needed exercise, and ought to walk for forty minutes every morning at a brisk pace, she had assumed that all she needed were a pair of trainers for her feet such as sportswomen wore. It was only when she got to the street that she realized that there was only sufficient space on either side if you wanted to seek shelter from the traffic, but nothing like a pavement on which you could walk along swiftly. She realized that it was impossible for her to walk on the street itself, where the traffic rushed past, made up of single and double-decker buses, lorries carrying heavy loads, Marutis and Hondas driven by the children of wealthy daddies as if they were piloting aeroplanes. And so, she had made it her habit to walk along the seashore which was some distance away. At one corner of the seashore were the hutments. The beach was their free toilet. As soon as she got to the beach, she could see people both to the left and the right, squatting down to relieve themselves. Between the two groups was an open space of about a mile, where she took her brisk early-morning walk.

The figure of Rama at the crest of the road made no real impact on her, except for hitting her in the eye as she went past it, sitting in the upper deck of a bus. She brushed the thought of it aside, thinking it was only a wave in the ocean-like Rama-frenzy which swept over the country at that time. Her early-morning walks continued. She rose from her bed as soon as she heard the morning call for prayers from the neighbouring mosque. As she passed the *gurudwara*, a hundred paces after she left her apartment-building, she saw a white-bearded old man, his eyes closed, seated in front of the Guru Granth Sahib laid open on its lectern. Another ten paces, and when she turned to the right, there was the road leading to the beach.

After the destruction of the Babri Masjid on the sixth of December, the entire nature of her walks changed. She walked twenty kilometres through the areas affected by religious riots in a procession for inter-religious harmony. She walked another ten kilometres for the sake of peace in the suburbs. Walks such as these. At the end of the procession for peace in the suburbs, a feast had been arranged in the spacious grounds of a school. A high-ranking police officer had been invited. He made a speech to the effect that to promote communal harmony, all Hindus and Muslims should meet together and share each other's food. Nothing else was necessary, he said. Everyone was surprised and delighted that communal harmony meant no more than this. The feast was delicious. And everyone ate well.

After that a mike was produced so that people could make speeches and arrive at a few decisions. A number of people spoke. One man said that his company would help to plant trees in that suburban area. Another declared that public toilets should be built and the beach cleaned up. When yet another started to put forward the view that the sea became polluted because of plastic bags full of puja flowers, coconut, and prasadam which were thrown into it, several people there protested that there was no need to mention this.

The police officer had been friendly, and she had spoken to him earlier about the sudden proliferation of shrines and orange flags, and also about the Rama figures with their threatening slogans. When the mike came near her, a friend whispered into her ear, 'Just speak about the environment; that will be quite enough.' At once, the thoughts that she had been focusing upon scattered away, and she only said into the mike, in a feeble voice, 'The rubbish bins ought to be kept clean.' Instantly, someone added, 'Women should come forward and take responsibility in this matter.' She retorted somewhat hotly that since there was neither male nor female in the matter of rubbish, everyone should take responsibility for keeping the place clean. The man proclaimed loudly, 'Oh, a feminist! A feminist in our midst!' Then he added dramatically, 'Please forgive me, Madam.' Everyone laughed at this.

Eventually, it was agreed that what that area most needed was an ambulance van, and a collection was made, quickly and efficiently. And with the practical decision that arrangements should be made for a cholera immunization scheme to begin the very next week, the meeting to promote communal harmony came to an end.

After some days, she began her walks once again. In the early morning many people could be seen, usually walking or jogging, slowly or at a brisk pace. It was the normal practice to greet whoever came towards you with a nod or a smile, or by saying 'Namaste', 'Good morning', or—if it were someone who had lived in the north for a long time—'Jairamji ki'. But now it seemed to her that the manner of greeting had changed. Instead of the usual 'Jairamji ki', some people seemed to roar out, 'Jai Sriram'.

When she reached the beach she found a group of people seated there, singing the bhajan, *'Hari bol, Hari bol, Hari-Hari bol; Mukunda Madhava Govinda bol'*. A couple of days later, another group settled themselves down a little further off and began to sing Christian hymns. After a week, five or six Muslim youths were seen walking about, singing something or the other. If she kept her distance from all these, she was forced to walk right next to the people who were defecating.

She remembered then that some distance away there was a small housing settlement with narrow streets and dense coconut trees. There would not be the nuisance of heavy traffic there either. After she had walked in those parts for a couple of days in peace and quiet, on the third day a dog growled at her through the still, unbroken darkness and she stumbled and fell down. Just then someone came towards her, calling out, 'Ei, Kalu, Kalu!' He looked at her as she was trying to scramble to her feet and said, 'This dog guards our street. Have you started walking here just recently?'

'Yes,' she replied in a low voice, rising to her feet. 'I started coming here some days after the Babri Masjid was destroyed.'

'That's what I thought. This dog won't attack anyone who is a regular walker here,' he told her. Then he walked on, warning the dog with a sharp, 'Kalu, no!'

After he had gone, she suddenly remembered the face that she had not so far recognized in the semi-darkness. It was the gentleman who had spoken about the environment with such urgency, and had put forward the proposal about the cholera immunizations.

The dog stood some distance away, looking at her and growling. Impossible to determine whether that low growl was friendly or hostile.

*Sadangai,* April–June 1996

# Glow

Squirrels as large as bandicoots were running about in Madrid's Retiro Park. These were not small mouse-like squirrels, grey in colour, with three lines smeared on their backs, said to be the touch and stroke of Rama's fingers. They were dark brown squirrels, their backs unlined, and they had fat, bushy tails. Squirrels which were not afraid in the least, but who stood opposite you and stared, lifting up their tails. People had told her about the rose garden in the corner of the park, which she would find a little further on, once the squirrels let her pass.

It was not the season for roses. There was yet a month to go before they would be in full bloom. When she set out to walk towards the garden which was still waiting for its roses, a drop of rain splashed against her cheek. In front of her, the squirrel which had been examining a nut was startled, and gave a quick leap. As she looked at the squirrel and laughed, the rain began to descend in fine needles. A gently stroking rain. At each step, a strand of raindrops glided past her head, ears, eyes, and hands. In her path, the squirrel, leapt about and surveyed the nuts that lay scattered there.

Wherever she went, she arrived well before the season for which that place was best known. Or sometimes, when the season was well past. Sometimes she saw trees and plants which were just thinking about blossoming; sometimes she saw them resting after they had bloomed; sometimes she saw the flowers that had fallen after a tempest or a sudden whirlwind. People might comment, 'If you had come in the right season, you might have played in the snow or made snowmen.' Or, 'You might have seen this flower. You might have seen the leaves of this tree steeped in different colours.' Even as they said this, sometimes there would be a sudden drizzle. They would say in surprise, 'Hey, what is this? Why this unseasonable rain?'

Unseasonable rain wasn't new to her, though. She had grown up with the story of a sudden fire when Tansen sang the Dipak Raga; the story of rain pelting down when Dikshitar said 'Varshya'; the story of Rishya Sringar; of the immediate arrival of rain when the virtuous women of Kural called it down. There was the further burden of images from the cinema when Nature becomes frenzied, and tempestuous rain falls at every crisis in a woman's life. Coming from a country where floods and famines followed each other, she was prepared to accept anything that was unseasonable or unusual. All she looked for were only small miracles. The miracle of water flowing out as soon as a tap is turned. Light coming on at the touch of an electric switch. Buses turning up as soon as she went to the bus depot. An electric train arriving on time. Being able to find a place on it. The telephone beginning to operate as soon as a rupee coin was thrust into the slot. The miracle of there being no stones in the rice. The miracle of milk not being watered.

She thought she could surely accept the yet unflowering rose garden and the unexpected rain. More strands of raindrops. Next to her, the squirrel leaping. It bounded forward for some distance, then stopped, as if waiting to show her the way. In between, a frantic ascent up a tree; then a descent. As soon as she drew near, another leap forward, with lifted tail.

It was a spacious park. She could hear it all at a distance: parents with their children, young boys and girls rushing about on their bicycles, the noise and bustle of people participating in Sunday games and performances, loud shouts from everyone greeting the sudden rain. The sounds rose and fell. Along the path leading to the rose garden, herself and a madly enthusiastic, fat squirrel. Just a little distance away, a bower covered with creepers: the entrance to the rose garden.

Accepting the strands of raindrops, she walked towards the bower, then stood underneath it, looking at the garden. Spreading into the distance were the yet unflowered rose plants and bushes. On one side were the grafted bushes. Creepers trained over trellises. Soft rustling of leaves, touched by the breeze on its quest for the scent of roses.

When she left the protection of the bower and walked on into the garden, once again she felt the falling rain. The squirrel had bounded away, elsewhere. She walked on, touching the leaves of the rose plants. As she followed the little pathways into the garden, she noticed a cement bench. She sat down on it. All around here were the rose bushes, dense as a wall. The rain continued to pelt down. Her face was awash with rain water. Her body cool and wet.

All of a sudden, the squirrel appeared in front of her, leaping, its tail lifted. With a leap and jump, it sat on the edge of the bench. Was it the same squirrel, or another? It was the very same colour. The same bushy tail. Why had it come to her? But why did she need to know this? A squirrel with a bushy uplifted tail sat next to her. That was all. No need to go any deeper than that. No need to disturb the roots. It was all evident to her eyes. If everything were to be turned into the beanstalk that Jack climbed, she might encounter the giant at the end. This. Now. This squirrel. She. This alone was real. The rain was real. The coolness was real.

By chance her glance fell on two people seated at another bench, some distance away. A young woman and a young man, seated sideways, gazing at each other. Their hands were clasped together. They sat there without making a movement. Their eyes were joined. The rain drenched them, falling on their heads and dripping down their faces. Their hair was wet and clung to them. Hers was heavy dark hair. Upon it, the raindrops were pearls. His was fine, feathery, honey-coloured; touching the back of his neck. Her thin dress, covered with a pattern of tiny blossoms, was drenched, sticking to her body. His trousers of coarse material, and his shirt with its flashy yellow flowers, were wet and tight against him. They were there in the rose garden. And they were not there.

Slowly. Very slowly. Her hand lifted and brushed the hair that was touching his cheek, to one side. As soon as her fingers touched him, he was startled and stunned for an instant, then pressed her hand against his neck with his face. He looked at her, his face aslant. She smiled. Then she laid her other hand upon his shoulder. They moved without haste, without tension, without over-eagerness. With patience, as if they had waited a long time for this; as if they had a long time in front of them. As if the rain and the wind that had touched the leaves of the rose plants had directed them, they moved in accordance with the wind and the rain, surrounded by the rose bushes.

She sat opposite them, within visible distance, the squirrel by her side, its eyes wide open as if in astonishment.

Scattering in all eight directions
*taka dheemtarikada dheemtarikida dheemtarikida...*

The rhythm of Bharati's line ran through her mind. Like a streak of lightning.

The rain came pelting down. She stood up. The squirrel ran, bounding along the ground, and climbed up a tree. She walked on, her body receiving the falling rain, and when she turned around at the last of the rose bushes, the two were clasped together. When a ray of sunshine fell upon them, ignoring the rain, the raindrops upon their bodies glowed suddenly.

# First Poems

She had made every possible effort to achieve wisdom. Ramakrishna Paramahamsa once said that those who wept continuously for three days would see God. So, although it was impossible for her to weep incessantly (for how could anything be pursued continuously in a house where they did not have a separate room each, a house where either her mother's rules or her father's voice drove her the moment she woke up until she fell asleep at night?), she had wept intermittently over six days. Yet no god had granted her a vision. Of course, she was disappointed. She didn't know what else a sixteen-year-old girl, who went about seeking wisdom, could do. She didn't understand anything clearly, anymore.

She believed she had not committed a single sin. But then, she wasn't sure whether some of her actions could perhaps be identified as sins. Once, when they were little, when she and her elder sister were given a slice of watermelon each, she hadn't eaten hers immediately. She had waited until Padma finished, and only then begun to lick her own piece of fruit. Then, when Padma pleaded, 'Ei, give me some, *di*,' she had retorted, 'Won't!', the fruit juice dripping down her face. Another time, she had scolded her mother silently, calling her, 'Saniyane'. Once, she imagined that her mother—who admonished her all the time to comb her hair, practise singing, drink up her milk, eat, sleep, and massage herself with oil—had suddenly dropped dead, leaving her orphaned. Once she had even read a 'bad' book three times over, before thrusting it into the fire which heated water in their bathroom. She wasn't sure how all these actions would be judged and accounted. If Chitragupta, in the attire of ancient kings, still kept the record of good and evil deeds for Yama, was there some other trustworthy individual who advised him about changing times? Especially about how greatly women had changed? Such questions often arose in her mind.

It was during this time, when she was seeking after wisdom in this way, and making every effort to redeem herself and the world, that the large-sized blue diary arrived at their house. Someone had given it to their family doctor, who passed it on to them. A diary produced by Nestlé and Company, which manufactured milk powder for babies. A diary full of photographs of mothers and infants, accompanied by notes intended for obstetricians.

She believed firmly that the arrival of a diary, which was connected with the creation of physical life, at a time when she herself was immersed in thoughts of life's transience, was a means by which God was testing her own steadfastness. 'So, stomach-ache for one *bhakta*, and a diary meant for obstetricians for me? Hm!' she said to herself, marvelling at the tribulations sent by God. She went into the puja room, looked directly at the Ravi Varma paintings of the gods ranged there, and smiled wisely. She had borrowed that wise smile from the actress Madhubala's lopsided simper. It seemed to her that when that smile appeared on her face, it filled it with light. But for certain reasons, she avoided displaying it in public. One reason could be that Amma, on seeing it, had asked once, 'What's the matter, do you have a toothache?' But then, how could people who lacked a passion for wisdom recognize the true nature of such a smile?

The blue colour of the diary was particularly attractive to her. She loved blue. Because the sky is blue. The sea is blue. The two-foot tall, flute-playing image of Kannan from Panrutti was blue too. She had a paavaadai of blue silk, as well. But because it was so much a part of this worldly life, she never included it as a reason for loving blue. Since the blue diary lay around, unused by anyone in the family, she appropriated it for herself.

When she sat in front of it and turned over its smooth, blank pages, she was suddenly filled with the desire to do what so many bhaktas had done before her. The desire to write poems of devotion. A couple of days later, she made an effort and wrote a poem with the title, 'Where is God?'

> Ask not where God is, innocent one;
> there in your own heart is God engraved!

The poem ended with these words and an exclamation mark. She wrote some more poems in pleading tones, asking that she should not be forsaken, and that she should be accepted as a bhakta. It struck her that her verses did not at all compare with the poetry of Tevaram, Tiruvasagam, and Tirupugazh. She was somewhat saddened by this. But a little angry as well. In their quest for wisdom, those poets had wandered everywhere, night and day, through forests, mountains, and fields. How could a sixteen-year-old girl, living in a city beset by thieves and full of dangers, wander about with the same ease? If she wished, she could wander about the garden that surrounded their house. She didn't have permission, anyway, to go much further on her own. Just because she had gone to see the film *Pasamalar* with her friends, Amma had upbraided her, saying the times were going from bad to worse, and that she did not approve of such outings.

Besides, for those bhaktas of old, God was a refuge and help at all times. He had turned fox into horse, horse into fox, carried sand on his head for a payment of *pittu*, and cooperated with them in all sorts of ways. But as far as she was concerned, it seemed that God wasn't being quite fair. He hadn't produced any miracle on her behalf. Not a single one. Couldn't he have worked even a tiny miracle, such as giving her the answer to a mathematical problem? This, for instance: a train is approaching at such and such a speed, another comes from the opposite direction at a different speed, at what distance do they cross each other? Or this: a bucket has a hole in it, and water is falling into it at a certain speed; at what rate will the water flow out, and when will the bucket be full? And not just that. When he could perfectly well feed a crying baby with the milk of wisdom so that it would write marvellous poems, why was he denying her the same milk of wisdom just because she was born in a country that was independent, in a town called Coimbatore, in a mosquito-infested hospital?

Whenever her thoughts ran in this direction, she would remind herself that a miracle had indeed happened in her life, just once. Her father believed strongly that girls could never be good at science and maths. She didn't quite know how he contrived to plant this idea firmly in her own mind. At any rate, she was hopeless at maths. At a mid-term examination once, they had been set a really complicated sum involving fractions. Even Stella, the only person in her class who

usually managed to get cent per cent marks in maths, couldn't deal
with it. The maths teacher had awarded them all zeros, and was just
about to demonstrate the sum on the blackboard. At that moment,
she glanced accidentally at her own answer paper. She had done the
sum correctly! Even the maths teacher, who had checked everything
twice over, had been amazed. She looked upon that incident as nothing
short of a miracle ordained by Shiva. She had rebuked him fondly,
'All right, so you've done the multiple fractions sum. Tomorrow we'll
be given the science question paper. Let's see how you deal with that.'
But Shiva didn't pass the science exam on that occasion.

Just at that time, their music teacher was teaching her and her
sister Padma the song, '*Vaaranamaayiram suzha valam vandu...
Surrounded by a thousand elephants he comes in procession.*' The
idea that a girl should marry no one other than God fascinated her.
At the same time they were learning about Akkamahadevi in their
Kannada lessons. Mahadeviakka too, had renounced everything for
the sake of Shiva. It struck her, though, that there might be a few
problems in accepting God as one's husband, when it actually came
to practice. In the first place, she was scared to think in what form
the gods might actually manifest themselves, even if they looked so
beautiful as statues, and in the paintings by Ravi Varma. In the second
place, it was N.T. Rama Rao who took the roles of Rama and Shiva in
the cinema, in those days. Suppose, after she had given herself up to
God, he then knocked on her door in the shape of Rama Rao? The
thought confused her. Very well, she could become an Avvaiyaar,
singing, '*Paalum theli thenum...* Milk and clear honey...' in the voice
of K.P. Sunderambal. But she was reluctant to pray for the gift of old
age, just yet. Somewhere in the corner of her mind, that blue silk
paavaadai unfurled, teasing her. Besides, she had made her mother
promise to buy her a parrot-green silk paavaadai for the coming
Deepavali.

But in spite of all this, she wasn't prepared to forsake her quest for
wisdom entirely. They had, in their house, a bound version of Kalki's
serial, *Sivakami's Oath*. She was extremely taken with the ending of
the novel. She wrote a poem about going to Chidambaram, dancing
in the presence of Shiva, and marrying him. She entitled it 'Truth'.
Tears welled up in her eyes as she wrote the last lines:

The incantation of your ankle-bells
ringing tirelessly among the gathered sages,
when you dance in Chidamabaram, having slain the demon,
I shall come to you, seeking refuge.

There were only two with whom she shared her poems and her feeling for God. One was Mickey, their black dog. The other was Kempamma. Kempamma was employed in the handicrafts and cottage industry which went on next door. Because she had no place to stay, she came to live in the empty motor-shed in the back of their house, bringing her tin trunk. She made herself useful to Amma in all sorts of ways.

Mickey was her friend. When she read out her poems to him, he would bury his face in his forepaws, and listen to her as he lay there, his ears drooping. Sometimes, he would lie down with his head on her lap as he listened, his eyes closed. Whenever her voice deepened with emotion, he would lift his head and look at her. It was under her bed that he slept.

She used to explain her poems in Kannada to Kempamma. Kempamma would listen patiently, and then give her certificate of approval: 'It's good.' Then she would sing Purandaradasa's Devar Nama lyrics in a very simple style.

Then it happened. That incident, one night. One night, at about eleven, they heard a voice yelling from somewhere behind their house, 'Ei, sule munde... Ei, you whore.' Within the next five minutes, Kempamma had suddenly burst open the back door which was not yet locked, flown inside the house like a whirlwind, and sought shelter under her bed.

When her parents went to the back door, they saw a man standing there, completely drunk. He shouted out, 'Ei Kempamma horage baare ... Ei, Kempamma, come outside.' He bawled out in Kannada, 'I am your husband. Out you come.'

When Appa tried to drive him off, he looked at him in fury and shrieked, 'Isn't one wife enough for you? You want mine as well, do you?'

Under her bed, Kempamma cowered like a terrified chicken. She was trembling from head to foot. But when she heard her husband's obscene words, she came out of her hiding place, went towards him with dragging feet, and said to him in Kannada, her voice betraying just a tremor, 'Don't talk a lot of drunken nonsense.'

In reply he gave her a kick in the stomach. When she sank down, screaming, 'Amma,' he hit her on her back.

'*Deva kaappaadu...* O God, help me,' Kempamma called out. Then thinking perhaps that it was wrong to summon God familiarly, in the singular, she called out again, '*Devaré kaappaadi.*'

He pushed her across the back steps and rolled her over them, tugging her by the hair. As soon as she tumbled to the bottom of the steps, he shoved her on to the lawn, parted her legs in an instant, and kicked her violently in between.

'Ha...,' screamed Kempamma, collapsing. It was *paurnami* at the time, the night of the full moon. The back garden was blooming on all sides with *arali*, *tulasi*, plantain, beans, snake-gourd, jackfruit. Moonlight fell in flakes, scattered over all this. In that light, Kempamma lay crouched and shrunken upon the lawn, like a hunted animal. Each second she called out yet again, 'Devaré... Devaré.' At last when he stamped hard into her ribcage, for the first time she raised the cry, 'Mickey!'

From within, Mickey came streaking out with the speed of lightning. Jumping higher and higher as he ran, with leaps and bounds, Mickey came running. He cleared the back steps in one vault, and lunged towards Kempamma's husband's throat. The man darted here and there in sheer terror, and finally hurtled across the back garden fence and fled.

Kempamma still lay face down upon the lawn, sobbing. Mickey went up to her and stood by her side, licking her head. Amma and Appa stood where they were, frozen and speechless. It had all happened within ten minutes.

Padma-akka and she were standing a little distance behind.

When her mother turned round and looked at her, she became aware of herself as a different person.

Amma looked at her and said in a low voice, 'Why did you come here? These things will horrify you.'

But she stood gazing at the back garden without making a reply.

For some time she wrote poems with titles such as 'Loneliness', 'Yearning', 'Dream', and 'Silence', with lines like, 'Loneliness until death; loneliness until the body burns away'. After that, there were no more poems recorded in the blue diary.

*Kizhakkum Merkkum,* 1997

# Parasakti and Others in a Plastic Box

Spreading out some rice mixed with ghee on the window-sill, and giving it a sharp tap with the back of her spoon, Amma called to the crows in Telugu, 'Krishna, raa.' What was so special about Telugu remained a mystery. Though Dhanam's father was transferred often, and to such different places as Assam, Ahmedabad, Orissa, and Bangalore, Amma's language to the crows never changed. Even in faraway Assam, the crows came flocking to her, as soon as she called, 'Krishna, raa.' Perhaps crows are united in this matter of language. Amma had taught this very same language signal to everyone who was close to her. Even Dhanam's younger brother Dinakaran's American wife's child by her first husband called out to the crows, 'Krishna, raa,' whenever he came to India. The window-sill her base, and scorning all border disputes, Amma had established for herself a world where crows recognized no difference among states and nations.

Yet, sometimes it seemed to Dhanam that although it appeared to encompass only these small things—a drop of ghee, a spoonful of rice, and a window-sill—Amma's space wasn't just contained there. She imagined that the tapping of the spoon against the window-sill drew to it everything that happened outside that window, too. It would seem to her that her mother's space wasn't confined to a single identifiable shape, but was ever spreading outward.

Dhanam's elder sister Bharati's marriage had taken her to America, and then ended in divorce. Bharati was devastated by this. She was greatly distressed; overcome by panic, fear, and shame. Every time she took a step, she felt as if there was no firm ground beneath her feet. Amma agreed to their father's plea, boarded a plane, and went to her daughter's aid. Ten days later, a long letter arrived from Bharati.

'Dhanam, Amma has arrived here. Two days after she came, the inland airline company on which she travelled telephoned, harassing her to accept a contract to make wild-lime pickle for them. Apparently, Amma declared it at the customs' examination. They must have tasted it as a check. As if this weren't enough, on the fourth day, when I came home from work, I saw that she had just finished stirring up some *paal-kova*, which she had made out of a couple of litres of milk. When I asked her about it, she said that she had seen three pregnant women in the neighbourhood. The paal-kova would be good for their health. Then she dragged me along with her, explained to them that these were milk-sweets, pointed out that they contained saffron, and left me to enlarge on the many wonders wrought by saffron for both mothers and children. (Amma has brought a small container of high quality saffron with her. She hasn't explained, to date, why she felt obliged to bring it. It's exactly like the lack of answers to questions about the wild-lime pickle.) Now I'm terrified that these women will invite her to be present when they give birth.

'There's plenty of sunshine here. I can guess that Amma's hands are itching to make *vadagam*. Do you remember how, in Bangalore, she used to wear a hat against the sun, and squeeze out vadagam? How she used to leave us both on guard, with an open umbrella tied to a stone beside us, to frighten away the crows? Do you remember how we used to imagine that we were like Valli and her friends when they were chasing the birds away, in that old play from Independence times, '*Valli's Wedding*'; and how we used to sing, 'O white, white storks'? What Independence struggle did we see; what after all did we understand by '*aalolam*'? It was that song that Amma taught us, wasn't it, that went, "You sparrows who come from elsewhere, who squat upon our land and peck at our fields, despoiling India..."? How furious we used to get as we sang those words! Even today, it seems to me, if Amma were to make vadagam, we could sing the same song with the World Bank and the International Monetary Fund in mind.

'My window here doesn't have a sill. I've put in a wooden attachment, though, to hold flower-pots. Amma lays out rice there, and calls, "Krishna, raa" every day. How can there be crows here? But from the second day, the squirrels began to arrive. Now, as soon as they hear the sound of the spoon tapping, they turn up, big as bandicoots. Amma's friends. Even amongst these, she's looking out for a couple of pregnant ones. Maybe she'll mix a herbal potion into their rice, who knows? When I think about it, it seems to me that this coded language in which Amma speaks to crows and squirrels is actually one which binds the earth and sky together. In a strange way, it's like *vajram*, cementing us together and keeping us from withering away.

'Amma hasn't asked me a single word about Kumarasamy. Nor has she spoken about the divorce. She carries on with her own business, making mustard seasonings, fragrant with ghee. If I am gazing out of the window, she nags at me to come and grind a chutney in the blender. Or, she will explain to me at length how a *poriyal* of finely chopped banana flowers, when soaked in buttermilk and cooked with a well-ground masala of onion, ginger, cumin seeds, and coconut, is very good for the health. How is this information useful to me here, in this town, where banana flowers are not to be found? But all the same, Dhanu, the backyard of Paatti's house in Coimbatore spreads out in my mind. How many banana trees stood there! In the front courtyard, by the threshold, there were traveller's palms with fan-shaped leaves. Do you remember that photograph of the two of us, sitting on the *thinnai* there? I can see it even now, my narrow face, hair combed flat, plaited with a fibre-ribbon and taken over my shoulder; all my teeth showing in a grin. I often wonder about the eucalyptus sapling that we planted together before *Thaatha* sold the house, and whether the present owners have let it grow and not cut it down.

'When I asked her to come and take care of me, I never imagined she'd create all these jobs for herself with the speed of a whirlwind. In a street close by, where they sell Indian groceries, there's a shop run by a Tamil. Amma has had a couple of conversations with him already, about Tamil Nadu politics. She is trying to break up the everyday routine and discipline that I need so much for my work. She irritates me no end. She makes me yell, "Amma, leave me alone!". All the same—you won't believe this—I've gained a whole kilo in just these ten days.

'Day before yesterday, when I came home Amma was singing "*Dikku theriyaada kaattil...* In the forest where I cannot find my way". After expanding on the line, "Flowers like fragrant embers in the heart", when she came to the words, "Weary of limb I sank down to the ground", Dhanu, I leaned against the door and wept. You sang that very song at school, at the Bharati song-competition, wagging your head and shaking your two plaits, this way and that.

'We went to visit the Sivanesans who work at the University here, at their home. During the conversation, Amma discovered that Tilakam Sivanesan's mother was her childhood friend Shenbagam from Vilaatthikulam. It seems Shenbagam's family were very much involved with the Self Respect Movement. Amma then sang the Bharatidasan song she used to sing with Tilakam's mother, "Rise up, you noble Tamil women, like many moons in a single sky! Arise and make good the humiliation to your finest heritage, the Tamil language!" Tilakam was completely overwhelmed. It seems that her mother died when Tilakam was still a child. She was so moved, and kept saying over and over again that she had not known all this about her mother.

"All the same, my mother has kept her belief in God," I told her.

"Amma, do you go in for elaborate *pujai* and all that?" Tilakam asked.

"I've only brought four idols or so in a small plastic box," Amma said in reply.

'When you open Amma's plastic box, you'll find a small Amman, a Sivalingam, Ganapati, Murugan, a baby Krishna on all fours, and some other gods. I really don't know, Dhanu, whether she has come here as a woman on her own, or whether she has rolled up the whole world and brought it with her in her bag.'

Once Bharathi was connected again to the squirrels, to the minutiae of her neighbours' lives, to food tasting of salt and tamarind and chilli, and to the Tamil songs that she had totally forgotten, their mother returned home. It was only later that they realized that she had actually met and spoken to Kumarasamy. Some members of his family came one day to bring back various pieces of jewellery, silver vessels, and such things. Amma served them an elaborate meal and sent them on their way. When Dhanam asked her, 'Why, Amma, did you ask them to return all this, then?', she retorted, 'All this belongs to Bharathi, doesn't it? Didn't we give it to her for her own use?'

Nobody spoke about Kumarasamy after that. A couple of years later, when Bharathi came home, having married a Gujarati, Amma gave her the jewellery. She sold the silver vessels, and gave her the money, to spend in India.

As Dhanam watched her mother calling to the crows, Amma turned round and came towards her.

'Have you eaten, Dhanam?'

'I ate a dosai at the restaurant before I came. I didn't actually plan to come here. That's why.'

Amma sat down to eat. Once she had begun eating, Dhanam asked her, 'What have you decided, Ma?'

Amma was quiet for a while. A month had gone by since Appa died. The owners of the house kept on asking for it to be vacated.

'Tell me, Ma.'

'What can I say? Your father left me in this state. How much I nagged him to build our own house! He always said, "Why do we want such a headache." Now he has left me to struggle alone, without a place of my own...'

'Why do you say that, Amma? You must stay only with Bharathi and with me. You can go occasionally to Dinakaran, if you want to.'

'That's a fine thing. When you yourself are having such a difficult...' she dragged the words out, hesitantly.

Dhanam's husband Sudhakar had tried to set up a business, and had overreached himself. There had been a huge loss, to the extent that all their savings were gone. It was this that Amma meant.

'That's nothing, Amma. I will take you home and look after you,' Dhanam told her.

'I didn't say no, now, did I? Do I need a mansion or a palace, after all? Rice for one meal, rice-water for the next, that's it. It is love that is important, *di*.'

'Don't all your things have to be packed?' asked Dhanam.

'What things do I have, di? I'll just put my four deities into a plastic box, and be ready to leave.'

But it was only when Dhanam and Sudhakar came to help her pack, having taken a couple of days' leave, that certain matters became clear. Everything that Amma possessed had a story: the shiny, dark red stone with stripes which she had picked up in Haridwar before Bharathi was born, the frying-pan that she had bought for eight *annas* when Bharathi was just one year old, the tiered standing-lamp with her name, Kumuda, etched on it, which had been presented to her when she visited her parents for the first time after her wedding. She went round and round the house in vain, unable to decide what to keep and what to throw away. It didn't look as if she would get rid of anything, easily—not the chest of drawers with a mirror that she had brought away after Paatti died, nor the dolls that Bharathi, Dhanam, and Dinakar had stored away, nor the bound volumes of serialized stories, nor the green trunk full of letters, nor the recipes for Siddha medicines and the cookery notes that she still collected. Like the rakshasa who would die if you crushed the bee that was hidden in a small box and placed in the hollow of a tree across the seven seas, Amma's very life was buried in each and every one of these things.

Dhanam and Sudhakar made a few quick decisions. For the time being, they rented a car-shed that was not in use, two houses away, and deposited all Amma's things there, carefully. And after that, Amma came to stay in Dhanam's house with seven or eight pieces of luggage—including the plastic box—and her vinai. That vinai had been packed with care every time Appa was transferred. A vinai that had been bought for Amma in Andhra, when she was only six years old. A vinai carved out of dark wood. She had made a cover for it out of an old sari, to keep it free of dust. There was not enough space in Dhanam's house for it to lie horizontally as it should. They had to lean it upright against a wall, supported by a piece of wood.

Amma looked for a suitable place, in Dhanam's atheistic household, to open her plastic box. In the end, the box with Amman and the other deities climbed on to one of a set of shelves intended for books, which they had fixed behind a door.

One evening, a week later, Dhanam sat close to the table at a window writing a letter, while watching the parrots as they alternately flew about or settled down on the fruit tree outside.

'Bharathi, Amma has come to my house now. But she is not at peace. There isn't the fuss and excitement of preparing meals every day, here. Until he can decide on what to do next, Sudhakar is mostly at home. Some bread and an egg, and his meal is done. At the most he'll make a *kichidi* with rice, dal, and vegetables all cooked together, and eat that. The regular cooking is only for Amma. A couple of times she tried to insist that Sudhakar should eat. Then one day I said to her, "Amma, Sudhakar will cook for himself whatever he needs. Leave him to his own ways. We must allow each other that much freedom, Ma."'

'"Is that what you call freedom? I can't understand it," she fretted.'

'As soon as she arrived, she was anxious to make all those things like rasam and sambar powders before the monsoons set in. Now, look, within one week, all these powders are ready in my house. And there are still three months to go before the beginning of the rains! Day before yesterday she went and bought a quantity of limes, chopped them up, and made salt pickle and hot pickle in two separate lots. Ginger *murabha* and ginger pickle have also been prepared. Because of something that I said casually during the course of conversation, she went out in the hot sun, bought a lot of greens, which she has now cleaned and kept ready. She thinks that we have to do so much thinking for our jobs and such, so she has boiled up some oil with hibiscus flowers in it, for massaging our heads. In anticipation of Sandhya's holidays from the Rishi Valley school, she has made fried snacks and packed them in a tin. Meanwhile, all sorts of divisions have been established in our house: good water (which Amma has collected) and ordinary water (which we have collected); vessels in which meat and eggs have been cooked, and vessels in which they have not; Amma's plates and our plates.'

'Of course, the plastic box for the gods is quite a small one. But within three days, this matter of Amma's pujai has expanded, spilling along the wooden plank beneath, accompanied by a brass pot, a plate for the camphor offering, a decorative *kolam* pattern, incense sticks, sandalwood paste, *kumkumam*, and flowers. Her jobs in connection with the gods keep on increasing: scrubbing them with tamarind and bathing them; offering them milk and raisins; dressing Amman in different skirts and *davanis*, and decorating her with sandalwood and kumkumam. The little girl from next door is roped in, because the milk and raisin *prasadam* needs a recipient. Then, because the little girl's mother's sister-in-law doesn't have any babies, Amma has to prepare a Siddha medicine for her. When Lingamma's husband, from the house opposite to us, has a headache, she'll grind up a mixture of dried ginger and pepper in milk, at nine o'clock at night.'

'Amma's gods can be contained in a small plastic box, it is true. She can pick up that box and fly wherever she chooses. But in order to return, she needs a place which contains the brass vessels etched with her name, Kumuda; her teakwood cabinet; her bureau with its wire-mesh doors; a place with window-sills. A place with a jasmine bower and a snake-gourd vine; a place where her vinai can be laid as it should be, horizontally. She might sing that Thevaram which begins, "Forsaking all other attachments, on your sacred feet alone my mind is intent". But Amma is one who is deeply bound to the earth. Even though she might float free like cotton-wool, she'll always feel the need to touch the earth again. Certainly, she could stay either at my house or at yours. But it is bound to be hard for her. She'll tell a thousand little lies: this one to hide that, that to hide this. It's not just that Amma needs a place to live; she must reign indisputably in that space. Because Amma isn't just an individual, she's an institution. Her need is not simply a small space in which she can keep her plastic box. The pity is, she is wandering about seeking after a realm of her own. And if you and I wish to do so, we could give it to her. The jewellery that you and I possess were all given to us by Amma. If we were to sell these, we could give her house back to her. The owners are still trying to sell it. Dinakaran can send her a fixed amount each month. In a couple of months, Sandhya will finish her schooling and come home. She is eager to go and stay with her Paatti. So with many long-term schemes such as learning English so that she can talk to your children, embroidering *salwar-kameez* sets that Sandhya can wear to college, giving music lessons, planning her autobiography, grafting roses, and setting out spinach plots, Amma will live happily in her own house.'

When she had finished writing, she looked up to see her mother seated in the easy-chair, gazing out at the street. The green parrots had ceased their restless flying about and were quiet, hidden among the leaves.

*India Today Annual*, 1994–5

# Vaaganam

There is surely a vehicle to suit each person's individual needs. A *vaaganam* appropriate to their status. A Nandi for Shiva. A peacock for Murugan. A Garuda for Vishnu. A crow for Saniswara, Lord of the inauspicious Saturn. A buffalo for Yama, God of Death. Even pot-bellied Ganesha, although he sits under the *pipal* tree, seldom travelling about, has a mouse so that he may not lack a vehicle. Those goddesses who hang about companionably in their husbands' chariots can't complain either, since they possess their own personal vehicles in any case. Bhagavati has her swan-chariot. Padmasini has her snake-chariot. Maheswari has her *rishaba*, her bull. And Minakshi has her horse. Besides, some of them, when they are not doing anything else, float about on red or white lotuses. Some of the female gods who want to engage in rather more forceful deeds will climb on to a lion and set off, holding on to its mane. But leave aside goddesses. Haven't many queens and princesses, in their time, mounted horses and elephants? There were even some who drove their own chariots. Epic heroines have travelled the skies in their *pushpaka* chariots. In English fairy tales for children, even witches fly about on broomsticks. Bhakyam's desire for a vehicle certainly had all these mythic, Puranic, and epic precedents. All the same, she did not have the good fortune to own one herself.

She could not remember owning any such thing as a tricycle or a pedal-car as a small child. It seems she was only ten months old when she had started walking, even without the help of a baby-walker. When she riffled through the family photograph album, she found photographs of every single boy from their large family, either on a tricycle, or sitting inside a toy motor-car. Of course, there were photographs of her as well. Holding a wooden doll. Or hanging on to the arm of a wooden chair with beautifully embroidered velvet upholstery. That decorative chair had stood as companion to all the females of their family, without distinguishing between young and old. Its back, arms, and legs had all been used by them, depending on how old they were. It was obvious that the family photographer held firmly to the belief that women were incapable of standing up on their own, and without the support of something or the other. Vehicles with wheels stood as companions to the men, from their babyhood. For women, on the other hand, it was always the teak chair, weighing half an elephant, placed firmly on the ground, absolutely immovable. There was a photograph of her maternal grandfather, wearing a suit and jacket, and leaning against his first black Buick car. After that, there were photographs of all her uncles, each in the same pose. From tricycle to Buick, a totally confident progress in the matter of vehicle ownership was apparent, as far as the men were concerned.

When her father's younger brother was promoted to Inspector, a motorbike arrived at their house, all shiny and new. When he rode around everywhere with *Chithi* behind him, and furthermore, took several photographs of her seated on it, there was a flood of criticism from the rest of the family. There were lengthy arguments about how to purify Chithi after she had gone and sat on a leather seat. Endless debates went on as to whether it would be better to wash the motorbike in cowdung water, or to bathe Chithi herself in cowdung. We heard that in the end, taking the advice of a *purohit* who could find relief for every kind of transgression, Chithi swallowed a drop of cow's urine mixed into something or other, and cleansed herself in this way. After she was cleansed once, there was no further contention. Chithi travelled by motorbike every day.

She had mingled with all the people of this town, accustomed as they all were to rushing to work by bus or electric train, fighting their way through the crowds despite the rain. If a fierce storm came pelting down, an umbrella was of no use. As soon as it was opened, it would give up the ghost and collapse, its ribs thrust inside out. Only a raincoat and cap gave succour at such times. The men would roll up their trousers as high as their knees, put their shoes into plastic bags, and set off towards the bus-stand or the railway station. Women kept special saris for the rainy seasons. Not cotton ones, but others made of synthetic material which dried quickly. These too would be pulled up, higher than their knees. If they were wearing a *salwar-kameez*, the salwar would be folded back to the knees. No one had the time to take notice of the thousands of women of different sizes and shapes rushing past in a throng, all of them wearing expressions that revealed their desperate anxiety to get to work. No one could afford to stop and ask a stranger who might be standing and staring, 'Haven't you got a mother, an elder or younger sister?' The crowds rushing onwards would just move on, knocking the stranger down without the least compunction. Bhakyam had grown accustomed to all this.

She stood in wait for the double-decker bus that she needed, and when it arrived, shoved and jostled her way inside, lost among the individuals who became mere symbols as the conductor pushed them along, saying, 'Oh, Umbrella! *Ei*, Yellow Sari! Arré, Black Trousers! Ei, Greyhead! Go on, move forward, move forward.' She got off at the railway station, looked for the flashing of the lights which indicated at which platform her train would be, climbed the stairs, ran across the bridge, climbed down again, rushed into the express electric train, sat down and looked through the window. Every single day.

The girls who attended the school that Maharishi Karve founded in Maharashtra had begun to cycle even in Bhakyam's mother's times. They even took part in bicycling competitions. In any case, the Maharashtrian style of wearing a sari is very convenient for cycling. There were advertisements in the magazines of those days, which featured Western women riding bicycles, in knee-length skirts. The women in her mother's family, though, had the good fortune of riding a bicycle only after their grandfather arrived in Coimbatore. The house that Thaatha chose was in a remote place, some distance away from town. A Raleigh cycle arrived at the house so that the uncles could ride to college, or run on various necessary errands. For some days it remained the exclusive property of the uncles. Later when Kamala Chithi learnt to ride it by holding on to the wall, and after she taught her younger sister Anandi as well, the cycle became everyone's vehicle. Kamala Chithi used to swing her leg over the crossbar, untrammelled by her sari. A swift charioteer, she was. A slender figure. Long, long legs. When Bhakyam went to Coimbatore, she went riding with her, hanging on to the carrier. Kamala Chithi stood straight up and pressed the pedals as she started up the cycle, then sat down as it gained speed. She went so fast that trees, plants, and houses all sped past her. Bhakyam imagined she was riding on a flying horse. A white horse that spread its wings and flew through the sky. She always climbed down from the carrier in a languor, as if returning from a different world.

Those cycle rides went on until her two front teeth were broken. After that, Thaatha bought the Buick. The chithis didn't drive the car, though. Very occasionally, when she went to Coimbatore, Bhakyam got the chance to ride in it. But it didn't give her the pleasure she once had, bicycle-riding with Kamala Chithi. The uncles never drove the car with the panache that Kamala Chithi had; they did not display any of her daring feats such as driving with both hands stretched free.

When she looked out of the window of the electric train, she could see people speeding past on motorcycles, jeeps, and cars. She loved looking down from the top of the double-decker bus. There was no lack of vehicles to look at: hand-pulled carts carrying heavy loads, water-lorries, rattling old cycles ready to be given away to the junk man in exchange for dry dates, racing cycles which you had to bend right over to drive, and cars which sped by in different colours and shapes, making different noises.

It was while she was looking out from the top deck that she saw it. That accident. A family of four were travelling on a scooter. Signalling that they were just returning from the shopping centre, a hugely swollen plastic bag in the hands of the wife who sat in the rear. The boy stood in front of his father, who was driving. The little girl was in the narrow space between her parents. A cheerful family, with smiles on their faces. In that instant, while she was watching, a bus rushing headlong at an uncontrollable speed collided against the scooter. Amidst the screeching of vehicles coming to a stop and the shouting of voices, the family lay, covered in blood. Held tightly in the little girl's hand was a yellow toy car.

That corner was always a dangerous one. Just the day before that, a boy on a motor-cycle had collided against a petrol-tank and died. When she looked in that direction, on her way home, oil and glass fragments lay scattered all over that area. Some distance away, a single chappal lay, upturned.

People said to each other, 'There are too many accidents. Nowadays, when you set off in the morning, you can't be sure that you'll return in the evening.'

It was only when her brother was a year old that a tricycle turned up at their house. A black one. After that, when he was four, a two-wheeler arrived in its turn. Painted all in red, with a slippery red rexine seat. Just right for a four-year-old. She got as far as touching it again and again with enjoyment.

But the dream kept returning to her. A dream of flying. A feeling of weightlessness as soon as her feet touched the pedals. After that, leaping higher and higher, riding her cycle into the sky. The pedals like petals of a flower.

As a matter of fact, there was only one occasion when she rode a cycle as a child. Having boasted to her younger brother that she could certainly ride the bike into the lane, she had climbed up the rubbish bin, managed various circus-tricks, dashed into the wall, and ended up in the gutter along with the vehicle. There was a sound of something cracking, as her left elbow smashed down. Even so, she got up and started riding again. By this time her elbow was a Banganapalli mango. There was an immediate outcry, 'If you go anywhere near that bike again, you'll see!', dire warnings that girls with broken arms and legs never got married; and finally permission was granted to her brother alone to ride the bicycle. Nobody paid any attention to her argument that nobody was likely to marry him either, if he broke a limb.

When they went to live near Guindy, she pleaded with her parents to let her ride a horse. There were many clashes of opinion within the family about her 'strange' desires. In the end, the horse too became a forbidden vehicle.

When she went to Delhi for further studies, there was a hidden desire in her heart to acquire a scooter. Her friend Manivannan brought round a brand new scooter and said, 'Come on, Bhakyam, let's go for a round on this. You must inaugurate it!' Not able to refuse, she climbed on behind him. He forgot to tell her the crucial detail that it was many years since he had driven a scooter and that he wasn't sufficiently knowledgeable about such things as brakes. Once they crossed the smaller lanes full of cows, buffalos, dogs, pigs, and bicycles without bells, they came on to the main road with fast-moving vehicles on either side of them. Like a bullock on the road for the first time, Manivannan lost his head. Suddenly, he braked hard, not knowing how else to cope with the heavy lorry that was harassing him from behind and the bus that was racing towards him at the same time. She was flung forcefully upon the gravel heaped beside the road, for repairs. There were abrasions all over her.

'Ayyo, don't you know how to sit at the back of a scooter? You have to hold on really tight. Get up now. Let's finish the round.'

She got up from the gravel and spoke to him without anger. 'Manivannan, don't you think so many war-wounds are sufficient for one day?'

Even today there were scars on her shoulder-blades and forearms, the size of the palm of her hand.

When she looked out of the windows of the electric train, or from the top deck of a double-decker bus, it struck her that there really was no place in the city for the green, black, yellow, and white, many-coloured and many-shaped vehicles that flashed past the eye so attractively. Morning, noon, or night, at whatever time you travelled in them, you experienced the trumpeting of horns, the choice obscenities in Hindi, Marathi, and English, and the extreme distress of crawling inch by inch on the main streets. The tunes played by some horns went through her to the marrow of her bones. When trendy people suddenly turned on a tape which said in an American accent, 'This car is reversing,' she was startled out of her wits. Some used a tape of a baby crying for the same purpose. Once, at some odd hour, she was walking down a street, lost in a dream in which there were no modern towns, when she heard the baby crying just behind her. It gave her a terrible shock.

The autorickshaws which looked like beautiful black and yellow samosas when seen at a distance, were enveloped in the smoke emitted by the bigger vehicles as soon as one boarded them. To ride along the main roads in an auto, breathing in the fumes escaping from heavy lorries, motor-cars, and buses, and to survive somehow, seemed like a battle of life against death. While the streets and lanes and highways stood covered in blood and filth and fumes, all these vehicles drove over them like a pack of demons.

When her brother was transferred to Kalpaakkam, he wrote and invited her there. 'Why don't you come and take a look at the sea? The fishermen hereabouts are my friends. One of them is a close friend, in fact. He has published a collection of poems. He puts out to sea in his catamaran, and recites his poems there. He says he wants to write songs for the cinema. Come and look at the sea from his catamaran.'

The house was beside the sea. The sand from the beach lay in heaps along the streets.

As soon as she reached there, she walked down to the beach with her brother and his children. At first her brother's friend was hesitant, saying, 'Women ought not to climb into catamarans.' But he was gently nudged towards poetry, and so they all boarded the boat. Against their rising sea-sickness he advised them to look up at the sky and not to watch the sea. They made their catamaran journey, looking up at the sky and listening to the fisherman friend's poems with their *e-le-lo* chorus, while the sea waves lapped at their feet.

As soon as they reached home, she had a sudden desire for a lime-juice sherbet. It was only when her sister-in-law said, 'Yes, of course,' opened the front door, and rode off to buy some limes that she noticed the bicycle standing there. Some time later her brother's daughter went off on the bike to borrow some books from a friend.

That night she said softly, 'I want to ride the bike too.' Her nephew and niece went along with her, with great enthusiasm. She had forgotten how to push it along and climb on to it that way. She leaned it against a corner, climbed on, and as she began riding it, the whole street seemed to shorten. The sand on either side seemed to leap towards her. The trees which stood at a distance, surrounded by a thorny hedge, seemed to rush forward, across the street. The chappals fell off her feet.

'*Athai*, Athai, turn it towards the sand. It will stop then,' her nephew shouted, running after the cycle.

She rode it on to the sand, and both she and the bicycle fell down. When they returned, her sister-in-law put medicine over her bruises. 'Is all this necessary, Akka?' her brother asked.

Stubbornly she set off outdoors the next morning, without making a sound, accompanied by her nephew and niece. She went around the area, followed by their encouraging shouts, 'Athai, you can do it. Come on, Athai. Press the pedal gently. Now steer the bike to one side.' For a few seconds she felt like a queen.

Without any decision on her part, a vehicle became hers. A vehicle without wheels, which would not pollute the environment. A vehicle which moved without colliding into anything, without raising a noise, or shedding blood. An electronic vehicle. A mouse vehicle. A vehicle which carried a computer. Mounted on this, she travelled great distances along the paths of communication. She glanced at many home pages along the Internet. She knocked on the home doors and opened many. She created a home address for herself there. Besides this, using the 'Geo-Cities' initiative, she went around the world, seeking a site and an address in many cities. At last she found an empty space in Paris, a city that is associated with cinema, romance, and revolution, and made herself a home there.

At the very threshold, in both homes, as a way of introducing herself to guests who were about to enter, she wrote about her relationship with different vehicles. She drew a picture of herself upon the electronic mouse, which she said signified herself on her current vehicle.

She, who was descended from all those who had chariots composed of snake, lion, swan, and horse, now had a vehicle of her very own. She began to seek the right electronic moment to destroy demons and meet the gods.

*Dinamani*, Pongal issue, 1997

# In a Forest, a Deer

It is difficult to forget those nights. Nights when we listened to all those stories. Thangam Athai, it was, who told them to us. They were not tales of the fox and the crow, nor of the hare and the tortoise. No, these were stories she herself had made up. Some were like fragments of poetry. Others were like songs which would never end. Stories which developed in all sorts of ways, without beginning, middle, or end. At times, at night, she would create many images in our minds. Even the gods and demons would alter in her stories. She would speak most movingly about Mandara. Surpanaka, Tadaka, and the rest would no longer remain as rakshasis, female demons, but be transformed into real people with impulses and feelings. She brought into the light characters which had seemed only to cling to the pages of the epics. As if she were stroking a bird with broken wings, with such gentleness she would portray them in words. I don't know what it was about them—the night-time, or the central hall of that old house where we lay, or the nearness of all the cousins—but those stories still keep circling and sounding somewhere in my mind, like the buzzing of bees.

In that house with its old pillars and central hall, I see Thangam Athai in several frames. Leaning against the heavy wooden door. Carrying a small lamp which she has shaded with the end of her sari; placing it within its niche. Serving a meal to her husband, Ekambaram. Pulling on a rope, one foot firmly placed upon the small parapet surrounding the well. Feeding the plants with manure.

Thangam Athai had beautiful dark skin. A face without a single wrinkle, as if it had been ironed smooth. Plenty of silver in her hair. There was an old-fashioned harmonium in Athai's house, worked by pressing a pedal. Athai used to play it. She would play different tunes, from the *tevaram* 'Vadaname chandrabimbamo' to the popular

'Vannaan vandaana', singing softly at the same time. Her long fingers which looked like the dark beaks of birds would fly over the keys of the harmonium as if they were black butterflies.

A shell of mystery surrounded Thangam Athai. There seemed to be a deep pity for her in the way the others looked at her with tenderness, or stroked her gently; it was there in the compassion flowing from their eyes. Ekambaram *Maama* had another wife. He always treated Athai as if she were a flower. Nobody had overheard him address her as 'di'. He would always call her Thangamma. All the same, Athai seemed, somehow, as if she stood a long distance away, behind a smokescreen. It was Muthu Maama's daughter, Valli, who pierced the mystery. What she found out was both comprehensible to us, and yet totally incomprehensible. According to Valli's mother, Athai had never 'blossomed'.

'What does that mean?' several of us wanted to know.

Valli was old enough to wear a half-sari. 'Well, it means that she never came of age.'

'But her hair is all white, isn't it?'

'That's different.'

After that we watched Athai's body carefully. We discussed among ourselves how a body that hadn't 'blossomed' would be. We couldn't understand in what way her body wasn't complete. Athai looked just like everyone else when she appeared in her wet clothes, after her bath. When she stood there in her knotted red choli and her green sari, she didn't look at all unusual. Valli's mother had said to Valli, 'It's just a hollow body.' We couldn't make out where the gap could be. We wondered if it was like the broken wing of a sparrow, a hollow that wasn't overtly discernible.

One evening they cut down a huge tree in the garden, which had died. At the last blow of the hatchet, it suddenly slid down to the ground amidst a rustling of leaves. When it was split across, there was a mere hole within. Valli nudged me at the waist and said, 'That's it, that's hollow.' But it was impossible to compare Athai's shining dark form with this tree, lying there facing the sky, exposing itself utterly, nothing inside.

What secret did that form hide? In what way was her body so different? In the hot summer afternoons, Athai would remove her

tight choli and lie down in the store-room. When we went and
snuggled close to her, laying our heads against her breast, freed now
from its confining choli, she would gather us up in a light embrace.
Held within the protection of her breast, her waist, her arms, it was
difficult to perceive any hollow. Hers was a temperately warm body.
She seemed like one steeped in feelings and emotions. Like a ripe
fruit full of juice, a life-spring flowed through her body. And often
those vitalizing drops fell upon our own selves. Through her touch,
through her caress, through the firm pressure with which she massaged
us with oil, a life-force sprang towards us from her body, like a river
breaking past its own banks. It was at the touch of her hands that
cows would yield their milk. The seeds that she planted always
sprouted. My mother always said she had an auspicious hand.

Athai was there when my little sister was born. 'Akka, stay by my
side. Keep holding on to me. Only then will I not feel any pain,'
Amma muttered, as we children were being swept out of the room.
When we came to the threshold and looked back from the doorway,
Thangam Athai was softly stroking Amma's swollen belly.

'Nothing will happen. Don't be frightened,' she said quietly.

'Oh, Akka, if only you too could...,' my mother sobbed, unable to
finish what she began.

'What do I need? I'm like a queen. My house is full of children,'
said Athai. Ekambaram Maama's younger wife had seven children.

'Your body has not opened...,' Amma wept the louder.

'Why, what's wrong with my body? Don't I feel hungry at the right
times? Don't I sleep well? The same properties that all bodies have,
this one has, too. It feels pain when it is hurt. Its blood clots. If its
wounds go septic, it gathers pus. It digests the food it eats. What
more do you want?' asked Athai.

Amma took her hand and laid it against her cheek.

'They turned your body into a bloody battlefield...,' she moaned,
holding that hand tight.

Valli's mother had told Valli that there was no medicine left that
they had not tried on Athai's body. If any physician came to town,
most definitely he would be asked to prescribe for Athai. It seems
they even tried English medicine on her. It seems that at times she
would take these medicines and fall into such a deep and heavy sleep.

It seems that for a few months they made puja with neem leaves and the sound of the *udukku* drum. In the hope that something might happen if she were suddenly startled, a dark figure wrapped in a black cloth once sprang on her when she was alone in the backyard. Screaming with the shock, Athai fell down, hitting her head against the washing-stone. The scar is still there, on the edge of her forehead. When the next physician came to her, it seems Athai cried out, 'Leave me alone. Leave me alone.' The evening after they had been to see a prospective second wife for Ekambaram, it seems Athai swallowed a mixture of ground arali seeds. They gave her an antidote, and somehow managed to resuscitate her. After that, Ekambaram had wept and said, 'I don't want anything for myself that will cause you pain.' Then Athai herself sought out a bride for him. And that was how Senkamalam came to live in that house. All these were details collected by Valli.

Without removing her hand from Amma's clasp, Athai stroked her head with her other hand. 'Leave it. Leave it now. Let it all go. Why think of my story at this time when you are giving birth?' she said. It was that very night that my little sister was born.

It was some time later, on one occasion when we were visiting her house, that she told us the story.

It was the rainy season. On one side of the living room, the *jamukkalams* had been spread and a few pillows encased in pillowcases with stubborn hair-oil stains were scattered about. And there were some pillows without pillowcases. These were made of heavy cotton in dark colours, stuffed with cottonwool. Here and there the cottonwool had knotted into lumps. These were not the pillows in daily use. They were kept for the use of the children of occasional visitors. Were the lumps and knots going to matter, after all, to children who played all day long and went to sleep with full bellies?

We could hear the sound of the kitchen being washed down. Then we heard the clang of the brass pot, the creaking of the door, the soft thump of the coconut-frond broom being banked against it. A tin box clinked. That would be the tin in which the kolam powder was kept. The kolam would now be traced upon the hearth. After that, having shut the kitchen door, Athai must come this way through the living-room. Not one of us was asleep. We waited.

As soon as she came by us, Somu began.

'Athai, won't you tell us a story... Athai?'

'Aren't you asleep, any of you?'

She stood there and watched us awhile, then she came closer and sat down. Kamakshi and Somu crept up to her immediately, put their heads upon her lap and lay on either side of her, gazing up at her. The rest of us leaned our elbows against our pillows.

Athai was tired. The sweat gleamed upon her forehead. She shut her eyes and thought for a moment.

'It was a huge forest,' she began.

'In that forest, all the animals lived together, happily. There were lots of fruit trees there. A small stream ran through it, to one side. If ever they felt thirsty, they would drink from it. Whatever any of the animals wanted, it was all there, exactly as they wished, in that forest. In that forest, they never feared the hunter. All those animals roamed about freely, never afraid that a sudden arrow might pierce them, or that they might lose their lives. Like any other forest, it was not without such things as forest fires, or trespassers coming from elsewhere to cut down the trees, or to steal the fruit, or even to shoot at the birds, or to strike at the fleeing wild pig. All the same, it was a forest to which the birds and animals had become accustomed. Indeed, they knew it well. They knew on which tree the owl would alight, and how it would hoot at nights when the entire forest lay silent; they knew on which stone the frog would sit and make its sudden croaking noise as if it were lapping water; they knew the places where the peacock danced.

'Everything went on like this until one day when a herd of deer went to drink water. As they walked on, following the water, one of the deer was separated from the rest. Suddenly it found itself in a different forest. It seemed to be a forest which had no pathways at all through it. There were marks on all the trees where arrows had penetrated them. Within the forest, a waterfall sounded with a loud flourish. The place wore a desolate look, as if there wasn't a soul about. The deer felt its whole body shudder with fear. Crying out loudly that this was not the place it knew, it wandered the entire forest, leaping about in its panic. It grew dark. The deer couldn't bear the terror of it. The waterfall's sound was frightening. In the distance, a hunter had lit a fire and was eating the roasted flesh of the animal he had killed. The deer could see the sparks from that fire. It hid itself. It sank down, exhausted from having gone round and round that forest, all alone.

'It wandered about in this way for many days. And then it was the night of the full moon. Moonlight filled the forest. Spread with moonlight, the waterfall had taken on a different form. A form that was no longer frightening. The moonlight touched everything softly, gently. Suddenly, as if a magic rod had been laid upon it, the deer's terror disappeared entirely. It began to like this forest. It began to learn all its nooks and crannies. Even though it was a different place, this forest, too, contained everything. There was the waterfall. There were all the trees and plants. Slowly, gradually, its eyes discerned all the animals and birds. It could see the beehives hanging from the trees. It saw the freshness of the green grass. The deer understood all the secrets of this new forest. And after that it walked around the entire forest without fear. The deer's terror had all gone and it was at peace.'

Athai finished her story. All the rest of the living-room was in darkness. Only this part was lit up. As we children listened to the story, we imagined that the dark parts of the room were the forest; we made friends with the deer, and now we too were at peace. Hugging our pillows, we fell asleep. As I fell back against my pillow with its rough cover of dark blue and yellow and black, and opening a single eye, looked upwards, half-asleep, I saw Thangam Athai sitting in our midst, leaning forward with her knees drawn up, her arms across her chest, and her hands clasping her shoulders.

*Unnatham*, October 1994

# Unpublished Manuscript

A stamped envelope with her name upon it lay on her desk. Her mother must have left it there. She had returned early from the university, then. When she peered through the slats of the wooden window shutters, she saw Amma, having changed into a comfortable salwar-kameez, walking across the lawn at her usual brisk pace. A salwar-kameez coloured like a golden-yellow beetle. She returned to the desk, picked up the envelope, and found Amma's note next to it, written in black with a broad-nibbed pen, saying, 'I'll be back at eight. Let's cook something together.' On top of the note stood a terracotta bird, painted red, with outspread wings.

She was somewhat taken aback by the words printed across the envelope: Muthukumaran Memorial Festival Committee. The Committee wrote that they were planning to bring out an anthology of the poet Muthukumaran's complete works, including those that had not been published thus far, in time for the Memorial Festival honouring him. They invited her, as an editor of a research journal and as someone who was closely related to Muthukumaran, to participate in the festival and honour it with her presence. They added that they had gone to some trouble to track down her address, and entreated her not to refuse their invitation. On the letter paper, above the Festival Committee's address, they had printed a photograph of the poet's face. Piercing eyes, tightened lips, heavy moustache, carelessly tumbling hair.

When she turned her head and looked through the narrow spaces between the shutters, she could see her mother at a great distance, at the edge of the green lawn, a yellow, honey-bee-coloured spot.

When she was a schoolgirl, there was a mirror in one of the inner rooms of their house. An oval mirror, set in an ornamental wooden frame. On either side of it were two small drawers with shining brass handles. A swinging mirror, on top of the chest of drawers in which her clothes were kept. She would tilt it halfway up, push it sharply back, and turning her head in a swift movement at the same time, look at herself, fierce-eyed. She was the three-eyed one. That look was a rehearsal for a future time when she would climb a stage and thunder against injustices, fixing her eyes on those individuals who were sucking the blood of the oppressed. Sometimes, she walked slowly towards the mirror from a distance, cultivating an expression of intense peace. This was her yogic look. A look calculated to persuade everyone to fall at her feet. Often, it seemed to her that, one way or another, she would attract everyone to her side in the future. Sometimes, during these rehearsals in front of the mirror, her mother's reflection would appear beside her, in a corner. Having just come back from the university, her big leather handbag hanging from her shoulder. Amma would look at her in the mirror, and smile. She would turn round to face her mother then, and laugh.

'Who are you today?' her mother would ask. She had many names to give in answer. Poets, artists, writers; all sorts. It did not matter which gender. If she were Lopamudra one day, she would be Nakkiran the next. One day, Avvaiyaar, the next day, Pari. Today, Bharati. Tomorrow, Akkamahadevi. One day, Veena Dhanammal. The next day, Tiger Varadachari. One day, Begum Akhtar. The next day, Bhimsen Joshi. One day, Siddheswari Devi. The next day, Paluskar. One day, Jikki. The next day, Raghunath Panigrahi. One day, Lorca. The next day, Sylvia Plath. All of them were individuals to whom Amma had introduced her.

Her mother was a professor at Banaras University. Because she headed the Department of English, she had many extra responsibilities. It was often quite late when Amma reached home. As for herself, as soon as school was over, she'd walk along the banks of the Ganga. Her arms outstretched like wings, her head tossed back, she'd run along, looking up at the sky. Sometimes, she would bump into a stranger. Nobody scolded her, though. '*Beti, sambhalke...* Daughter, look out,' they would say, smiling.

She knew all the secrets of the Ganga and its shore. She knew its crocodiles. She knew its filth and its pollution. She knew the people who dipped into its waters. She knew about the deception played on Yama, the god of Death, when a beloved child was pushed into the water and then retrieved. All the itinerant *bairagis*, the widows awaiting death, and the purohits performing their rituals belonged to the same river-bank that she herself walked along everyday.

Ten or twenty years before her time, women who had sung at princely courts in their youth could be seen in their old age leaning against the pillars of the small temples. Forgetting themselves, they sang *thumris* to melt the very soul. Sometimes, on festival days, they floated past in a boat, many of them singing together. One could tell, by their voices, who was singing. She had been told all this by the local people.

She had taken herself as far as the burning *ghats* where bodies were cremated. Once, she had stood and watched while a woman's body burned to the end. She didn't know whether it was a woman who had come to Kashi in order to die, who had lived out her last days in an *ashrama* on the banks of the Ganga. They had enshrouded the woman in a white sari. A fine drizzle came down. As she stood there watching, her clothes became wet. That day she wrote a poem. Her mother had read it and declared it was good.

At first she only wrote poems which kept strictly to the rules of metre and rhyme. Her mother had drummed Tamil grammar and poetics into her head. But, at the same time, Amma read modern poetry. When she asked why she too shouldn't break grammatical rules, Amma replied that one has to understand a rule first before overstepping it. How can there be infringement without there being a boundary?

Very occasionally, late at night Amma would sing from *Tiruvasagam*, the sacred poems by Manikkavasagar. She might sing from *Tirupulambal*, 'Utraarai nan venden, uur venden, per venden... I need no family, no place, no name...' Or, it might be some lines from *Tiruchatakam*, 'Vaazhginrai vaazhaada nenjame... You are alive now, lifeless heart.' Perhaps, she sang it for the image with which it ended, 'avala kadalaaya vellatthe... In the boundless sea of sadness.' For, Amma really loved the sea. Other than singing these sacred lyrics, she had never seen her mother making a puja, or going to the temple. Amma said she loved the tenderness of *Tiruvasagam*. She would exclaim in surprise at the effectiveness of repeated words. '*Nekku nekkul urigi urigi*... Melting, melting to the heart's core,' she would say over and over again, living the very words.

Amma's name was Tirumagal. Everyone called her Tiru. Sometimes, she would go and stand behind her mother's chair, entwine her arms around her neck and hug her, calling her, 'Tiru, Tiru'. When Amma lifted her head and looked at her, she would say, 'But you like repeated words.' And the two of them would laugh. At that age, her imagination was full of poetry and thoughts connected with poetry. She had named her gradually-forming breasts, '*Angavai*' and '*Sangavai*'.

As they walked along the river bank, her mother taught her many poems by several different poets. Amma asked her to consider how she could feel pleasure if she put her fingers into the fire. A favourite song of her own, in those days, was '*Tunbam nergayil, yaazheduthu ni*... In times of sorrow, taking up your *yaazh*, you...' Amma sang it perfectly. And as her mother sang it at evening time in a secluded place, the lamps tumbling across the Ganga in the background, a longing would seize her that one day a man should be struck by some deep sorrow which she alone would be able to assuage with the music of her yaazh. She'd tell her mother this. Her mother would laugh. Once, Amma asked her whether she had ever imagined a man playing his yaazh to her, dispelling her pain and bringing her joy. No, she answered. She should ask herself why, her mother told her.

Amma told her about the lives of many poets. How Bharati fed the birds with the rice that his wife, Chellammal, had actually borrowed; how he gave away a brand-new coat that had been tailored for him, to a beggar; how he took ganja; how he declared, 'Poetry is my life-work.' One birthday, her mother gave her a biography of Bharati written by his daughter, and a collection of his poetry. Amma also recounted to her in great detail, how Bharatidasan had shouted on the occasion of his daughter's wedding that he wanted a boiled egg immediately; how his family lived in one place and he in another; how he ran the journal *Kuyil*. She told her how Sylvia Plath killed herself by placing her head in a gas oven, and how Anna Akhmatova stood outside the Leningrad prison for many days. She spoke about them as if they were people whom she knew intimately, not as if they were lost in history.

When she went to bed at night, she stretched herself out and leaned against her elbow in the Ranganatha pose, and tried to imagine a man sitting opposite her, playing a yaazh for her delight. It was difficult to picture it in her mind. She tried to think of Bharati going next door and asking to borrow some rice. She imagined Chellammal taking the rice from him and happily feeding the birds with it. She wondered why something that seemed perfectly all right when done by a man seemed like an act of madness when done by a woman instead? Once, by a rare chance, there was a showing of the old film *Karnan*. Devika sang a love song in it, and during the entire time Sivaji Ganesan sat stiffly, one hand placed on his thigh. Perhaps, this was because Karnan was a warrior? Devika circled around him again and again, like a butterfly. Even Sivaji Ganesan's smile was like squeezing toothpaste out of an empty tube. If men can soften and dissolve and melt through *bhakti*, why can't they do so out of love? She decided firmly on the sort of man she could respect. He would have to know how to melt. 'Melting, melting to the heart's core.'

Among Amma's friends, both women and men, there were, in fact, several poets and writers. They used to gather at their house on Friday evenings. Poems were read out from different languages. And were translated. Certain lines would fix themselves in her mind. When she awoke in the morning, as she walked along in the evening, they floated gently in her thoughts like ribbons tied to her hair. Suddenly, they would weigh upon her like balls of lead. When she told her mother about it, Amma would say that poetry was like that.

The conversation and behaviour of the poets seemed very strange to her at times. There was a Bengali poet who would call out suddenly, 'Ma!' and fall at Amma's feet. One of Amma's students told her once that that poet was madly in love with Amma. When she asked, though, her mother said it wasn't true. The person he worshipped was an imaginary woman who existed only in his mind, Amma said. His appearances on Fridays didn't cease, however. That was because of the quality of his poetry, Amma declared. 'Is it similar to the way you like Appa's poetry?' she asked. Amma answered that it was easier to live with Appa's poetry than with a poet like Appa.

Her mother had translated her father's poetry into English from Tamil. When she spoke at conferences about poets writing in the Indian languages, she would mention Appa by name and read his poetry. When she did this, some people tended to exchange glances. Or they nudged each other with their elbows. But Amma never took any notice, and just continued with what she was saying.

Once she was immersed in her work, Amma would never get up. Nor cook. Not even bathe. Books and papers would be strewn around her. She'd tie up her hair in a tight knot at the top of her head, like the sage Narada. She'd simply answer 'M...m' to anything she was asked.

Once, at such a time, she had tried saying to her mother, 'Amma, I'm going to die.' 'M...m' her mother said. When told about it later, her mother just laughed and said, 'Truly?'

At such times, she would bring biscuits and fruit to her mother and force her to eat. She'd make tea as soon as she came home from school and take it to her. Amma would read out some part of what she had written. She'd read even some parts of her research papers to her daughter. Sometimes she understood. And sometimes she did not. But she liked the experience of hearing her mother read to her. She loved doing various jobs for her mother such as checking words in the dictionary, changing the typewriter ribbon, looking up references in books.

When her work was finally done, her mother would emerge from it with a radiance, like one coming out of a deep meditation. She'd sit down in the easy chair by the window and gaze outside. Often, by this time, dusk would have fallen. She'd appear in silhouette. She would have loosened her hair from its knot. A soft outline of light would run from her temples to the very ends of her hair. She loved her mother then, more than ever.

Amma would sit there for a while, then raise her voice and call out to her, using her full name, 'Senthaamarai...'

She'd come running to stand in front of her mother. Her whole face illumined by a smile, her mother would ask, shaking her head from side to side, ' Shall we cook something?'

She too would nod. Then, the two of them would debate seriously about what to cook. Not peas, they would take too long to shell; they hadn't bought any fish, so there was no way they could make a fish curry; not *parathas* either, the dough would have to be kneaded. Was there any milk or curd in the house? And so it would go on. As a matter of fact, there really wasn't any need for the debate. On occasions like this, most of the time they finally cooked egg curry and rice. Amma liked to cook with an eye for colour. She would spread the food out on the table: white rice, the light-red egg curry, orange-coloured carrot slices, a bright green mint and coriander *thuvaiyal*, and a curd *pacchadi* for extra whiteness. The very colours made one's mouth water. Any visitor who came to the house at that time was in luck as far as the food was concerned.

And very often, that visitor was Mohan Gupta. He would arrive bringing ice-cream or sweets. His plays had been staged in many cities. They had been much discussed and debated. His language, the structure of his plays, and his perspective on relationships had all given grounds for much argument. He would sit in Amma's room and talk at length. He'd leave late at night, at one or even two o'clock. Once when she went to ask her mother something, she overheard him.

He asked, in English, 'Tiru, can't I come and live here with you?'

'No, that's impossible,' Amma answered, also in English.

'Why, do you imagine that all men are like Muthukumaran?'

A long silence. After that Amma spoke again. Her voice had grown very soft. The words, in English, sounded just a little drawn out. 'I have struggled very hard to create this world for myself and my daughter, Mohan. You cannot even begin to imagine that struggle. My life has been even more dramatic than your plays are. In order to establish a home without a Muthukumaran, I... I... in that psychiatric hospital...' Amma's voice broke.

'Tiru... please...' Mohan's voice was hoarse.

Senthaamarai stayed outside the room. She knew that the 'M' that stood in front of her name came from 'Muthukumaran'.

It was some days after this incident that she found it. The manuscript. Amma had gone elsewhere, to a seminar. A student who usually lived in a hostel came to keep her company in the house. One day, she came home from school early, in the afternoon. While she was rummaging in her mother's bookcase, searching for an old book, she suddenly came upon the manuscript. In Tamil. Its title was *Tiru—vasagam,* Tiru's message. She took it out and began to read it.

How many times she read it then, how many times she read it later, she could never remember. She read it on different occasions and at different times. Each time it hit her like a forceful wave, again and again. Each time she became aware of different details in it. It was a story that wove together many incidents about her grandfather, his idealism, his gentleness, Amma's relationship with him, his friends, Amma's love affair. And it moved her to experience different emotions at different times: sadness, affection, anger, surprise, respect, desire. Each time a new emotion put out its new shoots. Reading some parts of it she had called out in pain, Amma, Amma. She had wanted then to turn her mother into a little girl again, and take her into her own lap. Certain lines, certain incidents from the manuscript, remained with her, like pools in her mind.

Amma had begun her story with a journey across a sea. Amma's father Ramasami decided to end his career in Malaya and return home to Tamil Nadu. After his wife died, he no longer cared to live there. He boarded ship with three-year-old Tirumagal. All that she remembered of that journey, Amma wrote, was her father's shoulder clad in rough *khadi* material, against which she always buried her head; his gentle hands surrounding her; the pitch black night-sky with its innumerable stars which she could see from the top deck; and the boundless sea.

Ramasami came to Chennai a couple of years after the end of the Second World War, bought a printing press and set up a publishing house. He held fast to certain principles of his own. He would only publish books to do with Tamil life, folk songs, many religions, the sciences, and school texts. He refused to publish books which laid stress on rituals and symbols such as the Friday fast or the power of the *tali*. He refused to publish books which made lewd attacks upon a particular caste or linguistic community. Often, just to keep the press running, he had to print handbills, greeting cards, wedding notices, and such things. Even in this he was obstinate. He would not take on handbills advertising black magic, or potions for charms and spells. He refused to print invitations to the coming-of-age ceremony for girls, nor for weddings with orthodox rituals. As she grew up, what she heard her father say most often was, 'We can't print this, sir,' Amma wrote.

A Tamil pandit who was also a social reformer was a good friend of his. This man once gave Ramasami a manuscript in which he argued that the only way to give widows a new lease of life was through remarriage. He invited idealistic young men to sacrifice their lives to this end. He was a good man; a man with a reputation for outspoken views. He was known as Sambasivanaar and Maha Panditanaar.

'Well, Ramasamiyare, how do you find my book? Quite revolutionary in its views, I think. Would you dare to publish it?'

Ramasami said quietly, 'No problem there. Of course I can publish it. But tell me, what is so revolutionary in saying that a widow can live a decent life only by marrying a fellow? We must help her to educate herself and find a job. If you say that she mustn't be condemned to wearing a uniform, without a *pottu* or flowers, then that's fine. But when you say that some man must come and give her a new life, it looks as if you are suggesting that we must always keep her under the control of a man. It's as if you are saying she can only shelter in his shadow. If she wants to, then let her marry. Let her marry someone whom she really likes. But why do you make out that he is giving her a new life? Why do you suggest that the man is making some sort of sacrifice?'

Sambasivanaar felt attacked. He was one who always wrote in praise of women. He maintained that women should never seek any kind of education which threatened their femininity. There were many who applauded him as a champion of women. Now, Ramasami had brought him down from his pedestal.

And after all, Ramasami had the right to speak to him in this way. The daughter of one of his own father's friends lost her husband. Ramasami was in love with this girl. Her face seemed always to wear an expression of unrelenting sorrow. Many of Ramasami's friends urged him to give her a 'new life'. When he approached her and declared his love, with no thought of a 'new life' in his head, she hesitated a little, and then said, 'I want to study. Will you help me to do that?' Of course, Ramasami agreed. Later he told Tirumagal, 'Your mother smiled then. It was as if a flower had just bloomed. All that sadness in her face was because she yearned to study.'

When his friends wanted to make speeches at the wedding, he refused to let them. 'Don't. You'll only go on and on about widow remarriage, and giving a new life to a widow. You'll repeat the word "widow" at least a dozen times. She'll be deeply hurt.'

After the wedding, he left her in a college hostel, and she continued with her further education, while he went off to Malaya. It was only after she completed her teacher-training course that she too followed him to Malaya, to live with him. During the time they were apart, they must have written a thousand letters to each other. Amma wrote that these letters were still with her.

Ramasami observed both the birthday of his wife, and her death-day. There was always a sweet along with their meal, to celebrate her birthday. On her death-day, invariably, he played a record of the song, 'Vaarai, ni vaarai... Come, will you not come?' At the turning of the song, 'Anbe, ni vaarai... Love, will you not come?' he would join in softly. This, Amma understood, was what a profound love should be.

Ramasami had another friend, Subayya Naidu. A Telugu by birth. But he was learned in both Tamil and Sanskrit, and had studied music in the traditional way. He knew several Isai Vellala artistes intimately. At evening times he would chew Thangapasapam tobacco, then begin on Tyagaraja kritis or javalis appropriate for dancing, humming them at first, before bursting into song. He would recite N.S. Krishnan's 'Kindanaar Kalakshepam' for Tirumagal. Once he immersed himself in Telugu, though, he could never bear to emerge from it. He often sang 'Rama ika nannu brova... Rama, heed me now' in Sahana raagam. He'd begin with the single word, 'Rama', drawing it out like a great sigh. After that he would sing, drawing out that 'Rama' again, lengthening it, shaking it about, making it resound like an Onkaaram, crooning it softly. As he began the line, 'Ika nannu brova raadha... Can you not heed me now?' he would start to plead. The kirtanai would reach its lowest pitch with the words, 'Daya leda?... Have you no mercy?' He would sing these low notes as if he were wandering in the subterranean world of paadaalam. Once again, he'd start to climb with 'Shri', his voice soaring upward to reach 'Rama'. Ramasami would listen and share in that experience totally.

This friend often asked, 'Should I sing only Tamil songs for you?'

'Don't, *ayya*. Sing in whatever language pleases you. Music doesn't have one language alone, ayya. There's a black man, Louis Armstrong, in America. He plays the trumpet. Jazz music, it is. When he plays, it is as if the entire life of black people were appearing before your eyes. He'll drag you off to all sorts of places...' So saying, he would play a record on the old gramophone that he had brought back with him so carefully from Malaya. They'd listen together, he and Subayya Naidu. If Amma were at home, she'd join them too.

Ramasami liked to cook. He'd make a *thuvaiyal*, grinding it fine, very fine, on the grindstone. He never allowed Amma to do anything other than very minor chores. 'You go and read, amma, 'he'd tell her. 'It is only now that you'll get the time to study.' Whenever distant relations of theirs came to visit, they would complain about her. 'Shouldn't a girl know how to cook at least? This one doesn't even know how to boil rice!' He was perfectly well aware that all this was preliminary to urging him to marry again, to acquire 'a woman to cook a tasty meal, to bring a mouthful of water in moments of need'. Without saying a word he would cook and serve them rice, fish curry, a *poriyal* of eggs. He would explain, 'My girl must study first. Cooking isn't such a big deal. When she is hungry, she'll cook for herself.'

And that is exactly what happened. It was only after her father became ill that Tirumagal began to cook. Sometimes she called him 'Appov'. At other times, it was 'Ayya'. If she wanted to tease him especially, she'd address him as 'Ramasamiyare'. Sometimes, he called out instructions from the outer room, while she cooked. Sometimes, he came into the kitchen and taught her there, taking on the less strenuous tasks for himself. She was studying for her M.A. in English Literature at the time. She was always rushing between home and college. And at that time, as an advisor to her father's publishing house, she recommended that they print Muthukumaran's poems. Ramasami did so. Then Muthukumaran began visiting their house.

She observed him from the first, and very soon could gauge the depth of her feeling towards him. It took him a little longer. He hardly noticed her at first. He kept aloof, as if to say, 'What do I have to say to a girl who is studying English Literature?'

Later, Senthaamarai would read with pleasure, again and again, Amma's description of a particular journey by rickshaw. Desire, it struck her, was like a wire, stretched out taut. Touch it at any point and its vibrations ripple in waves, spreading all along it, she came to realize later.

The rains came down suddenly, during the early part of that night. By the time Amma reached Mannadi, it was pouring down. She took shelter in the front portion of a house with a tiled roof. All around her, the rain fell off the tiles in long cascades. In front of her a screen of water; she could not tell whether it was rain or smoke. Suddenly, as if a painting were taking shape, Muthukumaran materialized out of the screen, and walked into the same shelter. He did not notice her. When he lifted his hand to push aside the wet, curly hair clinging to his forehead, his fingers grazed hers, touching her and yet not touching her. A fingernail barely flicked against her, like the touch of a feather. 'I cannot tell whether it was a sudden chill brought about by the rain, or an inexplicable mixture of heat and cold caused by the very first touch of Muthukumaran's hand, but my legs suddenly seemed to buckle,' Amma wrote. She wanted to take him in her arms that very instant, and lie with him in that narrow space.

Amma wrote that poets describe women in all sorts of ways, but it was only on that day that she herself understood how a woman looks at a man. He was wet through from the rain. His veshti and shirt were stuck against his body. Beneath his wet white shirt, his dark shoulders seemed to rise and fall in line with the folds in the material. His wet arms seemed to hang down from the short-sleeved shirt. On his hands, the raindrops lay like strings of beads. When he tied up his veshti and leaned against the wall, she could see his dark legs, grown sturdy from constant walking. Chappals with tyre-soles. His toenails were not properly cut. Some were misshapen. His feet spread out like fans. Their heels were streaked with cracks. Why do they always say that male gods have lotus feet? Who needs lotus feet? Do they bear the marks of dust and mud, of having walked, stumbled, fallen, played? Muthukumaran's feet were bound to the earth. They were shaped by the earth's movements. Those feet had many stories to tell. In direct contrast to such stories, there were his hands with their fine fingers. Tirumagal shivered.

It was only then that Muthukumaran looked at her properly. They exchanged some words. Later, he accompanied her home in a rickshaw. That journey was as if they were on their way to a supernatural world. As if they were gently flying, tearing through the rain. In front, the bent form of the rickshaw man as he raised himself slightly and then pressed down on the pedals, the rain pouring off his cap. His legs going up and down, rising and falling as he worked the pedals. The two of them inside the rickshaw, yielding to the driving rain.

Some weeks later, they made their decision.

When she told Ramasami, he did not object. He was aware of the emotions flooding through her. Perhaps he thought he should be careful before he said anything.

A little later, he said quietly, 'Tiru, it seems he is given to drinking.'

'But Appa, it's not as if he gets staggeringly drunk, is it? It could be that occasionally, when he is with his friends, he has a drink or two with them.'

'Amma, Naidu says that he even smokes ganja. Naidu and he are close neighbours, it seems.'

'But ganja isn't poison, is it? Didn't Bharati take ganja too? These are all common matters, nowadays,' she explained.

After this came a journey into violence. A journey that began only a few weeks after they were married. Amma had written in great detail about the path that the journey followed. Some of those details made one's blood run cold.

Amma was a lecturer at a college, in those days. A few of her research papers in English and a couple of her translations of poetry had been published already. As soon as her first article came out, Ramasami bought her a Remington typewriter. She'd sit in front of it whenever she wanted. They arranged a room for Muthukumaran's private use, in one part of the house. It had a large desk, topped with green rexine. Five different sorts of pens on top of it. Paper. A comfortable chair which would prevent backache. The windows were of stained glass, as in churches. She teased her father about it. 'Appa, Muthu is only a poet, not Jesus Christ, you know.'

Ramasami left both the printing press and the publishing house solely in her charge. Nor did Muthukumaran show any desire to take up any other responsibility than writing poetry. Her time was totally taken up with publishing, printing, and college duties. She cooked only when she was so inclined. As for Ramasami, he began to subsist on bread, fruit, and milk alone. On the days when she was hard at work, they tended to order their food from a hotel. Occasionally, she cooked only the rice.

Muthkumaran had a whole regiment of friends. They enjoyed listening to him as he recited his poetry loudly, and at length. And the poems, too, were certainly enjoyable. One of the errand-boys from the press was requisitioned to fetch the frequently-needed coffee, tea, and hot *pakoras*.

Tirumagal would have liked to have gone out with him in the evenings. He, though, preferred to stride along the beach with his friends. She thought that to stop him from doing so would be to deprive him of his independence. Instead, she went and sat next to Ramasami, and told him all about the printing press and her college.

Because she didn't really know Muthukumaran's background, she could not guess how he imagined a wife should be. He had told her once that his mother's name was Dhanalakshmi, and that he had been profoundly moved by the name Tirumagal. She did not know whether deep in his mind there was an ideal woman who would 'in times of sorrow, take up a yaazh', who bathed at dawn, wore silk, plaited her still-wet hair, and, with kumkumam ablaze on her forehead, woke him up in the mornings with steaming fresh coffee, and watched over him with delight as he feasted on jasmine-like idlis laid out on a banana leaf. But in some way he seemed to feel that he was not being treated as a husband ought to be.

In the early stages, the violence—like mistakes made in a fit of temper—did not exceed a certain limit.

'It's all right, is it, just to boil the rice? Who's going to heat up the *kuzhambu*? What keeps you so busy that you can't even feed a man who comes home hungry?'

'Muthu, is it such a big deal just to heat the kuzhambu? You could learn to do that. I've just finished my work at the press and come home this minute. I've still got to make notes for tomorrow's lecture. Just set out the plates. I'll have a quick bath and be with you.'

A muttering and a banging of the kitchen vessels. Then, a growl from deep within his throat. 'Are you a woman?' Again and again the same question was repeated, 'Are you a woman?' Later that night he would retract all of it. He'd lay his head at her feet in penitence and refuse to get up unless she forgave him. Sometimes it would all end in a poem. Or else in a fierce embrace. Or in deep sleep, his face against her breasts. Excess. Everything was in excess.

She began to find packets here and there, containing ganja powder. When she showed them to him, he would avoid her eyes. Never again, he would swear.

Senthaamarai was conceived. Ramasami watched over Tirumagal with the greatest of care. She had to tell him everyday, before she went to work, what she had eaten. He sent for sweets made with good ghee. An old couple in the street next to them made a living by cooking food for a few families. He arranged with them to deliver meals to their house.

'Why is he so bothered?' Mutterings from Muthukumaran.

'He's concerned for your sake, too. He says, "He works so hard at his poetry. Make sure he's drinking some milk."'

'Oh yes, he'd say that.'

His anthology of poetry had just received a prestigious award. His friends were constantly coming to see him. She would welcome them, and then retire to her room for a little rest. One day, one of his friends spoke up. 'You know, hospitality is the essence of Tamil culture. Here you are, married to such a famous poet. Don't you think you should attend to him and his friends? Instead, you seem to be insulting us.' The rest implied the same thing, in different ways.

Tirumagal listened to all of it. Then she said, 'You come here every day without fail, as if you didn't have your own families, wives, and children. You want to talk about literature. Very well, do so. I'm not stopping you. But who are you to give me your advice on hospitality? I might have all sorts of different things to do. I might be exhausted. Surely, your Tamil culture allows the time and occasion for a woman to get a little sleep?'

From within Ramasami called out, 'She's pregnant. Don't upset her.'

That night, the kitchen vessels rolled about. When she came to see what was the matter, he shoved her away. His eyes were red. The stink of alcohol and the stench of ganja filled the air.

'Muthu, what's this,' she exclaimed, trying to restrain him. He put his hand against her stomach and shoved her away.

'Don't you call me by name, *di*. Are you a woman? Don't you dare call me Muthu. Call me *Athaan*. Talk to me with respect. Are you a...?'

'Muthu, Ayya might be awake.'

'Why do you have to call on your Ayya for every least little thing?'

As he came staggering towards her, she tried to take him by the hand and lead him to their room. He shook her off.

'Why do you always have to be sitting in front of your typewriter? I am the poet here. If I were to sit in front of it, it would mean something. What is this rubbish that you are writing?' Before she knew it, he burst into the next room, knocked the Remington to the floor and kicked it hard against the wall.

She stood still, astounded.

When he came out of his drunken state, there was the customary plea for forgiveness.

In the days that followed, she could not look Ramasami in the eye when she spoke to him.

Senthaamarai was born. When she was wrapped in a white cloth and shown to Ramasami, he said, '*Thaamarai puu*... A lotus flower.' It was Muthukumaran who named her Senthaamarai. With the six-month-old Senthaamarai lying beside him, pulling at his shirt collar, having wet part of his bedclothes and his shirt, Ramasami died, very quietly. When they carried him away, it was Muthukumaran who wept the loudest. 'Forgive me, forgive me,' he entreated.

Ramasami had left the press, the publishing firm, the house, and everything else in Tirumagal's name. For some time Muthukumaran went about somewhat subdued. Six months later, the manuscript of another collection of his poems turned up on her office desk, plunging her into astonishment. She finished reading it that very same day. It seemed to her that a theme of violence ran through all the poems like an underlying thread. Even if one were to assume that it was a reflection of the violence that was indeed present in the world, here in these poems it appeared most of all in connection with representations of women. A penis turning into a knife and slitting a woman apart. Nipples being torn off, blood gushing out. Howling wolves and screaming, grunting pigs tumbling out of a womb. A penis turning into stone, thrusting into and shattering a *yoni*.

When she spoke to him about it at night, his expression changed. 'But we are publishing it, aren't we?' he asked.

'I can't answer that by myself. The publishing house has an Advisory Committee, doesn't it? I've sent it to them.'

'But the publishing house belongs to us, doesn't it?'

'The publishing house is mine, Muthu. But I can't make any decision on my own.'

'I belong to the Advisory Committee, don't I?'

'Yes, but when one of the committee members submits a piece of work to be published, he can't be on the committee that makes a decision about it. We have to co-opt someone else in their place.'

'So whom have you co-opted?'

'Manikkam.'

'How can you do that? He belongs to a different generation. He can't understand anything that I write. You could have chosen one of my group of friends, like Nellai Azhagappan.'

'The one who lectured me on Tamil culture?'

'You are simply not fit to run a publishing house. You should never go by your own likes and dislikes. The only thing that is important is the quality of the writing.'

'But haven't I judged the quality of the writing all this while? Even now, I have only given you my personal opinion. There need be no connection between that and our final decision to publish or not. Who was it, after all, who recommended your first book to Ayya? Have you forgotten?'

'No, I haven't forgotten, di,' he said savagely. 'You don't allow me to forget. Whatever I say, you answer, "These are Ayya's principles. Can't change them. Ayya wouldn't like it." It's always Ayya, Ayya, Ayya.' He screamed out the words. 'Was he only a father to you, or...'

Tirumagal didn't hesitate for even a single second. She stood up, took four paces forward, swung her right leg and kicked him hard in the groin.

'Ayyo,' he yelled, as he fell down with his hands pressed between his thighs, weeping.

She stood watching him.

When she turned away and stooped down to pick up Senthaamarai who had woken up and started to cry, something hit her hard at the base of her skull.

And when she opened her eyes again, she was lying down, her arms and legs bound down. She was attacked by one question after another.

'For how long have you had these violent feelings?'

'It seems you attacked your husband many times?'

'Do you hate men?'

'Who are the other women in your household?'

'Thaamarai,' she murmured.

The questions swirled about her, encircling her like battalions at war. For six months the warfare continued. Sometime later, Ekambaram, an employee of the press, came upon her accidentally while he was visiting someone else at the psychiatric hospital. He, and all the rest of them, had assumed that she was away, out of town. He brought along Subayya Naidu and the Tamil pandit Sambasivanaar to the hospital. And so she was discharged. Subayya Naidu took her away to his house. Fortunately, Muthukumaran had gone away to Kanchipuram about some business of his own. During her six-month absence, he had contrived to get his book of poems published. Ekambaram brought Senthamarai to her.

In the space of ten days, with the help of a lawyer friend of Ramasami's, she sold the press and the rights to the publishing house. She went to her college and collected all the references and certificates that she needed.

She thought carefully about going away to some distant place, and so she chose Banaras, where the lawyer friend's relations were settled. She sent away all their household goods in a lorry, and set off with Senthaamarai, two suitcases in hand. Amma had given an account of the day she left Chennai, in vivid detail.

'We set off very early for the railway station. Because it turned out to be the day of Annadurai's funeral procession. The streets were full of crowds. When I left in the rickshaw, sitting next to Subayya

Naidugaru, it seemed to me that all of Chennai had come to see me off. All that sorrow engulfed me, caught me in its jaws. As the procession moved on, a little further, women standing on the pavement beat their breasts and wept, saying, "Ayya, have you gone away? Have you left us behind and gone away?" I felt a heaviness in the pit of my stomach. Darting through the alleys, this way and that, when the rickshaw finally reached the station, the rickshaw man said, "Amma, here we are." Through the bars along the side of the rickshaw, I could see the station clock. Sadness churned in my stomach and then rose up and hit me in the chest. I pressed my face against the bars of the rickshaw. My throat choked as I raised my voice and wept.

"'What is it, Amma, what is it," the rickshaw man asked, panicking. Naidugaru was aghast. I wept for a long, long time, holding Senthaamarai close with one arm. After we boarded the train, I lay flat upon the berth, staring at the white-painted ceiling of the compartment and at the fan and the lampshades there, and I wept again. I remembered a poem by Muthu, about a railway journey. When I turned around carefully, trying not to disturb Thaamarai, there were sparks of fire flashing past the window, like tiny stars.'

When she finished reading the manuscript for the first time, she remembered that there wasn't a single photograph of her father in their house. In her memory, he was only the tickle of a moustache. There was indeed a photograph on the back cover of one of his earliest anthologies. It was faded and somewhat creased. One of the creases ran across his face, through the middle of his nose, and along the left eye. There was a hole made by an insect where the other eye should have been. So she could not picture him in his entirety.

When she finished reading it that first time, and when her mother returned home, she hugged her tightly. When Amma went to sleep that night, she went up to her and kissed her forehead. Amma woke up. Looking directly into her eyes, Amma asked, 'Have you read it?' She laid her head against her mother's chest.

Some months after that, Amma took her to the banks of the Ganga and told her the news as they sat there. Appa had died in the public ward of a general hospital, his intestines burnt out. Amma spoke of it in an ordinary tone of voice, as if it were a news item. His friends had lit the funeral pyre, Amma said. She moved a little closer to her mother. They sat there together, for a little while, quietly. Then they got up and began to walk on.

In front of them, a young couple. In the man's arms, a baby girl, about a year old, lay fast asleep. Her head turned towards his neck. Her soft lips nestled against him. The rose-coloured ribbon, bound about her lowered head, fluttered in the wind. The child's legs hung down, heavy with sleep. Around her feet were softly whimpering anklets. Every time her sleeping head drooped away from his shoulder, her father laid it back carefully with his free hand. Now and then she turned her head from one side to the next, rubbing her nose against him. Then he turned his head very slightly, and looked at her sideways, settling her more comfortably in his arms. Her legs swung then. The anklets whimpered.

Amma and she walked all the way behind them, and reached home at last. As soon as she entered the house, she went up to her room. She sat down at her desk and leaned against it. Her eyes were heavy. Slowly, slowly, starting with little sobs, she began to weep. When she raised her head at last, she found a framed photograph on the desk. It showed her as a small child, in her father's arms. An emerald green skirt. A red blouse. Her hair caught to one side, with a red ribbon around it. Amma stood next to him, wearing a red-brown sari, the colour of areca nut. His hair was just like hers, dense and full of curls. She looked straight ahead, wide eyed, her eyes streaked with collyrium. There were anklets around her dangling feet. Her bottom was pressed against her father's left arm. His right hand rested lightly against her thigh, on which the emerald green skirt was spread.

A couple of days later, when she returned the photograph, Amma said, 'Let it be with you.' So it remained where she could glance at it, every now and then.

She ought to attend the Memorial Festival, she decided. She would be able to receive that anthology in the right spirit. Just as she finished putting her acceptance into an envelope, she heard her mother opening the front door. A few minutes later, Amma hastened past her door. As if a gleaming yellow feather had floated past.

*India Today*, Women's Issue, 1996

# A Saffron-coloured Ganesha
## on the Seashore

The instant she was awake, she remembered that she had to go to Malad that day. She could get there on the number 210 bus. It was a double-decker bus, though. It tended to go rather slowly, meandering through the town, taking a circuitous route. On the other hand, if she walked for ten minutes she would reach Versova creek. She could take a boat across, climb into the bus on the other shore, and be in Malad within another ten minutes. There would be the extra pleasure of gazing at the beach as she walked up to the creek.

But first she made herself some milkless tea, added a couple of drops of lime juice, and as she was drinking it, arranged the books and papers that she needed, in her shoulder-bag. She bathed; put on a salwar-kameez with *batik* work in brown, spreading like spider-webs across a honey-coloured background, and leather chappals that would be comfortable for walking; and then set off with her bag hanging from her shoulder.

As soon as she came out of the building, she crossed the road and went over to the other side. She began to walk towards the creek. To the left of her were many-storeyed apartment blocks. In the spaces between their gardens, and between the pillars marking out the car-parks, the sea could be glimpsed in fragments. Pale-blue and grey, the sea tossed about, enshrouded in the early-morning mist. As she walked along, each fragment of the sea that she glimpsed was like a separate painting. There might be a fragmentary scene in which clothes billowed out from one end of a long line stretching out from the ribs of a building, while on the other side, the nose of a white boat came into view. Five or six paces later, if she looked again, there might be another scene, with a moss-green Maruti and a red Tata

Sierra in the foreground, and just a little behind, the back of an infant. The child might, perhaps, have thrown tantrums in order to come down so early in the morning, and would now be sitting on the parapet of the building, wearing a blue woollen cap and gazing out to sea. Beneath the parapet, the green lawn where his push-chair stood; beyond, the blue streak of the sea. Yet ten paces further, seen through red-flowered *gulmohur* trees perhaps, there might be a black dog lying stretched out on a low wall, panting, tired of running about; behind, a cluster of boats, their sails outspread. Such scenes appeared differently each day, and were engraved upon her mind. It was all a part of the delight of this walk.

The last two buildings had come up ten years ago. Before that, there used to be a big mansion there, with a tiled roof. Surrounded by coconut trees. Occasionally, there would be a dim light blinking away, in some corner. It had been nicknamed the Ghost Mansion, and many people from these parts had spent their school days telling ghost stories about it. Or performing plays there during the day, in which strong and ruffianly smugglers with moustaches, and moles as big as areca nuts on their cheeks, spoke to each other in the style of the Hindi cinema, saying, 'Let us meet tonight at eleven, at the Versova Mansion.'

After she had passed the last two buildings, she could see the sea, stretching out as far as the creek. In the high summer, bamboo poles were usually planted there, with fish hanging out to dry in the sun. When she turned towards the sea, she remembered that the day before had been the festival of Visarjan, when Ganesha is cast into the sea. Innumerable images of Ganesha lay strewn about on the shore, tossed by the waves, broken or whole, spread out or crushed, face-down, on their backs, to one side. Heads and crowns, legs and arms, paunches with trunks laid across them—all were scattered there. The seashore had the look of a battle-field when the war is over. As well as this, plastic bags which had been filled with puja flowers and immersed in the sea, flapped about everywhere. The young boys from fisher families who practised long-distance running there, every morning and evening, had to make sure the broken pieces of the images didn't obstruct their feet. Some picked up a few of the fragments, swam some distance into the sea, and sank them there.

This had become a yearly event. In the old days, the small clay idols of Ganesha used to dissolve away as soon as they were cast into the water.

'*Ganapati bappa morya, pudchya varshi laukar ya...,* Ganapati, come back soon next year', you could shout, and then forget all about it. Now, like many other things, Ganesha too had changed, becoming the proof as well as the declaration of the strength of certain political parties and individuals; or the convenient means by which the rich could spend their black money; or the symbol of any number of people who shouted out their views stridently. Now there were images, five to fifteen or twenty feet tall, made of papier-mâché laid over wire-frames. Innumerable quantities of these were made, in a variety of shapes and forms. Ganesha on a lotus, Ganesha with elephants on either side holding garlands aloft, Ganesha with Shiva and Parvati, Ganesha playing the flute, Ganesha dancing. A Ganesha to suit your own fancy. These had succeeded in obliterating completely the traditional images of Ganesha which used to come to mind, with his mouse, and his sweetmeats, and the song that went '*Kaiththala niraikani appamoda valpori...* With handfuls of fruits and sweets'.

At the Visarjan festival, throughout the evening and night, these new Ganeshas were taken out in a procession of lorries, accompanied by film songs, dances, camels, and horses, then loaded on to motorboats at different points, and immersed in the sea. And the next day, there was this battleground of a beach covered in broken and littered images that had refused to dissolve.

The procession had taken place as usual, on the previous evening. A number of Ganapati lorries had streamed past, accompanied by the ear-splitting rendering of songs suitable to a bachelor-god, such as '*Choli ke picche kya hai...* 'What's behind the choli' and the '*Ole, Ole*' one beginning with the line '*Jab bhi koi ladki dekhoon*' 'When I see a certain girl'. The fifteen- to twenty-foot tall saffron-coloured Ganesha which always came at the end went past at about midnight. A prominent textile merchant and other shopkeepers of that particular business area had arranged for this festival image of Ganesha. An image that had been coloured saffron with oil paint. The saffron Ganesha came, carried sideways in the lorry, because it was impossible to place him facing forwards. A seated Ganesha. The passage of this relatively unadorned Ganesha was a signal that the Visarjan festival was largely at an end. They would load him on to a boat, go far out to sea, immerse him and then return. Last night it had been a very long time before the saffron Ganesha arrived.

As she walked along, she saw fragments of images all along the beach. At the entrance of Versova village, lorries were ready, waiting to transport fish. The fisherwomen wore tightly-fitting cholis and saris of piercing blue, ripe red, green, and yellow, which were drawn tightly between their buttocks. Their hair was combed back into a knot decorated with a string of flowers, or sometimes just a single bloom. They were loading their baskets lined with ice blocks and filled with fish into the lorries, and then climbing in themselves. Full of the excitement and bustle of their trade.

As she walked past the lorries, one of the women smiled and gestured towards her as if to ask, 'Would you like to climb in, too?'. She, in turn, pointed to the baskets of fish and held her nose, as if to say, 'They stink'. They shrieked with laughter, calling out, '*Ayiga...*' Another woman waved a big fish at her, laughing and calling out as the lorry started up, 'If you marinate this in turmeric, chilli, and salt, and then cook it in a masala of coconut and *khas khas*, then you'll know!'

She hurried past the houses, the small shops, and the marketplace with its fish and vegetables, and reached the corner from where the boats plied. There wasn't much of a crowd there. Only a few Christian families, fisherfolk, waiting to go to the opposite shore, to the church there. A young woman held a tiny baby, bundled in yellow satin, in her arms. The baby slithered against the satin material, like a fish, as it turned this way and that. Laughing, the mother held it tightly, so that it wouldn't fall. Perhaps they were all going to the church in celebration of a family festival.

'Mariam, Mariam,' someone called out.

'Joseph is calling you,' one of the women said.

The woman called Mariam set off in the direction from which the voice came. In another couple of seconds everyone else congregated there. When she too went along with the others, she saw the saffron Ganesha image lying on its back in a cranny, along the seashore. Its body was broken in several places, and the wire-frame was sticking out. There wasn't merely a crown of thorns; the entire body was clothed in prickly wire. Clearly, it had not been taken out far enough, nor immersed in the real ocean depths.

After whispering together for a little while, Joseph and some of the other young men who were waiting to go to church started up the motor boat, put the broken Ganesha into it, and sped away into the sea. They could be seen going a long distance. The saffron colour sank into the sea like a shadow. After they returned, everyone climbed into the boat to go across to the other shore. Joseph's clothes were wet through.

'Why Joseph, you're soaking wet,' someone exclaimed.

'What could I do? After all, it is someone's deity,' he replied.

She became aware of a ten-year-old girl who wanted to come and say something to her, but was being stopped by someone else who pointed to her and gestured, 'Don't say it.'

She looked at the child and said, '*Tumi bola...* You just tell me.'

The little girl hurried to her, stood right in front of her and spoke up, her eyes wide, her head bobbing up and down, the rose-pink ribbon in her hair flying about. 'You know that wire, the wire inside the deity, it tears open the fishes' mouths. It cuts them up so that their mouths are full of blood and their stomachs are full of blood. And then...and then...the fish die if they eat the plastic bags. And float on the water...' She said all this at a gallop and then stopped.

She laid her hand on the child's shoulder, inclining her towards herself, and then looked towards Joseph. He was staring out towards the sea. The little girl stood close to her, leaning comfortably against her.

*Dinamani*, Pongal Issue, 1996

# A Rose-coloured Sari Woven
# with Birds and Swans

A Festival of India was going on at a school auditorium, fifty miles from Boston. A twelve-year-old girl had just made the traditional obeisance, and begun dancing to the song, '*Thiiraada vilaiyaattu pillai...*', 'Endlessly playful child'. Before she began, her mother had given an explanation in English: 'Krishna used to tease the *gopis*.' The little girl, born and bred in America, struggled with the dance gestures. Kannan's reed-flute often seemed to jut directly forward from her nose. She couldn't quite comprehend a Kannan who was given to such unhygienic habits as biting into a fruit and passing it on. She danced on that stage without any supporting images in her mind, of Kannan, his flute, the *gopikas* or the bitten fruit.

During the school holidays, there was singing and dancing all afternoon. An army of girls and boys danced together and sang, 'Mutthukrishnan, Beautiful One, how he cheated me, my friend!' When they sang the line, 'Stealthily he stole our saris while we bathed, tied them up in a tree, and hid himself, my friend', they could point to a tree and pretend to hide themselves, effortlessly. It was over the words, 'He returned the clothes, he guarded my honour' that they expressed their gravest doubts. There was a huge argument about what *maanam* meant. Then Murthy, a boy who was slightly older than the rest, said emphatically that maanam was actually a variation of *vaanam*, sky, and that they should point to the heavens as they sang that word. So when they sang, '*Aadaiyai tandaan...* He returned the clothes', they placed their hands across their chests as if indicating the top part of a sari; and at the following line, '*maanatthai kaatthaan*', they lifted both hands high up and pointed to the skies. After all, wasn't Kannan God? And heavenly beings live in heaven, don't they?

So isn't it right that he should guard the heavens? Images of Kannan became linked in their minds to the heavens. The hands that pressed against their shoulders could then point up towards the sky because of these supporting images; for no other reason. Body, song, play, and sky connected with one another easily.

On the instant that she landed at Boston from New York, Gita Ahuja told her they were attending the Festival of India.

She said hesitantly, 'What, straight away? Can't we go home and drop off the luggage...?'

Gita flared up at this. 'Your property will be quite safe in my car. And what's all this about a house and a home? You are always running towards a house. Do you think you won't have any protection at all if there aren't four walls about you? You want to raise walls on all sides of you as soon as you get to a place. Like the tomb they raised for Anarkali...?'

Climbing into the car next to Gita in silence, she wondered whether there would be another lecture about how she sat in a car. Gita always accused her of opening the car door and seating herself exactly as if she had climbed into a bullock cart. This was what she said the last time she visited. In spite of these words, though, the only food that Gita considered her own were maize *rotis* patted out by hand, and creamed mustard greens. Her meal was complete only when she had drunk a foaming tumbler of *lassi*, as tall as her arm. Even when they set out for a Mexican or Italian meal, she called it, 'roti-eating time'. She laughed when you pointed this out.

Gita's adopted daughter had been seated carefully in the child's car-chair fitted to the back seat. She was four years old. Gita had given her the name of a river, Alaknanda. She would say, 'She flows forever, untainted by mud or mire or moss. She has neither beginning nor end.' And when she was putting her to sleep in the evenings, it was Punjabi songs alone that would come to Gita's mind. She had chosen her from a Delhi orphanage, and adopted her as her daughter. When Alaknanda came home for the first time, she fell asleep on the withered thighs of Diljit Kaur, Gita's mother's mother. Diljit Kaur had covered her with her *dupatta*, and stroked her hair gently with her wrinkled fingers. 'Now she does some things exactly like my Nani,' Gita would say, in surprise.

Alaknanda spoke American-English. She called Gita's ex-husband, who had left her the previous year, by name, Peter. Gita said that it was specially for her that they were attending the Festival of India. She said that there would be many others there who had adopted Indian children.

After 'Thiiraada vilaiyaattu pillai', there was an old Hindi ballad. After this, a Hindi pop-song. And then a Gujarati *garba* dance. In the pavilion outside, there was a sale of snacks such as kachori, samosa, dhokla, idli, vadai, dosai, and tamarind-rice. Plaited hair with jewelled ornaments; coiled hair; saris, davani, Punjabi clothes.

She had aimed, through this American trip, to reach the very heights of computer-technology. She hadn't known what she would miss, or seek after, 'Thiiraada vilaiyaattu pillai', or idli, or samosa. There were things that were sunk deep inside her. Nothing tangible. They were only sounds, smells, images, and feelings, pervading her mind... The enchanting scent that used to meet her when she approached the *champaka* tree in the backyard of their Bangalore house. Creamy white flowers, half the length of one's fore-finger, known as Chinese champaka. If you fell asleep wearing those flowers, your pillow would get scented. The sweet smell that fills the air as soon as a jackfruit is split open. The knots and swirls and scatterings as Mali begins the opening *alaapanai* of his Kaapi raagam. The steam that hits your face as you open the lid of the water-pot, the firewood still burning underneath, and as you bend over it, *chembu* in hand, ready to pour out the water into a bucket. Drops of sweat blooming on Balasaraswati's forehead as she danced. Birju Maharaj's Kathak dance-leaps. The smell of cooking when a properly-soured batter is just spreading on a heavy dosai griddle. The smell of sesame in the chilli powder. The smell of gingili oil, unstrained, fresh from the oil-press. The tenderness of Bhimsen Joshi's Lalit raagam. The deep resonance of Gangubai Hangal's voice. Girija Devi's lilting tones. The kisses she and her lover had exchanged as they stood under a chestnut tree in a small village in Himachal Pradesh. The journey past her house every day, of bodies going to the cremation ground. Funeral fires burning at a distance. The voice of her Tamil teacher who had loved and read Tirumular, 'I nurtured my body; indeed I nurtured my life-source.' The poet Ghalib pleading, 'Lord, they have not understood me; they will not understand me. Give them different hearts. Or at least give me a new language.' Which of these things would her mind seek and at what moment? Would it seek after any of these at all? Or would it be soothed by Festivals of India?

People arrived in crowds. Several Americans who had adopted Indian children. They came with joy and enthusiasm. With their children, most often girls, like flowers. With poignancy the thought raised its head: were they girl babies who had been abandoned in rubbish bins or baskets? There was a sharp pang in her lower belly. Gita walked along, Alaknanda holding on to her finger, talking to everyone there. She was introduced as the visitor.

There was a baby girl in the arms of a young American woman who stood opposite them. She was called Rachel. Apparently it wasn't quite a week since they had returned from Mumbai. A six-month-old child. Dark skin, like silk. Her laughter came in ripples. As soon as baby Rachel saw the visitor, she put out her arms and leaned towards her. She refused to go back to her mother. Rachel buried her face in the visitor's chest, chuckling and laughing out loud. When she was petted in Hindi, 'Gudiya' and 'Sonu', she lifted her brow, showing her surprise. Suddenly, she laid her head on the visitor's shoulder. When her mother summoned her with a bottle of milk, she went to her, but put her arm around the visitor's neck, pulling at her too.

The programme continued on stage. And here was Rachel's merriment.

As the moments went by, she began to feel a certain heaviness climbing upon her chest. She felt as if she were an orphan, not yet claimed by anyone. A sudden self-pity. Weariness. But then, like an aeroplane in flight, a school song sung in children's voices, streaked across her mind: 'Treasure of the store-house of grace; daily I seek refuge at your feet.' After this, a voice sobbed, in A.M. Raja's very tone, 'Golden image, unsculpted by human hand, do you not know my mind?'. A folk song by S.D. Burman in Bengali followed hard on its heels. She had a sense of being caressed by warm hands. Once again, Rachel hugged her. She returned to her mother, but turned to look at her and sobbed, pouting her lips.

In her suitcase there was a sari of her mother's. A Banaras tissue sari. It was a light rose colour with a deep violet border. The whole body of it was covered in a pattern of vines in gold thread-work. The heavy end-piece was worked with swans and birds and vines. She asked Gita for the car keys. She lifted the door of the boot, opened her case, and pulled out the sari which lay at the bottom. She took her folding pen-knife from her purse, slit through an edge, tore away the heavy end-piece. She locked up everything once again, folded the piece of silk, and held it in her hands.

Her father had bought that sari, specially ordered and made by the weavers of Banaras, when he had gone there on business. He had given it to her mother, overriding the rules and customs of the joint family. And there wasn't an occasion when her mother had not worn it. It was a sari that had witnessed Sambanda Mudaliar's plays when they were performed in Madras. A sari that had soaked up the sounds of Vasavambal's harmonium music. It had spread itself out to the sound of Rajaratnam Pillai's Todi. A sari that had seen the film about Meera. A sari that was worn on Independence Day. It had travelled to Rishikesh and Haridwar. It had absorbed the coolness and ferocity of the goddesses. It had smelled the scent of flowers at weddings. When they toured Mysore once, it had visited the Brindavan Gardens and St Philomena's Church. It had been worn by many of her mother's friends. It was the very first sari that every girl in the family wore when she grew up. It lay in the wooden bureau, keeping company with neem leaves and southernwood. When her eighty-year-old mother wore it on the day of the final obsequies for her father, all the faces that wore forced expressions of grief changed. The children who had been restrained firmly began to jump about. Just as the whole of the Mahabharata was buried in Draupadi's unbound hair, so too this sari contained within itself a whole history. In its silken threads there was the touch of Ganga's waters. The winds from the mountains. The heat of the sun and the coolness of the moon.

When she went in, Rachel had fallen asleep in her mother's arms. She gave her mother her card and address, and spread the sari-piece over the child. Rachel moved gently in her sleep and snuggled down comfortably. With one hand she held on to the sari border.

May the silk threads of that sari fall on her soft body. May they stroke her. May the swans and birds and vines spread over her. And ground her.

*Uyirnizhal*, May–June 1997

# Wrestling

The milk was at the right heat, comfortingly warm. She added palm sugar and a mere touch of pepper to it. She brought a flask and poured it in. It was needed every time. As soon as the music ebbed away and the applause rang out, he would turn slowly towards her. The way he moved his head was deeply engraved in her mind. A thick neck with folds of skin just beneath the jawline. A thin chain clasped about it. His entire neck drenched in sweat as he finished singing. A red silk shawl just touching his shoulders. A shawl that Kripananda Varrier had once draped about him. He would turn his head towards her and raise his eyebrows just a little. At once she would hand over the *tampura* to a disciple, and pour the milk from the flask into a silver tumbler. She would say softly, as she held it towards him, 'It was wonderful.'

'Mm,' he'd say.

He'd drink the milk. And always, every time, there would be something slightly wrong.

'You could have put in less *kalkandu*, couldn't you?' Or, 'Should you put in the pepper by the handful?' Or, 'Not quite warm enough'. And so on, and so on.

He would grumble in a low murmur. But the *sishya* would hear, plainly. He'd look at her from the corner of his eye. The expression on her face never changed, though. 'Yes,' she'd answer, accepting it all.

As they returned home in the car, he would take her hand gently. He'd mention a particular raaga alaapanai, or a song, *swaraprastaaram*, or *niravel*, and ask, 'Did it come off all right, Shenbagam?'

It wasn't enough just to murmur, 'Mm.'

'Was it the way Ayya taught it?' he would keep on at her.

On some days she stayed silent. She'd look out of the window. She'd stare at the streets, the houses, the passers-by.

'Tell me,' he would insist.

At that day's concert there might have been a small mistake which no one else had noticed. When it was pointed out to him, his face would fall.

'Of course. You'd notice, wouldn't you? After all, you were Ayya's favourite sishya, weren't you,' he'd say, piqued.

His resentment would last until they reached home. Then, at once, his mood would change. He'd play a game of carom with the children. At supper-time he would lap up the garlic-flavoured rasam with relish. Later at night he would caress her gently. He'd take the tampura on his lap and begin to strum it.

'You sing, Princess,' he would say.

He would make her sing the very sequence where he had made a mistake that evening. While she sang, he would moan, 'Amma, Amma.' Sometimes, he would hit himself on the head with the tampura. 'Don't kill me di, you wretch,' he'd cry out. Sometimes, he would call out to his father, 'Ayya, Ayya.'

Then came that endless pacing to and fro. From one end of the verandah to the other. Sometimes, if she chanced to wake up during the night and open her eyes, he would still be walking up and down on the verandah. Softly, she would walk up behind him and touch him. At once he would reach behind him with his arms and clasp her to him. She would stand there, her face and breasts and shoulder pressed against his back. Sometimes, after a while, he would walk back with her and lie down by her side, holding her close. And at times they would make love. He would put all his efforts into bringing her to a climax, making sure that she was satisfied, asking her again and again. But at other times, he would spread his mat on the verandah and lie there by himself. He would keep on humming the song he asked her to sing. In the morning his army of disciples would turn up. And surround him.

'*Anni*, Annachchi needs some warm water.' 'Anni, Ayya is asking for coffee.' 'Anni, some pepper rasam for Annachchi.' The requests came to her continuously. He used his students like a screen behind which he disappeared. If she confronted him directly, he would not look at her. But by the evening, the crowds would melt away. His usual jokes and teasing would begin. This always went on like a kind

of game. But a game without a referee. A game without set rules;
a game which the players themselves were not aware of playing. A
game in which there was neither victory nor defeat. A game in which
winners became losers, and losers winners.

Ayya's portrait hung in the reception room of their house, garlanded.
Kadirvel Pillai was 'Ayya' to everyone who knew him. He was a
performer who came of a long and renowned line of Isai Vellalar,
steeped in the knowledge of their art. He used to say that when his
mother danced, wearing her diamond eardrops, an *addigai* studded
with rubies about her neck, her eyes touched with collyrium and her
lips stained with betel juice, all of Kumbakonam was ravished and
entranced. As a boy, he had seen her dancing through the streets,
when the deity was taken out in procession. He used to say about
that occasion, 'I remember that the street was quite wide, Shenbagam.
Even today, I can picture Amma in her arakku-red sari and green
choli, dancing the *navasandi kavuthuvam* at the cross-roads. Men
walked on either side of her, carrying gas-lit lamps on their shoulders.
There were such crowds there! And it seemed to me then that as
Amma danced along the street, it grew wider and wider.'

Many years later, when he went to visit the place, the same
crossroads with gutters on either side seemed altogether to have
shrunk and narrowed in size. He used to say that without the
adornment of Amma's dance, the street was shown up in all its
nakedness.

Ayya's mother, Kanakambal, went all the way to Chennai to see
Gandhi, taking the young boy with her. Crowds had gathered along
Chennai beach, wave upon wave. She stood for several hours there,
her hands gripping Ayya's shoulders as he stood in front of her. She
didn't say much on their way home by train. But the next time she
danced she wore a plain hand-woven khadi sari. When the temple
administrators admonished her for it, she put them in their place,
saying, 'Ask me which *shastra* says I must only wear silk! I am not just
a street-acrobat, ayya. I'm a woman with sensibility, who eats salt

with her food.' Later on, when she came to know Ramamirtham Ammaiyaar well, she went with her to many meetings of the Self Respect Movement. By the time Ayya was ten years old, except for Vakil Govindaraja Mudaliar, the coming and going of other men to their house ceased. Mudaliar was a fine Tamil scholar. During the evenings, he would chant verses from Tevaram and Tirupugazh to different raagams, Ayya sitting beside him. It was then that Ayya's musical training began, on a regular basis.

Amma's dance performances became more and more rare and finally ceased altogether, when the law banning the dedication of *devadasis* to the temple was passed. It didn't seem, at that time, as if she took much notice of it. She led a busy and cheerful life teaching Ayya the subtler points of music and holding many vigorous discussions with his gurus. Mudaliar, though, would still ask her on some evenings to dance to a particular song, interpreting it through her *abhinayam*. He had already made his will, arranging for Kanakambal to have whatever she needed by way of land and property. The evening that a messenger came to tell them that Mudaliar had died of heart failure, Kanakambal stood for a while quietly, leaning against a pillar. Their lifestyle did not change. They continued to live in relative comfort. Ayya was perhaps seventeen or eighteen at that time.

Mudaliar and Amma had once taken a photograph of themselves at a studio in Kumbakonam. Mudaliar sat up straight in his chair, his hands spread over its arms on either side. She stood behind him, slightly to one side, her arm just seeming to graze the back of his chair. Her other arm hung by her side. That picture was hung in the left hand corner of the narrow corridor running the length of the main room of their house. Kanakambal did not move it. When her health failed her later, and when she was bed-ridden, her eyes roamed about all the time. It was perhaps the photograph she looked for, Ayya thought, the photograph which she would have glanced at constantly as she went up and down the corridor. But instead she beckoned him and asked him for the box that held her *salangai*, her dancing bells. As soon as he brought it to her, she lifted the bells and laid them against her side, as one would a baby, stroking them so that they chimed faintly, making a sound as soft as a baby's whimper. The next morning she died.

Ayya spoke about his mother as if he were telling a story. The photograph which Mudaliar and she had taken together hung in his room, still.

When Shenbagam was about five years old, her mother brought her to Ayya. After her father died, her mother had made a living by cooking for several families. Her Amma loved to sing. She always hummed the Bhupalam raagam in the mornings and the Nilambari in the evenings. But life did not afford her the opportunity to study music properly. She never failed to attend a *kachcheri* at the temple. All Shenbagam's own memories of those early years were deeply associated with music. When the knife-grinder called out 'Knives sharpened' and then laid the knife against the whetstone, its 'kr kr' would seem to her to have its own melody and rhythm. She'd call her mother and tell her so. Then, her mother would seat her on a wooden stool, oil her hair, place a *chombu* of water in her hands, and begin to massage her scalp. She, meanwhile, would paddle her fingers in the water, making a splashing noise, 'salak-palak'. Paddling her fingers twice towards herself and four times on the opposite side, she would ask, 'Amma, guess what song this is?'

'Who can tell, di?'

'Don't you know, Amma? It's *"Vara vina"*.'

'Oh, all right.'

'And this? Salak, salak, salak, palak, palak, palak.'

'I don't know, go on with you.' Amma would rub her head hard.

'*"Orumaiyudane ninadu"*, Amma. Can't you tell?'

Amma would burst out laughing.

Everyone in town knew about Ayya's music and his character. One day, Shenbagam's mother took courage in her hands and brought the child to him. Ayya came out and sat down on the *thinnai* in the verandah, and asked her, 'What is it, amma?'

'You must teach this girl music.'

'It won't work out, amma. Send the child to school. Let her study there and make her way. Music means hard work. You have to give up your life to it. Impossible for her to do, amma.'

Ayya went away inside.

Amma didn't leave, though. She kept on standing there. When he came out, two and a half hours later, Ayya was taken aback.

'Haven't you gone yet? What is this, amma?'

'Please teach her music. Let her stay with you here. Let her be like your own daughter.'

Ayya looked at Shenbagam. She could still remember the clothes she was wearing that day. A checked, green cotton paavaadai with a black border. And a yellow blouse with puffed sleeves. Amma had combed her hair back, and then taken a bunch to one side, tied it with a ribbon and encircled it with flowers. No chappals on her feet. She stood with her legs planted firmly apart, and stared back at Ayya.

'Let's see, sing me a song,' he demanded.

Amma had primed her well before bringing her. At that time, Ayya had written and set to music a song in which Sita, as a young girl, asks who, in reality, are her parents. It was a moving, melodious song in Anandabhairavi, beginning, '*Bhumi yen thaai endraal... If the earth is my mother...*' Ayya himself had sung it in the temple, twice. She sang that song as she stood there, her arms folded. Looking straight ahead, she sang, making no movement at all with her body. Ayya was silent for a moment after she finished. Then he said, very tenderly, 'Come here.'

She went up to him swiftly. He lifted her up and sat her next to him on the thinnai. He stroked her head. Then he looked up at her mother. Before he had finished speaking to Amma, she was fast asleep, her head on his lap.

He used often to talk about it, later on. 'You put your head on my lap and fell asleep, as if you had somehow arrived at the very place to which you were destined to come.'

After that began the unending music practice. Ayya's son Shanmugam was four years older than she was. She was made to sing with him. Within two months her mother went away to Delhi to cook for a south Indian family. She sent money regularly from there. She came to visit her once a year. She'd ask Shenbagam to sing to her, then. And she lived until the time of Shenbagam's own first kachcheri. In every other way, she grew up as if she were Ayya's daughter; and Ayya's wife became her mother. Nagammal had a fine knowledge of Tamil literature. So one could say that she learnt music from Ayya and literature from Nagammal.

Ayya needed his drink, a whole bottle of it, every evening. He would sit down to it either with his musical friends, or by himself. It was during those sessions that he told his stories, passed on gossip, tried out the latest lyrics. It was at such a time, too, that he spoke about his mother.

But it was with Shanmugam that all her singing, her talking, her quarrelling, and her peacemaking took place. Shanmugam tended to be rather lazy. He took his daily practice very casually. He was offhand at lessons, as if to say, 'My Ayya's music is mine by right; who else can claim it?' He seemed to be under the impression that his father's talents had already entered him through his very blood, and without any effort on his part. So he never exerted himself. When she and the other pupils woke up at four in the morning and began their voice-improving exercises, Shanmugam never joined them. And as if to prove that such disciplines were not necessary to it, his voice flowed abundantly, like a clear stream.

Ayya began to teach her to play the vina, since she needed to learn to play an instrument as well as to sing. He never allowed her to do such kitchen chores as chopping vegetables or cleaning vessels. He said her fingers would become worn out. If Nagammal was ever unwell, he never expected his own pupils to do the household chores. He managed everything himself, with the help of Shanmugam. She was never allowed to do anything other than to lay the banana leaves for meals, and to bring drinking water. He looked after her fingers to that extent.

'She is going to become really lazy,' Shanmugam would grumble. 'Why don't I start learning to play the vina as well? Then I won't have to do any of these chores either, will I?'

'Why do you try to compete with her, da?' Ayya would ask him.

When Ayya wasn't looking, Shanmugam would give her a knock on the head. Or he'd pull her plait when she was singing, and make her lose her concentration. It was a great game for him to watch her face all twisted up as she wept. All the same, it was he who climbed up the mango tree to pluck the fruit, who brought green cucumbers from the garden, who stole jaggery and coconut from the kitchen during the afternoon when Nagammal was asleep. All for her.

She was somewhat scared on the day she came of age. She went and stood by a window in one of the rooms at the back of the house, all alone. She was aware of a heaviness in her thighs. Would they isolate her for three whole days? Would she be allowed to sing? To touch her vina? To read the books in Ayya's room?

She also remembered her mother who was somewhere far away, in Delhi. Amma had spoken to her about all this on her last visit. She had left a cotton half-sari with Nagammal before she went away, a sandalwood-coloured one, with a print of purple flowers. The same one that she wore now as she stood there. But she must sing! She must play the vina! She must take the fat books in Ayya's room and place them on her lap like kittens, and riffle through their pages.

Ayya came there after a while. She started to cry when he walked straight up to her and laid her head against his chest saying, 'My dear Princess.' Heaven knew how he intuited her state of mind. 'You are anxious, aren't you, whether you can sing, or play the vina, or touch books?' he asked.

She nodded.

'Silly girl! What connection is there between this and all that? Who told you to come and stand here all by yourself? Anyone may touch books or the vina whenever they please. Come out now.' He took her hand and led her out of the room. He spoke to Nagammal, who was busy at her work, 'Nagu, don't tell her to keep away from the others. You know I don't like that sort of thing.'

'Of course,' said Nagamma, smiling at her. 'I didn't tell her. She went away by herself. She wouldn't come out, however much I asked her.'

He spread out a *jamukaalam* in the front room and handed her the tampura. He summoned Shanmugam and all his other pupils. They sang together as usual. They also noticed she was wearing a half-sari. And so this event too flowed into all the other events of her life, causing no sudden rupture.

When Ayya chose her out of all his other pupils to sing with him at a kachcheri for the first time, there was some resentment on Shanmugam's part. He accompanied them to the concert, but he did not sing. He assumed that Ayya had arranged it that way, deliberately. Just two days earlier, someone had come from elsewhere, one afternoon, to invite Ayya to give a performance. Shanmugam had invited him to sit on the thinnai, and then disappeared inside and forgotten all about him. When Ayya emerged two hours later, the gentleman was still sitting there. Seeing Ayya, he greeted him respectfully, and mentioned that he was very thirsty. As soon as Ayya realized that he had been waiting for two hours, he stormed inside and shouted out, 'Shenbagam!'

Shenbagam, who had been sitting in Ayya's room, looking at some books with Shanmugam, heard the anger in Ayya's voice and came out.

'Did you call me, Ayya?'

'What is this, amma, do you just ask a man to sit down in the thinnai and forget about everything else? He's come all this way in the mid-day heat. Shouldn't you ask him whether he wants anything to eat or drink? What were you so busy about, in there?'

Shanmugam came out then, and said, 'It was I who asked him to sit down, Ayya. I'm afraid I forgot about him. It didn't strike me that it was going to be an important kachcheri. Judging from his clothes, I'd say you are not likely to get more than half a coconut out of it.'

Ayya took the towel off his shoulder and flung it at him. He went inside and brought out a chombu of water and a platter of fruit and snacks. He placed it on the thinnai, saying, 'You must forgive me. My son forgot to tell me you were here.' He agreed to sing at the kachcheri.

After the man had left, Ayya came inside and said to Shanmugam, 'A musician ought never to be arrogant, da.' Shanmugam didn't reply. He merely looked at Shenbagam, raised his eyebrows and curled his lips.

It was for that very kachcheri that Ayya chose Shenbagam, out of all his pupils, to accompany him. He made her sing together with him, and at the end of the programme, he asked her to sing a couple of kirtanai on her own. The concert took place in a small village. They had just completed laying a main road, and it was in celebration of this that the concert was held. Apart from the microphone, and the small lights surrounding them, there was no other evidence of electricity being used there. None of the lamps shed a garish light. If anyone stood up and walked away carrying a battery-operated torch, its circle of light entrapped a few white shirts, or brightly coloured saris and cholis, or the cheeks of babies pressed against thighs, as they lay fast asleep. Between the audience and the performers on stage, a bridge was established within the very first minutes. Crossing it again and again, the two could touch each other. When Ayya had finished, there was no applause at all. Then, an old gentleman came forward and said, 'Ayya, we have sat here this evening, spellbound by your music. I am now in my eightieth year. I have no idea whether there is such a thing as another birth or not. But if there should be such a thing, then I pray that I should be born a child in your household. I want to go on listening to your music.' Then, having learnt about Ayya's usual ways, he held out a bottle towards him. Ayya did not refuse it. But from the presentation platter that held his fee, he took only the half coconut, saying, 'Please buy some sweets with this money, and give them to those children who never cried or made any trouble tonight.'

That night, as their bullock cart went slowly along the road that wound its way among fields and woods, Ayya said, 'Shanmugam, don't think I asked Shenbagam to sing tonight in order to punish you in any way. There is no connection at all between this and what happened the other day. Shenbagam has outstripped the rest of you and gone a long distance ahead. She has worked that hard.'

After that Shanmugam began to practise fiercely, like a demon.

Ayya began to make arrangements for Shenbagam's *arangetram*, her first public performance. It was held at a school in their town, on a modest scale, without much flourish. He did not forget to invite her mother. But Shenbagam had a secret that would take Ayya by surprise at the arangetram. She had composed a *varnam* describing a peacock dancing amidst a dense forest, set it to music as a *raagamalikai*; and she sang this in place of the usual invocation to Vinayakar. It contained her own signature in the line, '*Kadirvel Nagamiruvar magal Shenbagam manam magizha...* That the heart of Shenbagam, daughter of Kadirvel and the two Nagams, may rejoice.'

As soon as they returned home, Shanmugam asked, 'Isn't it a sign of arrogance, Ayya, to sing without praying to Vinayakar?'

'No, da. Hers is the pride of knowledge. You need that too, da,' said Ayya.

Amma deeply appreciated that special signature and its reference. Her name was Nagavalli. When Shenbagam invoked the two Nagams,

she bound herself to her mother once again. It was as if it made up
for all those years of cooking in other people's houses. But she wasn't
there for Shenbagam's next kachcheri.

Shenbagam was invited to give at least five or six kachcheris in a
year. Meanwhile, Shanmugam too began by singing together with
Ayya, and then went on to take the stage alone and to give his own
solo concerts.

One couldn't say at what instant exactly the deep bond between
them became established. Perhaps, without their ever realizing it, it
had been burgeoning deep within them. When Ayya spoke to her
about getting married, she never said a word. 'You mustn't marry a
man who will stop you from giving performances,' he said. 'He must
respect your music.' Neither did she reply when he asked her whether
he should look for a bridegroom from her own community, or what
he should do. Shanmugam intercepted her in the corridor as she
came away from this conversation.

'Shenbagam, how can you even think of looking for a bridegroom
elsewhere? You've got to marry me.'

An intense happiness rose up within her. Quickly she went up to
him and held him tightly. She stroked his bare chest with her face.

When they told Ayya about their wishes, he did not reply to them
immediately. Nagammal, however, hugged her with joy. Then Ayya
said to Shanmugam, 'Why don't you let it be for a couple of years?
What's the hurry?'

'Now that it's been decided, why should we put it off?' Shanmugam
asked in his turn.

'Let her grow up a bit,' Ayya said.

For a couple of days, Shanmugam and she went around with long
faces. After that Ayya agreed to fix their wedding date. Then two
months passed as they touched and learnt each other, astonished and
delighted each other. They were overwhelmed by their joy, wave upon
wave. Not a single new song was practised. During the third month,
she had an invitation to do a kachcheri in a different town. After she
had accepted by telegram, she decided on her programme, and then
sat down with Ayya to discuss it. He suggested a few changes. He
promised to teach her a couple of new pieces.

While they were eating, Ayya told Shanmugam about the new pieces, and suggested they learn them together. Immediately Shanmugam asked, 'Is Shenbagam going to give concerts?'

'What do you mean? What else is she going to do? Cook?' Ayya asked sharply.

'No, Ayya. But why should she go rushing about everywhere? Let her sing as much as she wants to, at home. These concerts will only exhaust her. Leave me to do the running around. Let her rest at home.'

Ayya continued to eat without saying a word. Later, when she went into his room with his drinking water, he spoke to her brusquely. 'Go on, go on. Run your household. Have your babies.'

She stood there quietly. Her eyes filled.

'Why are you crying, wretched girl?'

'Will you teach me the new pieces?'

'We'll begin tomorrow. Go on,' he said, without anger.

He never stopped teaching until he died. The outside world claimed that Shanmugam was the true heir to his music. Awards, degrees, presentation shawls, and citations kept on coming to him. The days when he and Shenbagam sang together gradually faded away. Along with the concerts came the pomp and show of success. Shanmugam entered the huge world of acolytes and sycophants as well as of true artists. Shenbagam lived with him. She stood close by him. From where she sat behind him, she handed him his milk. But somewhere, at a place invisible to the eye, they continued to be as wrestlers, locked in their struggle.

'Anni, could you give some hot milk, please, with turmeric powder in it?' asked Somu, the sishya, coming into the kitchen.

'Why, aren't you feeling well?'

'I coughed a couple of times, Anni.'

The bangles were still on his wrists.

It happened about three years earlier. While Shanmugam was away from home, Somu pestered her to teach him the varnam she had composed, and Shenbagam did so. He sang it at a small function a little later, citing her as the composer. By chance, a famous *vidwan* happened to be in the audience. He had made it an unswerving rule that no woman should be on stage with him while he performed. Apparently he had ridiculed the boy later, saying, 'What is this, appa, you've started to take lessons from a woman, have you? Do one thing. Get a couple of bangles for your wrists.'

'Bangles won't be a problem, Anna. Look, I can get a pair straight away,' Somu replied. And he went off in haste to the jewellery shop and returned, wearing a pair of silver bangles. Later, Shanmugam scolded him for showing up the vidwan in that way. But Somu refused to remove the bangles.

As Somu was drinking his milk, another pupil came in haste to tell them that Rangasami had arrived. Within the next instant, Rangasami himself walked right inside the house.

'Shenbagamma, a terrible mistake has happened,' he said in consternation.

Shenbagam came out of the kitchen into the main room asking, 'Why, what's the matter?' She invited him to sit down, and sat down herself.

'I've been out of town for a whole month. I fixed Shanmugam Anna's concert date, and then went away. I asked the man working under me to arrange for the orchestra. He's somewhat new to all this and doesn't understand all the conventions. Not realizing what he was doing...he's gone and engaged women artists... Both the violinist and *ghatam* player are ladies. What shall we do?'

'When it comes to music, what does it matter whether the artist is a man or a woman, sir? In our Ayya's family, the women played all manner of instruments, *mridangam*, *kanjira*, everything. Even in those days, when they used to say that it was not necessary for women to sing *raagam*, *taanam*, and *pallavi*, the women of his lineage would sing *raagams*, and even go on to *swarams*. This is our Ayya's son. He won't say anything. Please go ahead.' With these words of comfort, she sent him away.

Meanwhile Somu stood by, fingering his silver bangles.

Shanmugam climbed on to the stage, his brocaded shawl glittering, greeted the audience, and sat down. A look of surprise crept across his face as his eyes swept over the accompanying artists on either side of him. By this time, Rangasami began to introduce the musicians.

Shanmugam began his first song, and paused for a moment at the point where Somu could join in with him. But just then Somu appeared to be looking elsewhere and not paying attention. A second time, Shanmugam contrived to pause, creating an opportune moment for Somu to join in; but the boy did not seem to notice. A split second later Shenbagam leaned towards the mike in front of Somu, repeated the line that Shanmugam had just sung, and joined in with the melody. Her eyes blazed into his, as Shanmugam turned towards her, startled. Her entire face was illuminated as she smiled. A huge applause rang out from the audience. Shanmugam looked at her as if he had been caught in a tight hold and wrestled to the ground at a totally unexpected moment. In an instant, Somu took away the tampura from her hands and moved the mike in front of her. Shenbagam led into the next line herself.

Perhaps Shanmugam was perspiring in spite of the air-conditioning in the room. He removed the shawl that was draped around his shoulders, laid it aside, and began to sing with Shenbagam.

*Kalachuvadu*, 14 June 1996

# A Rat, a Sparrow

When she turned around in her sleep and opened her eyes, the rat's face was right next to her cheek. And when she screamed out loud, leapt to her feet and stood there shuddering, the rat too, startled by her scream, jumped on to the window and sought shelter there. It lifted its nose and stared at her as if to say, 'How you terrified me with your scream!'. Every time it tried to move, she screamed again. Finally, it sat right where it was, motionless. And she stood frozen in front of it, staring at it all the time.

It is difficult to be friendly with rats. Most particularly so with this one. It must surely have been this one. A rat which tended to eat up only the autobiographies in the top shelf of her bookcase. Because the covers of the autobiographies had been nibbled completely at random, their titles stated starkly, *My His* or *My Autobiog* or *My St* As for one of them, entitled *The Autobiography of a Donkey*, only the *Donkey* remained. When you looked up at it, beneath the smiling photograph of the author, you could only see the word 'Donkey' in boldly-inked letters. Although many people might have thought the word appropriate to the author, one could not say whether they would have wanted it to be left to the rat's judgement in the end. It struck her that even if the author had called himself a donkey in false deprecation, he might object to its being emphasized in quite this way.

It was because of this that as soon she heard the sounds 'krk, krk' the following night she flashed her torch along the top shelf. The rat was sitting on the autobiography, and had begun nibbling its way around the 'Donkey'. It looked down at her. It seemed to her that it was laughing. Her tongue rolled into a scream. Her friends, knocked out after their customary Saturday celebrations, woke up. They chased after the two-inch-long rat. It scuttled into the bathroom. Paramvir followed it inside with a coconut-frond broom, and locked the door behind himself.

'Param, don't kill it. Just make it faint.'

'It's just two inches long. Do I know how to hit it so that it just faints?' he replied from within.

'If, after thou hast given it chase, it still does not die, what wouldst thou do?' asked Susan in pure Tamil. She was from Paris. Paramvir's girlfriend. She had attended a three-month intensive course in Tamil, and was here to do some research on female deities. According to her, Lakshmi sitting at Mahavishnu's feet and stroking them was not an indication of being dominated by him; she was only instilling in him the energy and strength he needed to succour the world and to create whatever was necessary. When asked why someone with so much energy should not stroke her own feet and take on Vishnu's work herself, she said, 'Thou givest me cause for laughter.' Now she stood there exclaiming 'Aiyako' in response to the loud noises of Paramvir's battle with the rat inside the bathroom.

Paramvir emerged, with the rat lying prone on the coconut-frond broom.

'It's only fainted,' he reassured her. He let it go on the street below, and then returned. The caretakers of the building were somewhat disturbed by the sight of a Sardarji with his hair bound up, coming downstairs at one o'clock in the morning, carrying a rat on a broom. The next day, they avoided looking directly at her.

Just as she had fallen asleep peacefully, assuring herself that when the stunned rat opened its eyes, it must surely have walked off into a world without autobiographies, here it was again, sitting right next to her cheek.

But was it the same rat? When it recovered from its swoon, did it come straight back here? Or was this one its mate?

Many people had forewarned her that the big city was full of rats and bandicoots. Because it was artists and intellectuals who told her this, it was reasonable for her to assume that they were referring metaphorically to the human inhabitants here. Besides, when she and Amulyo spent their very first night in this city in a flat which belonged to Gita and Sukhdev, with its single room, its kitchen smelling of mustard pickle, and sweaty clothes hanging up on the line, the rat-image had struck her as particularly appropriate. The kitchen was really like a rat-hole. And it was on that night that she had her dream.

Skyscrapers on all four sides, like mountains. Narrow streets. If you enter a building looking for a place to stay, they turn into rat-holes where you cannot even stand upright. Everywhere there are people lying either on their backs or on their sides, sitting with their heads on their knees, talking together, laughing. A woman returns home from her office. Very casually she enters her rat-hole. Voices, as if from heaven, tell her of the comforts of their flats. ...When she tries to take hold of a rope in order to raise herself up conveniently, it turns out to be a rough, abrasive rat's tail.

She must have called out in her sleep. She opened her eyes. Amulyo was peacefully asleep. He was one who was truly blessed with the gift of sleep. She shook him awake.

'Amul, Amul!'

'Ha...,' he said, waking up with a start.

'Amul, I had a dream.'

'Mm.'

'A frightful dream, Amul. I went cold all over.'

Amulyo sat up and drank from the water bottle. He poured some water into a glass and gave it to her. When she had drunk it, he said, 'Tell me.'

When she finished describing the dream, he laughed.

'How do you manage to dream in such beautiful images? It's complete with symbols and everything. And for all that, you don't even agree with Freud.'

She hit him on the stomach. 'You are a goonda, a loafer. You are a Kumbakarnan who sleeps all the time. You are a rascal.' A blow accompanied each epithet.

He lay back, still laughing. She climbed on top of his stomach, her legs on either side of him, and took up the posture of the Destroyer of Demons.

Amulyo caught hold of her raised hand. Very gently. Her eyes filled. Tears came too, to his eyes.

He glanced at the shelves above them, blackened with smoke; at the aluminium vessels that could be discarded at any time they chose to pack up; the kerosene stove; the roach-powder scattered at the edges of the walls; the kitchen drain only ten feet away. Then he looked at her and was silent.

She touched his navel gently.

'It was only a dream, Amul,' she said.

She remembered the spacious backyard of her grandmother's house in Coimbatore. Certain images are inextricably linked with certain places. Her image of her Paatti was inseparably linked with that house. Paatti who had borne children from the age of thirteen. Paatti who had cooked vegetables and stirred *halva* in great big pans. Paatti who had told stories from the Ramayanam as she massaged her puny grandchildren—including herself—with castor oil, firmly, firmly. Paatti with her tongue like a whiplash. Whose every word had stung.

Animals always surrounded Paatti, like the cattle which stood about Krishna, enchanted by his flute.

One hot summer afternoon, Paatti woke up with a start. She went to the backyard. A monkey sat on the wall behind the well, making the most frightful noises.

'What's the matter, da?' asked Paatti.

'Urr,' it replied.

'Paatti, don't go near it Paatti!' she and her cousins, Chithi's children, called out.

Paatti looked at the monkey steadily. Then she went to the room next to the bathroom where the firewood was stacked, and brought an empty coconut shell. She dipped it into the water trough and filled it. She went towards the monkey and held it out, full of water. It grabbed the coconut shell from her and drank it down in a single breath. Having drunk three times from her shell, it leapt away, swirling its tail.

'It was thirsty,' said Paatti.

The house was full of black and white and brown cats. At least a dozen of them. After a row of children had eaten their meal, followed by the men, when Paatti stretched out her leg and sat down to eat with the women, the cats would come, swarming about her.

'Miaou,' one would say.

'It wants an *appalam*,' Paatti would translate.

They were cats which had acquired a palate for appalam, rasam, rice, roast-potatoes, and so on. She would give ghee-rice to a cat that had just survived the delivery of a litter of kittens. When the morning milk arrived, the cats too had their share.

'Would you like to keep a cat?' asked Amulyo.

'Mm. No. What about you? You keep a dog at home, don't you?'

'It's really wrong to keep animals locked up in these cage-like places,' he said.

'Children too,' she agreed.

After the rat-dream, there had been other rat-*darsanams*, manifestations. Rat legends. Rat experiences about which Sukhdev and Gita told them. As she watched a cinema show, munching popcorn, Gita had felt a sharp nip at her foot. The very moment after she shook her foot and looked up again, Sukhdev was shaking off his foot, too. When both of them looked down, they saw a huge bandicoot running away. Both their feet were bloodied. Several injections later, full of righteous indignation, they had approached a journalist friend and asked him to make a report about it. He, however, had shed a patient smile and informed them about the experiences of the cinema critic of their paper. For some reason, this woman had missed the preview meant for the press, and went instead to the cinema theatre where the picture was being released publicly. As she was writing her notes, she felt her dupatta being pulled. Apparently, she took no notice of it, but held her pad against the armrest of her chair, and went on busily making her notes. When the lights came on for the interval, she bent down and saw a rat on her lap! When she stood up and screamed, the other spectators calmly watched the rat running away and commented, 'Such a lot of fuss, just for a rat!' Then someone sitting next to her told her an elaborate rat joke. There was a girl who learnt judo. She learnt karate. She learnt *kalaripayittru*. One day, she saw a rat running across her kitchen floor. She screamed out loudly and climbed on to a chair. He cackled loudly, 'ke-ke-ke-ke', as he told her this.

One does not know whether a bandicoot ever bit his feet.

She knew a story about a Rat Prince. Once, there were three princes. Two of them chased one away from the land. After many trials and tribulations, he meets a princess. When she kisses him, he turns into a handsome prince. When she grew up a little, she added a postscript to the tale. The Rat Prince became a handsome Human Prince after the kiss. The princess, though, became a rat. What a wonder! No prince came forward to kiss her. Not even the Rat Prince.

After Gita and Sukhdev had gone abroad for a year, they had taken over the flat and this rat had come to do battle with them. Often, there is a particular symbol which stands for a big town. Just as the Big Apple stands for New York. It struck her that only one symbol could possibly stand for this city: a Rat. Rat city. Rat people. People who stayed as rats, even after a kiss. There might be a whole history behind this rat cowering by the window. It might be a rat which was bored with many *yugas* of life as a rat, weary after eating so many autobiographies; it might be hoping to change after a kiss from her.

She got up and pushed the window shutter outward with a long rod. The rat sprang up and ran outside.

When Amulya returned home from his trip the next day, she told him all about the rat. He suggested they buy some rat-poison. She thought that this was, after all, a literary rat. It shouldn't die in agony. There were any number of ways to die other than by poison. Come to think of it, she had a nonsense *ula*, a song of praise, in her possession. It was an ula composed in praise of a Tamil Nadu leader. In fact, one sect of the now-divided party had circulated a rumour that this ula had been sung to the leader hours before he died, and that there was definitely a connection between the poem and his immediate dispatch to the hospital. She thought that if this rat ate the ula, it would certainly die. But would it die without writhing in agony? She wanted to laugh.

'Why, do you have a book which will put an end to it or what?'

'Look here, don't make fun of Tamil. All your books are rotten ones which even a rat won't eat.'

'What's this, a "linguistic state" dispute?'

'Well then, should any idiot who can't even pronounce 'zh' make fun of Tamil? What's all this Tamil, anyway? It's Tamizh, Tamizh. Say "zh."'

'Zh,' said Amulyo, pronouncing it perfectly.

'Is it enough to say it just once? Say after me: *Vaazhaippazham vazhukki kizhavi nazhuvi kuzhiyil vizhundaal.*'

'Look, I didn't get a sleeper, so I've sat up all night. Why can't you teach me Tamizh—see, I said Tamizh—after I've had a cup of tea at least?'

They said that this was a city where all sorts of people lived. But it was clear that several among them were marked off as Madrasis. There was a certain friend of Amulyo's. As soon as he saw her, his mouth would grimace a little. '*Namaskaram* ji,' he would say, grinding away, with the idea that if you added '-am' to a word, it became Tamil. 'Sambaram, rasam, tea-am, coffee-am, *puri*-am, *chappati*-am...,' he would say in a rapid volley, and then ask in a drawl, '*Kya* ji?'

After he had done this a couple of times, she questioned him, full of concern, 'Vijay, you poor man, have you had this speech defect since you were a child? Is there no way to correct it? How you have to struggle to speak!'

Vijay was taken aback. He stumbled, 'No, no. This is... Madrasi...'

'Oh, I see. I was feeling sorry for you all these days. You see, we don't speak like that at all.'

Vijay looked at Amulyo as if he were seeking help.

'Well, Vijay, what will you drink? Tea-am?'

'Tea,' he answered in a subdued voice.

There was another friend who insisted on telling jokes after having downed three pegs of rum. 'I'm going to act like a Madrasi,' he proclaimed loudly. Before the others could stop him, he had turned himself into a Madrasi. He rolled back his shirt sleeve. He pretended that there was a leaf in front of him, scooped up a handful of food and sucked at it with a loud hiss. Another scoop, another hiss. Then a series of rapid movements as if he was shovelling the food into his mouth. Finally, he thrust out his tongue and licked off both the inner palm and back of his hand. He laughed at his own performance. Nobody else laughed with him.

Vijay went up to him and whispered something. He looked at her and said, grinning away, 'It was only in fun. I like the temples in Tamil Nadu very much. Then dosa, vada, idli,' he drawled, stressing the 'd'.

'*Saniyane*,' she said, meaning, You wretch.

Only Amulyo understood what she said. He gave the friend his bag and sent him on his way. When Vijay left that day, he didn't say, 'Namaskaram ji,' but gave her a hug and said limply, 'Good night.'

She was in a sudden frenzy. She wanted to embrace the plantain-leaf seller in that part of the city where most of the Tamil people congregated. When she heard a certain Tamil accent, she felt as if the Tambaraparni had burst its banks and come flowing towards her. Dosai, idli, rasam, *idiaappam* and Chettinad chicken curry seemed to her like the very staples of life. Suddenly at night, or in the afternoon, or in a crowded bus or train as she was wiping away her sweat, a long-forgotten song would come to mind, sharp as a lightning of pain. She heard the Kaavadichindu song her grandfather used to sing in the terrace at night, looking at the stars and pacing about with his legs held apart,

> This rotten body is of use to no one—
> like a broken sieve, oh parrot,
> always it brings pain.

That frenzy held her in its grip until she reached the Tamil library. There, when she saw the brightly coloured book-covers, all of them portraying women either on their backs or lying prone, her legs began to buckle.

It seemed that the overseer of the library would never take his hand out of his veshti. Heaven knew what buried treasure he had there. As soon as he clapped eyes on a woman, his hand went into hiding. He spoke vociferously about Tamil culture, gesticulating with his other hand.

'We are safeguarding a whole culture, amma. For the sake of Tamil, I've had stones thrown at me.' He displayed a bald patch on his head. 'We are making great efforts to have a statue of Bharati placed outside here, and another of Tiruvalluvar. I've also put forward the idea that we should cover all the walls here with *kural* couplets. As soon as you walk in, a kural should catch your eye immediately. It should hit your eye. Say you've just come in. You see a kural right in front of you:

> She who worships none other than her husband as her god
> Says 'Rain' and instantly the rain falls.

What do you think of that, amma? Your hair would stand on end, wouldn't it? You'd be thrilled. We must praise our women, amma. We have competitions at singing kural, tevaram, and all that. If women win, we don't give them prizes at random. We might give them a pedestal oil-lamp. Or we might give them a book about the role of women in Tamil culture.' He leaned towards her. 'It's simple, amma. Our entire culture is in the hands of women, amma.'

His voice revealed his tranquillity at having given over Tamil culture into women's hands. She thought to herself, if his hand were ever to emerge from its own cultural search, then some of Tamil's cultural burden might be placed there too.

Outside, just by the door, a singer attached to the Sabha where all south Indians came to learn various arts, was talking away.

'They've got rid of me. Did you know that?'

'Is that so? And why?'

He rapidly undid the buttons of his crisply-starched shirt and displayed his bare chest.

'I don't have a sacred thread.'

The two of them bought an extremely potent poison. They smeared it on bread and placed the pieces in corners of the room. She put one piece behind *The Autobiography of a Donkey*. Heaven knew which particular piece of bread it ate. It lay dead, modestly, in a bag made of soft blue material. She felt a shock. Would it have suffered a lot? Might it have been in agony? Certainly, it had tormented them. Wrecked their sleep. Ruined their books. It died alone and in agony, in the blue bag. Amulyo went and shook it out on the seashore.

This rat would not act in obstinate resistance like the one they had once seen. One evening at the beach a man had walked ahead of them, carrying a rat-trap. The tiny rat peeped out of the trap, squeaking. He placed the trap facing the sea and opened its door. It saw the sea in front of it and was paralysed. It refused to come out of the trap. Squeaking aloud it clung to the bars. The man who had brought it there tilted the trap. He shook it hard. He banged at it. The rat obstinately refused to come out. Not knowing what else to do, the poor man settled down by the trap as if in penance, waiting desperately for it to come out. When they left the beach and turned around one last time, the rat still had not come out, and he still sat there waiting, so that he could take the trap home. It didn't seem as if the rat appreciated the man's obstinacy either. Both man and rat-trap were silhouetted against the fading light of the sunset. In front of them, by the horizon, apartment blocks rose, like mountains.

Some days after all this, there was the advent of the sparrow. Standing in the balcony which could only accommodate one person comfortably, she looked down on the rubbish heaps below and the children sitting there defecating; then turned her gaze towards the old theatre opposite. An old Hindi film was showing there. The balcony doors stood open, perhaps to compensate for the breakdown of the electric fans. Through the heavy black curtains a song sung by Mukesh for Raj Kapoor came floating towards her. It was then that it fell, brushing against her shoulder. Startled, she moved, leaned down, and saw that it was a sparrow. A baby sparrow. One wing was broken and crooked. Inside its beak, its mouth showed, red as a berry. She was afraid to touch it. She filled an ink-filler and dropped water into its mouth. It opened its eyes. She carried it inside on a piece of cardboard and laid it in a corner. At night she covered it with a net basket.

When she lifted the basket in the morning, the sparrow shrieked. It circled about, calling out 'ki-ki-ki'. It tapped the ink-filler with its beak. Before she could recover from her shock, two birds alighted on the balustrade of the verandah parapet. Swiftly they flew down, and thrust little worms into the baby sparrow's mouth. With little relishing squeaks, it swallowed. Then it snuggled down once more.

In the afternoon, flying lessons began. One of the sparrows flew up and down, down and up; first slowly then rapidly. As soon as it stopped, the other one took over. The baby sparrow rose to its feet, raised itself into the air with its crooked wing, then fell. Until five in the afternoon the parent birds went on trying, incessantly. The baby sparrow gave up its attempt at flying and began to walk about. At last, the parent birds left the baby sparrow in her safekeeping, and flew away. The older birds came back for some days, but disappeared after that. The little sparrow could not fly further than five or six feet. It made its home against the first iron bracket of her book shelf. Unlike the rat which laid siege to the books stealthily in the middle of the night, this sparrow cast its droppings all over the books on that side, in broad daylight. One day, she knelt in front of it and sang, 'Sparrow, little sparrow, do you know what has happened? My husband has gone away and not yet come home.' The sparrow squeaked 'kerk', making its protest clear. It was greatly attracted to red things. It shed its droppings most generously on books with red covers. When they came in late at night after a long time away, as soon as they opened the door, it called out sharply from the corner of the book shelf, expressing its disapproval loudly.

When she opened the window nearest the bookshelf, it immediately went and perched against the bars. As she gazed out at the buildings covered in factory smoke, standing out against a background of stench and noise, it was the little sparrow in the foreground that caught her eye. A sparrow that opened its jewelled eyes and looked outward.

When she rested her head against the window bars, and everything behind the curtain of rain turned into shadowy lines, the sparrow perched next to her. She narrowed her eyes and looked sideways, and the sparrow filled her vision. Behind it, the ash-coloured city extended. Like a city that was placed upon its head. Like a crown.

One day, after she had stood for a moment with her head against the window, eyes closed, she opened her eyes again to find the baby sparrow gone. She searched throughout the flat, calling out, 'Kutty, Little One!' She came out into the verandah, calling loudly, 'Kutty', when it peeped out from a hole in the outside wall of the apartment building. She could just catch a glimpse of its broken wing. As she stood there wondering anxiously how to save it from the clutches of a kite, or an eagle, or a vulture, it rose gracefully upward and then flew back into the hole. Another time it rose upward, demonstrating that it could fly. A third time, while Amulyo and she stood watching from the window, it rose high into the air, flew up and down harmoniously, and then disappeared into a tree that stood at a distance of fifty feet. There were several other sparrows there.

As far as the eye could see, there were long rows of buildings, with no space in between. Unrepaired walls, displaying their cracks. Curving lines of cement covering some of those cracks. Some walls tarred over, to prevent rain water from seeping through. Many-coloured clothes hanging on hooks extending from the verandahs. Green leaves sprouting from flower-pots on window sills. The city lay like a rakshasa, displaying all this. And in the branch of a tree that had somehow struggled its way up in the midst of it all, a little sparrow.

And then one evening, a little later, this happened. Street lights and shop lights and neon advertisements had all come on. The street was an ocean of traffic. Roaring double-decker buses; autorickshaws with their incessant noise as they wound their way in and out; impatient scooters and cars. An absolute deluge of noise. Amulyo entered the traffic stream, ran, shoved, pushed, and reached the other side. She got halfway across the street, and was stuck on the stone barrier, one foot wide, that divided the street into two. Amulyo stood on the other side, beckoning with his hands, 'Come over.' All around her, huge advertisement lights flashed, without even a foot's interval in between, assaulting her eyes. A red double-decker bus, with violent blue, yellow, and green lettering rushed past, practically scraping her back. Terrifying vehicles, stopping, screeching, and then overtaking each other. She sprang forward a couple of feet, then fell back again, frightened by a furious black car. Car horns practically squealed into her ears. Her face, her neck, her armpits, and her thighs were all streaming with sweat. And then a woman came next to her, holding a couple of empty fish baskets at a slant. She caught a whiff of smell from the baskets. With the one hand which was free of the baskets, the woman caught her by the waist. Holding her baskets high up to stop the traffic, the woman dragged her along. As soon as they reached the opposite verge, the fisherwoman left her at Amulyo's side and went on her way.

As she stood gasping for breath on that pavement covered with spittle, waste, cigarette stubs, vendors, and gutters, a place where all the city's noises seemed to gather and overflow, he suddenly appeared in front of them. In the city's language, he was a *bevda*, a drunk. The city behaved with kindness towards bevdas. If they stretched themselves out to sleep in buses or in trains, nobody shook them awake. 'Bevda *hai*... He's only a bevda,' they would say, and walk past, excusing him. Once, a bevda boarded a bus at midnight and obstinately refused to buy a ticket from the conductor. He stood there, shouting in Hindi, 'Drink, drink, drink; drink in the evening, drink in the morning; drink at day, drink at night; drink, drink, drink.' The conductor himself bought the man a ticket. The bevda said, 'Wake me up at the temple,' crashed down and slept. There were temples all along the way. A wayside shrine to Sai Baba every ten feet. At which temple should he be woken up? 'Poor old bevda,' said the conductor.

The bevda came near her, and she realized he was middle-aged. When he was just about ten feet away, he slithered down, gently and in slow motion, on to the pavement. Nobody took the slightest notice. They just started walking around him.

He tried to get to his feet as she and Amulyo went up to him, but failed. He held out his thumb and forefinger, two inches apart, and smiled radiantly, saying, 'It just got a bit too much.' They helped him to his feet and made him sit up, leaning against a wall. 'Are my chappals on my feet? Place them in my hands. Otherwise, these rascals will snatch them and make off.' He hugged the chappals as soon as they were in his hands, and closed his eyes. A peaceful smile on his face.

When they reached the bus-stand, they joined the long queue. She leaned against the lamp-post nearby and started to laugh. A second later Amulyo joined in. They could not stop laughing.

*Kalachuvadu* Annual, 1991

# Journey 3

As soon as the summer began, Amma would start planning the food-offering to Mariamman. When she began announcing twice a day, like a news broadcast, 'It's absolutely burning hot. We must make a food-offering to Mariamman,' Mythili would start to get excited. Because this short excursion was a special annual event. It always took place soon after the school holidays began. A little tour undertaken just by Marudayi who worked in their house, Marudayi's daughter Minakshi, and Mythili.

The Mariamman temple was at the Majestic. Amma undertook all the preparations for the offering, but would never go to that temple herself. Marudayi interceded on their behalf and worshipped Mariamman who prevented diseases like small-pox. 'She is their deity, you see,' Amma would explain to Mythili. Amma herself went to the temple of Kannika Parameswari at Malleswaram's 8th Cross Road. On each of the nine days of Navaratri, Kannika Parameswari was offered a different adornment. Turmeric, sandalwood, kumkumam, *javanti*, jasmine buds, orange sections, *kadali* bananas, *kanakambaram* flowers, and finally a silk sari. Crowds surged in the temple at evening puja time. Amma usually took Mythili with her. When the screen parted to reveal the goddess in all her adornments, Amma would be transported. Folding her hands, she would begin to sing softly, '*Amba, ninnu nera nammidi... Mother, in you I have faith.*' But it seems that the goddess who received all these adornments didn't have the power to prevent small-pox. Only Mariamman, who wrapped a bright red cloth about herself, daubed herself with kumkumam, and had huge staring eyes, had that power. And there had to be a Marudayi to act as a messenger from them to that Mariamman.

The preparations for the offering would begin with the question, 'Marudayi, have you had your cleansing bath yet, this month?'

Once the discussion about Marudayi's state of ritual purity came to an end, a date was set for the food-offering. On that particular day, Marudayi would turn up at their house at earliest daybreak. She would finish all the household chores at top speed and have a bath under the tap in the backyard. She'd call Minakshi who was usually running around the extensive back garden planted with oleander, southernwood, and *kasi-thumbai* plants, and mango, jackfruit, plantain, papaya, and drumstick trees. 'Ei, Minakshi, come here,' she'd call out, and give her a bath too. Minakshi had curly hair. It spread out, flaring, before falling down her back. Marudayi would pour water over it, add shiyakai and scrub hard, while Minakshi screamed and screamed. She'd hold her firmly between her thighs and bathe her, while the little girl struggled to free herself, shouting, 'Let me go, Aya, let me go.' Sometimes Mythili, who was watching from the back door, would be called and bathed too.

After her bath, Marudayi went into the empty garage to change her sari. There were some saris which she kept only for special occasions, such as the bright green Chinnalampati sari with the imitation zari border, or Amma's old blue silk with its red border which almost hit you in the eyes, or else a glowing yellow handloomed cotton with black checks. She emerged from the garage wearing one of these with the same black blouse with red spots which went with all of them. She'd have fastened a *paavaadai* on to Minakshi—red with yellow dots, or purple with green stars—beneath her navel. The blouse above the paavaadai always stood a little short of her waist. Mythili often stood by the door to the backyard, waiting for the moment when Marudayi would emerge from the garage, with wet hair, her face covered in turmeric, and a big kumkumam spot on her forehead, holding Minakshi by the hand. In the back garden full of mango trees and plants, the very first rays of sunlight just beginning to glint, Marudayi would stand, looking like a woodland sprite. Next to her, Minakshi with her curly hair fanning out about her, a tiny sprite.

A big earthenware pot to cook the pongal offering. Another pot containing the rice, jaggery, coconut, bananas, and banana-leaf. Amma would have kept everything ready. By this time, Mythili too would have had her oil massage and bath, been dressed and adorned. She would stand next to her mother, her wet hair loosely plaited in order to allow it to dry, wearing her favourite green paavaadai, with a black velvet choli. Hers was a 'bodice-paavaadai'. The bodice was attached to the skirt and concealed the waist. She used to pester her mother, demanding a *naadaa* paavaadai, which tied around the waist with a string, just like Minakshi's.

Because Mythili and Minakshi were going with her, Amma would tell Marudayi not to take the bus. She gave her the fare for a *jutka*. Every year the return fare by jutka went up, from twelve annas to a rupee, a rupee and a quarter, and so on, until it was as much as two rupees on their last journey. Amma always added some small coins to the jutka fare. For Minakshi and Mythili to buy sweets.

Every time she said to Marudayi, 'Marudayi, you won't take the child *that side*, will you?', emphasizing '*that side.*' When she said 'the child', she meant Mythili. Apparently the other child, Minakshi, was at liberty to go to *that side*.

Marudayi would declare, 'I won't do anything like that, 'Ma.'

*That side* was a place to be relished. A place that also aroused fear and excitement. A place where roosters, their screams rising and falling, or sheep calling out 'me-e-e-e' as they were dragged along, were sacrificed, skinned in an instant, and cooked. A place where she and Minakshi stood with clasped hands, their eyes wide, their mouths gaping open. A place where the two of them walked about, asking each other about pain, blood, and death. Sometimes they would get piping-hot chicken *pillau* on sewn-leaf plates, the chicken meltingly soft, with cinnamon, clove, and pepper. Mouths watering, they would blow and blow on the rice, and then eat it.

When there were so many buses going to the Majestic, it didn't seem right to Marudayi to take a jutka. On their very first journey, just as soon as they had turned around after waving goodbye to Amma and the baby, Marudayi asked, 'Shall we go by bus, Mythili?' After that, it became their regular practice.

All three of them would set off along the street leading to the Pillayaar temple. The bus-stop stood on the main street, before they reached the temple. It was right in front of a shop with a placard announcing, 'Ganesh Butter Stores.' They could see the proprietor seated there, sometimes. He looked as if he himself had consumed all the butter in the shop. When her *athai* came to visit them from Trichur, she taught Mythili little songs. She taught her to dance, too. One of the songs she taught her went, '*Aanatalaiolam venna taraameda, ananda Sri Krishna, vaay mudukku...* We'll offer you as much butter as an elephant's head, joyous Sri Krishna, shut your mouth...' Every time she tried to imagine a person who ate as much butter as an elephant's head, the proprietor of Ganesh Butter Stores would come to mind, holding a flute. As she approached the bus-stop, her walk took on the rhythm and tempo of a dance sequence her athai had taught her, where she entered the stage from one side singing '*Aanatalaiolam,*' swinging her arm like an elephant's trunk.

When he saw them, the proprietor would ask, 'Off to the Mariamman temple?'

Aanatalaiolam, aanatalaiolam...the tune and the rhythm running through her head, 'Yes,' she'd say.

'Come here.'

Aanatalaiolam, aanatalaiolam... She'd go up to him, with Minakshi.

He'd pick up two small packets and give them to the girls.

Aanatalaiolam, aanatalaiolam... 'Thanks, maama.'

As they waited for the bus to come, they licked the butter. Until the bus arrived, 'Aanatalaiolam, aanatalaiolam' filled the mind.

They had made a pact that on the outward journey, Mythili would have the window seat, and that Minakshi was entitled to it on their return. As soon as they reached the temple, Marudayi would make a hearth out of three stones and begin to cook the pongal. The two girls would hold hands and wander about, taking a look at Mariamman now and then. Once the offering was made, they would eat some of it, distribute the rest, and then leave. Amma had made it clear that they need bring home only the kumkumam prasadam.

It was only after this that the money saved by taking the bus rather than the jutka, was squandered—in the shops spread all around the temple, loaded with hot, spicy fried peanuts smeared with chilli and turmeric; jujube fruit; ripe tamarind; parrot-nosed mangos; and sweetened balls of gram. Everything went into their stomachs. After that came sweet, sticky *javvu mithai*. The mithai-man held the sticky mass on a long stick. He could make whatever you asked from the sweet stuff—elephant, cat, peacock, rabbit, or deer. A rose-coloured sweet. The more one licked at it, the sweeter it tasted. Sometimes they bought glass bangles and put them on. As they licked away at the sweet, the bangles jingled up and down. Then came the journey home. As they got off the bus, lime-sherbet from the corner shop, with ice-cubes afloat.

When they reached home, the kumkumam prasadam was handed over to Amma. And Amma would place the kumkumam on the foreheads of all three of them, saying, 'Mariamma, keep us safe, di, Amma.'

After that, the cross-questioning session would begin, starting with, 'Where did you pick up the jutka?'

On the days that the proprietor of Ganesh Butter Stores had seen them, Marudayi would say, 'We went by bus to Mallechpuram Circle, Amma, and found a jutka there.' On other days, she'd answer that they found one at the 8th Main Road corner, or even at the next street. In every case, though, the jutka man would not have had time to turn into the 8th Main Road on the return journey. He was a man in a terrific hurry, insisting on dropping them off at the corner of the road and making off immediately. What sort of jutka-drivers are these, Marudayi would complain.

'You haven't eaten any rubbish, have you, only plain sweets?' Amma would ask.

She and Minakshi would shake their heads vigorously in denial. Sometimes, even as they did so, their stomachs would be rioting. The spicy gram and ripe tamarind and javvu mithai would all be in collision inside them. Belching from the lime-sherbet, she and Minakshi would run towards the toilet in the back garden. And so the journey to the Mariamman temple would end. Every time.

When her younger brother was four years old, he insisted obstinately on going along with them. On that occasion, Amma gave Marudayi the round sum of three rupees. As soon as they came out of the temple, Marudayi bought them javvu mithai, and as they were licking their elephant, rabbit, and deer, she said, 'Mythili, there's a Tamil film running at Central Talkies. Shall we go?'

'M...m,' Mythili murmured in assent.

Thambi was primed to reply properly to Amma's catechism. He learnt to repeat correctly, in telegraphic style.

'How did you get to the temple?'

'Jutka.'

'What did you see there?'

'*Mari saami.*'

'What did you eat?'

'Pongal.'

'And what else?'

'Orange drops.'

There was a huge crowd of women waiting for the afternoon show at Central Talkies. When Marudayi had bought six-anna bench-seat tickets, taken them to the toilet, and then ushered them inside, the film started straightaway. Because they were seated so close to the screen, they had to crane their necks upwards to see. The faces on the screen looked gigantic. In a very short time, it became apparent that the hero was up to something wicked.

'Corpse of a fellow,' the *maami* next to them cursed.

'You're in for an evil time, da. Your wife is a chaste woman, da, a *pattini*,' another woman put in.

'Look at your face and your chin! You'll go to hell,' Marudayi commented, cracking her finger joints.

After the interval, just when they had finished their ice-lollies, and the film started again, Thambi began to whimper that he wanted to go to the toilet. Marudayi led him outside. When she came rushing back, she asked the neighbouring maami, 'What's been happening, maami?'

'I tell you, this lecher has gone and fallen for that whore of a woman,' the maami answered.

'Look at the way the slut is showing her teeth. Her mouth is wide and her cunt is wide,' said Marudayi.

In the end, the man who had done wrong returned to his wife, and the audience roared its approval, 'That's right, come to your senses, now!'

They came out, caught their bus, and arrived home. As usual, Amma touched their foreheads with kumkumam, and then asked, 'Where did you find your jutka?'

Out of the blue, Thambi announced in his shrill voice, 'Amma, we went to the cinema.' Then he added, loud and clear, 'A lecher fell for a whore. That slut's mouth was wide and her cunt was wide.'

After that the excursions to the Mariamman temple ceased. Amma began to set aside some money in a yellow cloth, for Mariamman. And with many prayers that Mariamman should not get angry, nor mind that the money was going into the safekeeping of the modest Kannika Parameswari, the offering was deposited in the *hundi* of the Parameswari temple.

Whenever their numerous uncles and aunts came to visit them, Mythili had the chance to see many films such as *Guna Sundari*, *Kanavane Kankanda Deivam*, *Tuukku Tuukki*, and *Manohara*. But without Marudayi's and the other women's special commentaries, her heart was not in it.

*Sadangai*, July–September 2000

# Forest

It was not real forests that Chenthiru had in mind. Rather, forests from the poems of Ahanaanuuru. Forests where the waterfall fell sheer, like milk, flanked by granite rocks on either side from which beehives hung. She wanted to go away to a forest. To a forest far away, leaving behind the noise of traffic, the sounds of conversation, of people walking about, of electrical gadgets in the house.

There were those who teased her: was this an attempt at *vanaprastha*, they asked. Others ridiculed her saying, 'Oh Forest, come come! Oh Home, go away!' *Brahmacharya*, *samsara*, *vanaprastha*, and *sannyasa*—must all these happen at separate times and stages? Must one enter the next stage only on the completion of the one before? Why could they not all be mingled together?

Her father used to work on a coffee estate. He was chief accountant to the owner of a number of coffee estates. She and her younger brother normally stayed in Bangalore with their mother. When they went to their father during the school holidays, their afternoons were spent running about the coffee plantations, among the pepper and cardamom plantations which lay along the densely-forested mountain slopes.

The estate workers always warned them, 'Watch out. These are places where bears roam about.'

It seems when her mother started her labour pains, and they were taking her to the hospital which was some distance away, she actually had to get out of the car halfway. They had hurried her out, and brought her to sit under a tree with widely-spreading branches; within ten minutes of their doing this, Chenthiru was born.

'As I was walking through the forest one day, I came upon you lying under a tree. So I picked you up and brought you home. Who told you that your mother gave birth to you?' It became a game for her father to tease and provoke her until she was in tears.

She would go to her mother each time, her eyes full of tears, asking, 'Is it really true, Amma?'

'Oh yes; very true. You were just lying there; he picked you up and brought you home. He's the great Janaka-raja himself, don't you think?'

When her younger brother was a little older, he began to make fun of her as well. 'Ei, you're a girl who was born under a tree!'

But by that time she had learned not to cry. 'Why, the Buddha too was born under a tree, you know; didn't you know that?' she'd retort sharply.

'So, you'll also go off in search of a *Bodhi* tree, will you?' he'd mock in his turn.

She declared to Tirumalai that she was the selfsame girl who was born in the mountain woods and played there as a child. Tirumalai could not agree. He claimed she was building up an imaginary picture of herself as a huntress who lived in the forest. Given a chance, she'd start thinking of herself as Valli, singing aalolam songs in the mountains, he teased.

What had he said, after all, for her to want to run off to the forests as if she were venturing into a life of austerities? He certainly was prepared to accept her as a partner in his many-branched business. If he saw himself as king of all that, he certainly considered that she was his queen. If his other business partners couldn't quite see it that way, how could he be faulted? Surely, she must realize that he too regretted this state of affairs? Should she just bundle up her goods and set off? Run off to the forest? Quite true, during the years when he wandered here and there, struggling to leave behind a mundane life and to make some real progress, she gave him her unreserved support. Did he ever deny that? But the situation was different now, wasn't it? Just because she had been asked to distance herself a little from business matters, did she have to make these preparations as if she were renouncing everything? Besides, what sort of goal was the forest, anyway? Was it just waiting there, to be her sanctuary, did she imagine? Wasn't her behaviour like that of someone who dreams that she is in the ancient epic world?

Anyway, even in epic times, a woman only went to the forest meekly accompanying her husband. It was the epic men who went on their own, to hunt or to destroy demons. As for women, they could only be in the position of Sita, accompanying Rama who assented immediately when his father ordered him into exile in the forest. A woman's visit could only be like that of Damayanti, walking by the side of Nala. It was most appropriate for a woman to be a *rishi-pattini*, spouse of a sage, journeying along with her husband. If she did go there on her own, it could only be as the seductive Menaka, putting an end to a sage's meditation. For a woman, a forest is a place where she cannot find her way. Everything there—trees, deer, flowers —is bound to mislead her and make her lose her direction. For a woman, the forest is a means of punishment. To send her there is to cast her aside and make her destitute. So argued Tirumalai.

The time has come to re-write the epics, she replied, smiling. Is that why you are making this trip, he asked. For that as well, she said.

There had been a reply to her application to the official in the Forestry Department. She now had a letter which said she could stay at the government guest house in the forest. A letter of permission on cowdung-coloured paper. She showed it to him. He exclaimed in irritation. He complained that she had made all her decisions herself, informing him only at the end. He said she was behaving as if he had banished her, in some sort of way. Arguments and counter-arguments. Threats. Entreaties.

After all this, he said, 'The bus-stand is very far from here. Let Annamalai drive you there in the car.'

She agreed.

Annamalai went with her. While they were waiting for the bus, he said, 'Anni, you don't think badly of me, do you?'

'*Che, che*, it's nothing like that, Annu. After all, you work with your brother. You have to do as he asks, don't you?'

She climbed in as soon as the bus arrived. She put her head out of the window, and waved goodbye.

She thought of the notebook with its camel-yellow covers and its blank white pages, lying there in her suitcase among her clothes. She had bought a dozen dark-leaded pencils. A pencil sharpener. An eraser.

The wind traced the first sentences as it went along its way.

The horses yoked to the chariot ran as if they were clashing against
the wind. The opposing wind struck hard against their bodies. The
trees on either side seemed to come running along with them. The
journey had been decided upon all of a sudden. All these colours and
sounds of the forest fill my mind as if they were bridal gifts from my
parents' home, Sita said to Lakshmana. He did not answer. He merely
folded his arms together, and faced windward. As soon as the chariot
stopped and they climbed out, he told her of his brother's command.
When Lakshmana told her that hereafter the forest was to be her
dwelling place, Sita looked hard at him, and spoke up. This was not
something new to Lakshmana, Sita said. It had become his brother's
main duty to doubt other people's purity; to put them constantly to
the test. He was suspicious of everything. He cross-questioned
witnesses. He called upon the sun and questioned him. If Surya
protested that he could bear witness only to the times when he was
present, how could he speak for the times when he wasn't there, then
Rama flung his barbed questions at the moon. And when Chandra
said I can only give you a guarantee for the nights when I am in the
sky, after all I am not in the sky on *Amavasya* night, Rama immediately
summoned Fire as the final test of one's purity. Didn't Lakshmana
himself experience this? How firm he, Lakshmana, had been in his
celibacy! How radiant his body! The moment he touched the musical
instrument known as *kingri* by the forest dwellers, who had not been
enticed by the music which rose from it, gently at first, like a fine
fragrance, then falling like an uncontrollable torrent? Did Lakshmana
remember the Gandharva girl? Indrakamini, from the assembly of
Indra himself? She who, having failed to arouse Lakshmana's lust,
scattered her broken bangles and her earrings all over his bed in
order to discredit and defame him? Was it not Sita herself who had
seen them when she came to clean his room, and who then went
running to tell Rama about it? The headman of the village was
summoned and all the women living there were asked to try on the
earrings and the repaired bangles. The ornaments did not fit a single
woman there. Rama then asked whether there was anyone left among
the women who did not partake in the test. The headman said, 'The
only one who has not done so is Sita Devi herself.' When she tried
them on, they were exactly right for her. It had been Indrakamini's

plot all along. Surely, he must remember the reply he made to his brother's unjust accusation? Did he not dive into the fire with a newborn child of one of the forest dwellers, emerging unscathed, and thus establishing his purity? She was weary of these purity tests. This forest was not new to her. Nor was it a place she disliked. But before he left her, Lakshmana must look carefully at her lightly-swelling stomach. He must make sure to tell his brother she is with child. Otherwise, there will be preparations for yet another ordeal by fire. There are some whose minds cannot travel in a straight line. As for the king of Ayodhya, his mind was entirely warped.

The chariot began its return journey. The sound of the horses' hooves could be heard for a long time before silence reigned in the forest once more. She was alone. The gusting winds covered her body with dust. She was alone. Gazing at the stream that flowed in front of her. Thinking of herself. Thinking of her own birth.

As the stylus finished writing that last sentence on the palm-leaf, a shadow fell. Sita looked up. The sage Valmiki was standing in front of her.

'What are you writing, amma?'

She stood up and bowed to him. 'A life-story,' she said, 'Sita's *ayanam*.'

'Isn't the Ramayana that I wrote sufficient?' he asked.

'No. In the ages to come, there will be many Ramayanas. Many Ramas. Many Sitas.'

He picked up the palm leaves in his hand and asked, 'Is this not the same Sita I wrote about?'

'You were a poet of the king's court. You created history. But I experienced it. I absorbed into myself all manner of experiences. My language is different.'

'And where will this story be launched?'

'In the forest. In the minds of forest-dwellers.'

It was not a particularly large room. But it was arranged in such a way as to invite one to stay there. There was a sense of warm comfort about it, like the feel of a hot-water bottle that soothes away one's pain. A small bed, covered with a spread of handloomed material, bark-brown, scattered with deep red flowers. Next to it, a table and a chair. A bathroom with just the essentials. More important than anything else, that window. A window right in front of the table. It had shutters fitted with slats that moved up and down, and which opened outwards.

When the bus dropped her off, it was already the very last moments of dusk. They told her she would have to walk a little, to reach the government guest house. A small boy offered to carry her suitcase. In the fading light, she walked along a path through the trees, the boy showing her the way; by the time she arrived at the guest house, it was totally dark. As soon as she introduced herself, an attendant there opened the room for her. While she looked about her, the attendant leaned across the table, stretched out his arm, and pushed the window outwards. Suddenly, there in front of her was the forest, enshrouded in darkness. A wide forest, where the branches of trees hung in festoons like snakes, or stretched upwards like the necks of giraffes. Strange and unrecognizable noises. Right in the middle of the window, as if it were strung upon a fine thread, a moon—the colour of well-thickened milk. In her mind a song echoed, in Raghunath Panigrahi's voice, throbbing with life: When I look for you, must you run away? Why do you turn away from me, white moon?

The attendant went away, having asked her about her evening meal.

Still watching the moon, she sat down in her chair and leaned her arms on the table. Then she climbed on to the table and sat there, her legs hanging down sideways, and turned her head to watch the moon, and the forest spread with its light.

Before she went to sleep, the camel-yellow notebook found a place on the table, with the dozen pencils and the rest on its back. Through the slatted shutters of the window, now closed, the moon shone in many fragments.

A pond filled with lotuses. Each lotus as wide as a mother's lap. Each lotus made up of a thousand, thousand petals. As he walked past, surrounded by his retinue of soldiers and bodyguards, Ravana glanced at the pond with its floating lotuses. Their colour and form attracted him, enticing him to pluck one at least. Handing his bow and arrows to one of the soldiers standing by, he waded into the pond, his silk garments dragging in the water, when he heard a child's voice saying, 'I will kill you. I will kill you.' Thinking it must be a myna-bird, he looked about the pond to see if any were about. Not a single water-bird which spoke with a human voice was to be seen. Each time he touched a lotus, the same voice spoke up again. He couldn't make out from which lotus the voice actually came. He plucked all the lotuses he could reach, and gave them to Mandodari when he reached home, telling her about the voice that he had heard. The entire floor was covered in lotuses. Mandodari sat down and opened the lotuses one by one, gently smoothing them out, petal by petal. As she opened the innermost petals of the very last flower, there, right in the heart of it, she saw a girl baby. The baby looked up at Mandodari with her dark eyes, and said clearly, 'I will kill Ravana'; but the next moment she smiled widely, and began to babble, lapsing into meaningless baby-noises. Mandodari's stomach churned. She placed the baby in a box made of bamboo. With two maidservants in attendance, she walked to the seashore. She waded in among the waves and put the box out to sea. It floated onwards, riding on the waves.

It went a long way and at last touched shore. The first person to open the box raised an outcry; others thronged about him, and the baby was handed over into the safe keeping of their headman. That headman was Janaka. He gave the baby the name Sita.

Sita came into being, in touch with flower and earth and water.

Rama, as soon as he was born, caused grief to a living creature. Kosalai determined that they would serve venison at the feast celebrating the child's birth. Under a green tree there rested a male and female deer. The doe looked troubled. 'What has happened? Didn't you find any green leaves? Are you thirsty?' asked the buck. 'No, I'm not thirsty. But I hear the sound of hunters coming near. You'd best run away,' said the doe. Then, to the hunters who approached them, she offered, 'You may kill me if you like.' But they killed the buck instead, saying, 'It is the flesh of the male that is the best.' The doe then ran to Kosalai and pleaded with her, 'Please at least give me the skin of my dear partner. I will gaze at it and assuage my sorrow.' But Kosalai said, 'I intend to make a beautiful kanjira with that skin and to give it to my baby boy to play with.'

Each time Rama crawled up to the kanjira, tapped it with his hand, played with it and made it resound, the echo would make the doe's entire body quiver. Each time it wailed with grief, saying, 'Kosalai, one day you too will suffer this pain of loss.'

Sita tied the palm leaves together and looked up. Some distance away, Valmiki was telling Lava and Kusa about the *putrakameshti yagna* which Dasaratha performed for the begetting of children; and the births of Rama, Lakshmana, Bharata, and Shatrugna.

As soon as she woke up in the morning, she felt an urge to walk until her legs were weary. She put on some sturdy shoes. When she came out of her room, she happened to see the guest house attendant. She asked him to bring her some tea, and sat down outside on the verandah steps. Dark green, light green, and palest green stretched away in waves as far as the eye could see. In a cleft where two greens collided, light red rays of the sun played hide-and-seek, appearing and disappearing.

The tea arrived.

She took it and began to drink, blowing on it again and again. The scent and flavour of tulasi leaves were soothing to her. When she returned the cup, she questioned him about the extent of the forest, where the tracks began, and where they led. She decided upon an easterly direction, and began to walk as if she were hastening to greet the sun.

Many paths branched off, one from another. As she walked further and further along, the densely-spreading trees spread out like a shadow above, completely hiding the sun. Sometimes, suddenly, a single ray of light sparkled like a diamond and sped along the leaves. And was hidden again.

Suddenly, something cool touched her. In front of her there was a stream. Before she could reach it, however, she was surprised by a peacock flying low, dripping its blue and green tail-feathers. And before she could recover from the shock of it, it touched the earth, walked about, and then, in an extraordinary instant, spread out the full extent of its tail, and began to dance, hopping from one foot to the next. A dance for her alone. The peacock danced, watching her, and moving about in a small circle. Beyond it, the stream.

She sank to her knees in front of the peacock and began to weep as she sat there. I don't understand, peacock. I don't know my goal. Is there a goal at all? I know how to overcome the obstacles that stand in my way. But I don't understand the quest. What do I seek? And how? Do I even seek? How much further is it going to be? Even though I have come so far, the burden has not eased from my body. I want to feel light. As soon as my toes press against the earth, as if I were propelling a swing forward, I want to feel myself rise up into the air.

The peacock continued to dance.

Oh peacock, peacock, peacock, peacock...

She heard voices coming towards her from a distance.

'Ayiga! *Tya morala bag.*' Startled by the sight of the peacock, a group of women exclaimed in Marathi, 'There will surely be a drop or two of rain at least, look at the peacock dancing!' As they approached, their bundles of food swung from their hands. They washed their faces in the stream. They shook out the cloths which were tied about their heads and wiped their faces. When they saw her, they showed their surprise. Opening their bundles, they invited her to join them.

She went and sat by them. Thick rotis made of millet flour. A bright red thuvaiyal, made of coarsely ground garlic and chillies, roasted groundnuts, desiccated coconut, and rock-salt. One woman broke off a piece of roti, put some of the tuvaiyal on it and gave it to her. Another took an onion between the palms of her hands, squashed it, and gave her half. Yet another laid four or five green chillies on her share of roti.

With the ease of long-familiar friends, they asked after her and told her about themselves. They told her their names: Minabai, Rukminibai, Savitabai. The millet-flour roti went down her throat to the savoury accompaniment of the thuvaiyal, between bites of onion

and chilli. When they had finished eating, Minabai took some tobacco
leaves out of the drawstring bag at her waist, placed them in the
palm of her hand, and began to roll them with her thumb.

'Would you like one?' she asked Chenthiru.

'No, I'm not used to it. Do you know that it's not good for your
health?' Chenthiru remarked.

'*Ravde Bai*. If it isn't good for the health, then why has that Dev
put so much flavour there?' Minabai asked in her turn. She spat out
the spittle that had gathered in her mouth.

Chenthiru's mother used to say exactly the same thing. Her mother
used to chew tobacco. Wherever they went, her eyes would rove in
search of a betel-leaf and tobacco stall. 'My mouth feels bland and
numb,' she'd say. If ever Chenthiru protested, 'You don't need that,'
she would retort, 'If I chew tobacco, why do you get so annoyed?'
Chenthiru's father never said anything. He, after all, smoked cigarettes.
'Call it quits,' Amma used to say in Telugu. Amma had travelled
about with her parents and lived in several places with them. She
used to say she had acquired her tobacco habit in Kerala and her love
of music in Andhra. Her father had said, 'They say that in certain
places in Andhra some women smoke great big cheroots. It's just as
well, Chendu, that your mother didn't pick up that habit.' Amma had
returned, 'It's not too late, you know. Just bring me a box of Havana
cigars from Cuba, I'll smoke one and show you.' In this, she and
Tirumalai's mother were exactly the same. There was a period of
time when Tirumalai's mother suffered from ill-health, and Chenthiru
refused to allow her to buy tobacco. Tirumalai's mother would keep
opening her betel-box, looking inside it and fretting. She'd take
Chenthiru by the chin and plead with her, 'Listen, princess. If you
like you may starve me. Only don't punish me by keeping me away
from tobacco.'

Rukminibai lit her *bidi* and began to pull at it. 'Ei, don't blow your
smoke all over me,' said Savitabai, moving away. She went a little
further off and lay down, pillowing her head on her arm. A foot or
two away from her, Chenthiru lay down as well.

Savitabai asked 'Chendiyabai' what she was doing in these parts.
When she replied that she had just come away on her own, Savitabai

proceeded to ask her a series of questions: Was she married? Did she have children? Where was her husband?

Rukminibai, who had finished her bidi, scolded Savitabai. 'Ei, Savitabai! Are you looking for a second wife for your husband or what? Firing off all these questions, one after another!'

'Oh yes, as if Chendiyabai is of an age to get married now! And as if all that drunkard needs is a second wife!' Savitabai sat up, loosened her hair, and tied it up again.

Chenthiru laughed and rose to her feet. She told them that her children were studying abroad and that she had left her husband and everyone, and come away just to be by herself.

'Is that so? Very well, then,' they said, and made ready to go. They told her that if they were in the vicinity of the guest house, they would most certainly come and see her, and then they walked on at a swift pace.

The peacock had disappeared a long time ago. Only its dance continued to unfold in her mind, green and blue.

She began to walk in the direction of the guest house.

Tirumalai's trademark was actually a peacock. A peacock in profile, spreading its tail on the ground. Tirumalai's father ran a small business in *vibhuti* and kumkumam. A *swamiyaar* who was like a guru to the family had given them the symbol. When she first met Tirumalai, he was carrying packets of vibhuti and small tins of kumkumam in a cloth bag, the colour of a peacock's neck. He had brought these materials which had been ordered by the members of the Women's Association who met regularly at her Periamma's house in Bombay. He must have travelled quite a distance on his motorbike. He was exhausted. He asked for some water to drink. She brought him a glass of cold water, and another of lime-sherbet, just as her Periamma had told her to. Completely relaxed, smiling, he asked her, 'Have you come on a sightseeing visit?'

'No, I'm here for my further studies.'

'What will you be studying?'

'M.Sc. Textiles.'

'Do that.' He put his glass down.

'And what do you do?' she asked him.

'I'm in trade. With my father. I studied up to my B.Sc. But my father's health wasn't up to it. So I became involved in this business. My younger sister is studying for an MA degree.'

'Where?'

'Oh, she is here too.'

Her aunt came in and asked, 'Well, Tirumalai, why couldn't you have brought your mother and sister with you?'

'Amma is not very well, you see.'

'What do you mean, she's not well? It's a whole year since I saw her,' she complained.

'She's just tired. I'll bring her one day,' he promised.

'This is Chenthiru,' said her aunt.

'Yes, we chatted,' he said. Then he said goodbye and left.

It had only been a casual conversation. But the thought of him remained in her mind. A very tall figure. Dark skinned. The darkness of his pupils seemed to shine against the whites of his eyes. A moustache which very slightly hid his mouth. A finely-sculpted body. His buttocks were modest, and didn't protrude or swell out. The back of his trousers did not bulge in an unseemly way, but fell somewhat loosely, with a fold. It was her opinion that a man's bottom should be tightly muscled and well-knit.

She wrote to her father about him. She said that she liked the fact that he worked independently, for his own business. She wrote that his unflashy, simple lifestyle really attracted her. Her father, surrounded by coffee-blossoms that were bursting open, could not make any sense of vibhuti and kumkumam. He didn't see what was happening to her.

By the time she finished her M.Sc., she had become totally familiar with him and his family. She wrote to her father again. He immediately telephoned her.

'What Chendu, is this all about love?'

'Mm.'

'Does he have a moustache, this man?'

'Mm.'

'Tell him you have a great big bow in your house. Tell him unless he bends and breaks it he can't marry you.'

'Go on, Appa.'

'What does he look like?'

She sang softly, 'His body is like the green mountains ...'

Her father laughed.

The trees spread their shade above her, so she did not feel the excessive heat of mid-day. She walked on at a fast pace. Nowhere was the peacock to be seen.

Whenever she crawled in the courtyard, the baby Sita's eyes fell upon it. That huge and heavy bow. She first learnt to walk by leaning against it and holding on to it. Ever since her earliest memories, she knew of it as Shiva's bow.

All hours of her day were spent playing in the forest. She knew all its secret places: the mountain springs where the water was as sweet as honey, the ponds full of water-lily and lotus, the trees where ripe jackfruit lay, burst open, the streams where the deer came to drink, the rocks where the beehives hung, the best places to rest, where the trees gave their most dense shade.

One day she decided to stay at home and help her mother. While her mother was resting, she brought fresh cow-dung and began to pave the wide courtyard. When she came to the place where the great bow lay, she lifted it with one hand in order to spread the cow-dung underneath. She had just finished and was replacing the bow when her father came by. His eyes widened in surprise.

He lifted her to her feet, her hand still full of cow-dung, and held her close.

'With one hand, my daughter has lifted up the bow that no one else could carry. Only a man who can bend and break it shall be fit to marry her.'

She turned around and gazed at the bow.

Of course, she married the man who alone could break the bow. But he was not someone who was unknown to her. One evening when she went to the orchard to pick fruit, she saw a young man standing among the fruit trees. They looked at each other, the two of them. When he opened his arms, she walked into his embrace, without even knowing what she was doing. Then she freed herself, exclaiming that if her bangles broke in his tight clasp, she would not know what explanation to give at home. After that she ran homewards. Her mother asked her why her eyes were red, why there was that drawn look on her face. She said that however angry her mother was going to be, she would accept it; take whatever punishment she thought fit to hand out, even if it went to the extent of driving her away from home. With complete honesty she said that she had met Rama in the orchard, and been embraced by him. Her mother consoled her, saying that it was certain that the very same Rama would break the bow and marry her.

He broke the bow. He married Sita.

It was time to light the lamps. Sita rose to her feet. Lava and Kusa came running in with their bows. Breathlessly they told her about chasing after a deer, far, far into the forest. They had been surprised, shocked, by the beauty of the deer, and the terror in its wide eyes. You must let the deer be; let it run, you don't have to chase it, said Sita.

The tea that arrived in the evening was fragrant with ginger. That morning's long walk had left her feeling pleasantly tired. The hot tea was as comforting as a poultice. The languor of her afternoon nap hadn't quite left her.

She found that she had to speak to Tirumalai almost immediately after she returned to the guest house. He said he had tried to reach her by telephone three times, and had been anxious when he was told she wasn't there.

'Why should you be anxious? I went out intending to walk a little while. But I found I had gone a long way.'

'Why do you have to wander about like a ghost, a *pisaasu*? See if there is a tamarind tree close by you. That's the right place for you.'

'So I am a tamarind tree-pisaasu, am I?'

'Yes, a stubborn pisaasu. A beautiful temptress of a pisaasu. Have you eaten?'

'Mm. I saw four or five men when I was out walking. I swallowed them up in one gulp.'

'Yes, you're quite a one to do that. Isn't it enough that you've swallowed me?'

'I swallowed you, yes. But I couldn't digest you.'

'And why's that?'

'Too much fat and impudence, you see.'

He laughed. Then he said, 'Valli and Kaarmegam both telephoned.'

'What about?'

'Kaarmegam needs to go to Canada, he says, next week. He said he hoped to see his sister. Then Valli rang to say she's expecting him there. Both of them said they wanted to speak to you.'

'Shall I put the receiver down, now?'

'Why?'

'It's getting too expensive, isn't it, this call?'

'So when do you plan to come home?'

'I don't know,' she said. Once again she said, calling him by his name as she did when they were alone, 'I don't know, Tirumalai.' She could hear his sharp intake of breath at the other end.

'What on earth is going on in your mind?'

'I need to feel easy. I need to feel light.'

'Come home. Come back, amma.'

'No, I have to do it on my own...'

'On your own, in that forest?'

'Yes. *Even if it is a forest path, Even though it is beset by robbers.*'

Silence.

He would call every day. He would plead with her to go back. She put on her shoes and began to walk westwards. Apparently, she had begun to walk early, when she was only ten months old. When she was eleven months, and they were visiting her Periamma in Bombay, she had walked across the street and gone off to Shivaji Park all by herself. She could remember to this day the young boys dressed in khaki clothes, doing their drill. She had never forgotten how she stood on an ant-hill, how the ants had bitten her, how it had hurt. If ever anything happened, she always set off walking at a swift pace. The family teased her, 'The ants are biting her feet. That's why she's off.' On both occasions when her parents died, she had walked and walked until her feet were swollen. Tirumalai, and her younger brother who had come home from abroad, had caught up with her and insisted she return with them.

Everywhere she turned, there were ant-hills. If she went in a slightly different direction, or went away on her own, there were ants biting her feet. She wanted to roam at will in several cities and in desolate forest interiors. She wanted to sleep wherever a ledge was available to her. Watching the dark sky with its sparkling stars, she wanted to sing aloud, raising a voice from her very underbelly, without any particular aim, addressing no particular god, 'Diamonds encrusted in an indigo sari are the stars you see at midnight , di' She wanted to sing, in the Kaavadichindhu raagam, just for the pleasure of the sound of the words, and for the sake of its rhythm, 'In the forest of time, in the tree of the universe, a bee buzzed; calling itself *Kali-shakti*'. She wanted to dive into whatever pond she chose, and rise from it.

Tirumalai's father used to sing:

His stomach dropping, his hair whitening,
his teeth rattling, his back bent,
his lip hanging down, one hand on his staff, he comes—
to the sound of women's laughter.

He'd go on, melting, melting as he sang,

When my woman weeps and wails, when Yama's messengers gather
around,
when the waters spill out of the body, when my life is ending,
come to me swiftly, upon your peacock.

All visions and all quests are allowed only to those who are old enough. And only to men. As for her, she had to give a thousand explanations. Make excuses. Or become a devotee of Kannan or Shiva. She must seek sanctuary, repeating, '*Mere to giridhara Gopala*', or the Varanamayiram, or the words, 'She worshipped at the Lord's feet'. Then she could reach liberation, *mukti*, at once. And become one with the light. Those journeys in flower chariots were only meant for male bhaktas. Tukaram could hope for it. Not Janabai. As for herself, she hoped for neither visions nor for heavenly chariots. She only hoped to achieve a sense of expansion. An expansion that knew no boundaries.

Tirumalai's father was a humane man. A man of integrity. If Tirumalai questioned something, he'd say, 'I've given my word,

Thambi.' It was a sentence that came to his lips every day. Tirumalai's mother suited him, like a lid that fits a jar. It was under her supervision that the vibhuti was made. As soon as Chenthiru and Tirumalai were married, the father gave up his position as head of the business.

Tirumalai teased him, 'Why, Appa, have you gone and given your word to anybody that you will give up all your responsibilities as soon as your son gets married?'

'Yes, I have,' he said, 'I promised your mother.' Then he called Chenthiru to him and said, 'Look, amma, people tell this story. One day, a thorn entered Dasaratha's hand. He felt a terrible throbbing pain. While he was suffering like this, Kaikeyi came to him and gently, very gently, drew out the thorn. At once he gave her his word: he would grant her wishes, whatever they might be. Just so, whenever your mother-in-law massaged my back, or rubbed oil into my head, or pressed my forehead when I had a headache, I too have given my word, I don't know how many times. Now she's nagging me to make good my promises. Now she wants to travel, and see the sights in Kodaikanal, Ooty, Kuttralam and all those places.' And he laughed.

'Shameless man,' said Tirumalai's mother, laughing along with him.

She worked tirelessly alongside Tirumalai as they gradually turned the business in the direction of masala powders, and then expanded it to include silk material and readymade garments. For fourteen years they struggled in the jungle of commerce, as if they were competing in a race, running to touch the boundary line. Now their business had reached as far as Canada. For the past eight years they had also gone into the totally unknown field of leather goods. She herself had seen to the expansion of their sales: suitcases, handbags, shoulder-bags, wallets, purses for holding small change. There was talk of making her an equal partner in the business. It didn't come to anything. At once she was seized by a frenzy to walk. To walk a long, long distance. The rejection was not a reason. Only the signal.

In front of her, the sunset unfolded like a silent drama, spreading different colours in the sky. The crimson ball which had been sinking very, very slowly was suddenly not to be seen anymore. Its remains were in the skies. She wasn't aware of the passage of time. Then she heard the sound of voices.

Rukminibai and Savitabai were approaching with their water-pots. They had no more drinking water left in their homes, they said. She walked along with them. Just nearby, there was a small water-hole full of water. The water was still and clear, almost as if it had been reined in. Moonbeams lay scattered upon it. Amidst the scattered light, the moon could be seen, clearly outlined. The water held it captive there. As soon as Rukminibai dipped her water-pot into the well, the moon dissolved into fragments and spilled all over the water. When the water-pot was held upright again, there was the moon, within its narrow mouth. Savitabai too lowered her water-pot and lifted it out. Again the moon floated in her water-pot. The water in the well became motionless once more, and lay there with the moon.

She began to walk back towards the guest house with Savitabai and Rukminibai. The moon accompanied them, floating in their water-pots. Along the way, she said she was thirsty, and at once Savitabai poured some water into her cupped hands; the moon remained within her hands for a moment, then partly slipped down her throat, and partly drained away through her fingers. When she looked at the moon within her cupped hands, drank the water, and then looked again, Savitabai laughed.

'It's gone, Bai. If there's no water, there's no Chandrama either.'

True. In all the open courtyards of all the little houses of the forest, there must be innumerable moons in water-pots and little puddles of spilt water. Perhaps, if you put out a small vessel, a moon as big as a small coin would float there, who knew? Moons that float so long as there is water. Moons which approach with every scoop of water, and hurry off as the water drains away. A moon brought down from the skies. And then its extension. She felt a coolness pervade her body. She was a woman who had feasted upon the moon. She had eaten her fill, and returned the rest to the skies.

As soon as they reached the guest house, the other two said goodbye, and hastened away. In the dining room, her meal had been placed ready for her, under covers. After she had finished, she went to her room and switched on the light. Then she sat at her table.

The larger part of Sita's life was spent in the forest. The forest of her childhood where she had played, plucking fruit and flowers and leaves, was a miracle, hiding many, many secrets deep within itself. Later, it was a refuge and an asylum for her and her husband. A place where many experiences became possible. Sita was then an entirely innocent girl. When she saw herself in the clear water of the pond where she first went to bathe, she came running back to Rama, to tell him the moon and a swarm of bees were inside the water. Rama had to return with her and point out that it was her own face she saw; what she thought was a swarm of bees was her own long curly hair that flew about her. It happened another time too. On that occasion, the face she saw in the clear water was a radiant one. It was filled with grace. She went off in haste to pick a quarrel with Rama. She said that he lied when he spoke of his faithfulness to his only wife; she accused him of keeping another woman hidden somewhere. Once again, Rama went with her, and asked her to look in the water. Immediately she saw the beautiful woman. I will show you the woman's husband, he said, and came to stand next to her. When she saw Rama's reflection next to the woman's, she recognized herself. She was ashamed.

It was in a forest, too, that she was imprisoned. And now, it was a forest that was her sanctuary.

With what intensity, with what childlike obstinacy she had thought of Rama alone, in her forest-prison! And what was it that Rama had declared publicly, the very day the war ended? When he sent word through Hanuman that she should come to him, attired in her best clothes and ornaments, had she not replied that she would rather come in the clothes she had always worn in Ashokavanam? Even when they had insisted on adorning her, her heart had not been in any of it. There was a big stone beside her, where she sat under a tree. She had often thought, when her whole body felt shrivelled, when she longed for the day when she would be rescued, when she would at last be home in Ayodhya, how useful that stone might be, to grind sandalwood into paste. When she confided this to Hanuman, he tried to pull it out of the earth right away. But the elder statesman, Jambavan, intervened to say that one must never take back a gift. This land has been given over to Vibhishana, he said, and that she must not take anything without requesting for it properly. She was a girl who had longed for a deer, and for fruits and flowers. She had given up the comforts of royalty. She had made the forest itself her companion. Out of all the kingdom of Lanka, she had only asked for a stone. She wondered whether he implied that she had not behaved with the dignity of a royal princess, and she felt ashamed.

At the great battlefield strewn with the dead, her legs entwined and buckled. She thought of the many who had died to rescue her sole self. It seemed to her that Rama was treating her like an exhibit in front of the crowd. She had been alone for so long in Ashokavanam, totally protected from public gaze; now she had to come out into the wide-open battleground, in the midst of all the men standing there, battle-stained and weary, and in front of the thrusting crowds who had gathered there to gaze upon her. She arrived in her best attire and ornaments, as if she had not suffered in the least, as if she were now proclaiming aloud, 'Look, I am a redeemed woman.' But it became apparent very soon that all that adornment had not been for the sake of delighting Rama. He told her that all eight points of the compass surrounded her, and that she was free to go in any direction, and with whoever she chose. The battle had been fought in order to defend his honour, he said, not to rescue her. She could choose to live with anyone: Lakshmana, Bharata, Vibhishana, Sugriva. The Jambavans who had reminded her to behave as a princess did not raise their voices then. He who was so aware of the pride of his lineage, did he forget that she too belonged to a proud clan? Had she not herself made it necessary for him to wage a battle, because she was so aware of his pride? Otherwise, would she not have sat on the shoulders of Hanuman, who thought of her as a mother, and left Lanka when she could?

Hanuman set fire to Lanka. All Rama could do was to light a fire in his wife's heart.

Her very first words to Lakshmana, who greeted her after those long days of parting, were, 'Lakshmana, light the fire!'

Even after she finished writing about it, that moment was like a weight upon her heart. A little way off, Valmiki was telling Lava and Kusa the story of Ahalya and her deliverance from the curse that had been laid upon her. How many changes there are, while an event becomes gossip, and then turns into story! Ahalya's heart had hardened into stone. Only when she worshipped Rama's feet did it melt again and fill with the essential waters of the fountain of life. But, Sita thought to herself as she rose, there is even more miracle and drama in turning a stone into a woman.

East, west, north and south, she had walked in all the directions, many times. As she walked and walked, she felt a prickling sensation at the base of her spine, as if something were trying to grow there. At night it spread all over her body, and rocked her to sleep. Eastwards, past the stream, they told her, was a small waterfall. One day she set off to meet the waterfall. It was a restrained little cascade. Like washed hair, left loose to dry. As she sat down to look at it closely, she discerned a face at the edge of the water. Its body glowing like gold in the sunlight, a deer was drinking. It drank some water, then shook its head, and looked all around. It stooped to drink again. The next time it lifted its head, it spied her. It leapt, startled. Then, like a yellow whirlwind, it was gone.

She went quietly to the edge of the waterfall, and lay face down at the place where the deer had drunk. Holding in her stomach, she reached out and drank, just as the deer had done. The water trickled through her, in some hitherto unknown path. As soon as her thirst was quenched she turned over, face upwards. Above her, the sky. Pale blue. Her dupatta caught in the wind, flew upwards, and covered her face. She gazed up at the sky through it. Her eyes were heavy with sleep.

...She was running to catch a train. Why were all the roads made of mountains and deep gorges? A deep fear arose within her, as if someone was chasing her. She heard horse-hooves. Horse-hooves, in the middle of the town? She reached the railway station. She hung on to the metal handle and climbed into the train. Her breath came fast. Even before she could sit down, they had reached the next station. When she looked out of the window, she saw her father sitting on a bench, a little distance away.

'Appa, Appa, how did you get here?'

'I'm waiting here, just for you.'

'For me?'

'Yes.' Her father straightened his glasses with one hand, smiling at her.

'But I can't get off, Appa.'

'Why not?'

'There's all my luggage, Appa.'

Appa smiled. He stretched out his hand towards her. His hand was still in that position when the train began to move.

'Appa, Appa...'

Suddenly, her father, who couldn't sing a single line in tune, mimed as if he were keeping time with a *sapplaakkattai*, and began to sing, jumping up and down. The song came from Appa's throat in the voice of her first music teacher, Ramachandra Bhagavatar. In the background was the sound of the vinai. Purandaradasa's Devarnama.

'*Naaneke badavanu, naaneke paradesi?* ...Am I really destitute? Am I truly a wandering beggar?'

The railway station moved along with the train.

Ramachandra Bhagavatar was blind. He used to go from house to house giving singing and vinai lessons. When he first came to their house, Amma asked him, 'Sing us a song.' A streak of a smile spread across his pockmarked face. He tuned his vinai and began to sing, accompanying himself. '*Naaneke badavanu, naaneke paradesi?* ...Am I really destitute? Am I truly a wandering beggar? I who have been gifted with that rare treasure, Purandaravittala himself, how can I be destitute? How can I be a wandering beggar?' It was a song composed in Sindhubhairavi raagam, a ragam that has dazzling highs and lows, twists and bends. But in this song there is no technical wizardry, only a straight and sliding path.

He always arrived on holidays, just when she had finished eating and was considering a nap. A young boy usually led him by the hand. Annoyed at having lost the chance of an afternoon nap, she'd shake out her skirt and sit down for her lesson. In loving tones he would ask her in Kannada, 'Why are you so cross, amma?' All those memories and details fell, one on top of another, thud after thud, as mere words, reflections; linked, dissolved, floating. In pieces, fragment by fragment. Just as Appa sang, outside the window.

Appa, who had for so long been jumping about and singing, began to stumble like a blind man. The train gathered speed. The station had stopped in one place. Appa was a mere dot in the distance, his hands groping in the air. Only the song still sounded in her ear, 'Naaneke, naaneke.'

Her face pressed against the window bars, she stretched out her hand. 'Appa, Appa... '

She heard a voice calling out, 'Bai, Chendiyabai.'

She woke up with a start. Rukminibai, Minabai, and Savitabai—all three stood there, leaning down and looking at her as she lay there.

'*Kai jaala* bai? ...What happened?' asked Minabai.

She sat up then.

They said they had been searching for her. They wanted to invite her to their homes. Their families and husbands had gone elsewhere. All four of them walked along together. Chenthiru had not quite recovered from her dream. It was as if she were still in an extension of it.

Savitabai's house had more space than the others'. So they went there. Savitabai switched on the lights. She opened the back door.

Her house was spotless. To the right side of the single room there were two trunks. In the left-hand corner were an oil stove and a firewood hearth. The back door was half-open. Beyond, there were banana trees. Clothes drying on bushes. Minabai and Rukminibai ran to their own homes to bring various things. They returned in a short while. By that time, Savitabai had lit the stove and made tea. All four sat down facing each other, and drank the tea. When she asked what they were celebrating, they said it was nothing special, that they tended to get together now and then, just like this. Savitabai teased Minabai and Rukminibai, saying it was very rarely that their husbands left them and went anywhere, here or there. Their sons and daughters were all married, they were grandmothers. Even so, their husbands always held on to them, wherever they went, she teased.

'Be quiet,' Rukminibai chided, affectionately. She removed the lid of a small aluminium dish she had brought with her. Fish pieces spread with masala, yellow and red. Savitabai lit the firewood hearth, placed a shallow pan on it, and poured in some oil. Minabai went up to it and began to fry the fish. Savitabai sliced onions and chillies and put them together on a plate. Rukminibai lit the kerosene stove once again and put the chapati griddle on to heat. She took the millet-flour dough which Minabai had brought with her, rolled out pieces of it, placed these on the griddle, and began to cook them, frequently dipping her hands in water, and patting them as they baked. It fell to Chenthiru to grind the thuvaiyal. While she ground it, she watched Rukminibai who was humming a song under her breath. When she strained to listen, she realized they were the words of the saint, Bahinibai, 'Arré sansara, sansara'. Life is like a griddle on which you are cooking baakri; it is only after you have burned your hands that you get your baakris, the song went. The rhythm of the song was completely in accordance with the pace at which Rukminibai was making the baakris.

When it was all done, Savitabai pulled out a tray, on which a dough of wheat-flour mixed with oil lay covered with a cloth, and placed it in the middle of the room. She took out the puranam, a filling of mashed channa dal, jaggery, and coconut. The fragrance of cardamom filled the air. As if they were well rehearsed at this task, all four began to pat out the puranpolis, dipping their fingers in oil every now and then. Savitabai briskly fried them in batches, as they were patted out. The smell of roasting coconut and jaggery pervaded the room.

Savitabai arranged all the puranpolis in a neat pile and covered them. The other two went quickly into the backyard. She could hear water being drawn from the well. Chenthiru wiped her hands on a towel and stood up. The other two returned, wiping their faces with their sari-ends, which had been pulled tightly and tucked in at the waist. Savitabai went toward the back door. Minabai drank a tumbler of water. Before Chenthiru could have a drink, Savitabai had returned. When Chenthiru went to the back of the house, Savitabai came with her to show her the privy. By the well was a bucket of water, and a piece of soap on the parapet of the well. She splashed the cold water on her face, again and again. When she squeezed the soap, spread its lather all over her face and splashed it with water once more, she felt cool, comfortable. She wiped her face with her dupatta and looked ahead, where the banana trees, the shrubs, and the neem tree in a corner, were all like outlines in the dark.

'Chendiyabai... ' The invitation came from the house.

Inside, all three of them had knotted their hair back tightly. Tattoo marks shone on the forehead and chin of their well-scrubbed faces. They all stretched out their legs, and leaned back against the wall, relaxed and easy. As soon as she sat down with them, Minabai set the plate of fried fish in the middle. Rukminibai took a couple of bottles out of a bag. 'Palm-toddy,' she said.

The other two women put the glasses out.

'Is Chendiyabai used to drinking palm-toddy, though?' Rukminibai asked.

There was palm-toddy on the night they went to the Murud-Janjira Fort. They had gone with their friends and their children, in two cars, to Alibagh. And from there to Murud-Janjira. The fortress was right in the middle of the sea, a fortressed island, once in the possession of sea-pirates. The boatman hurried them into the boats which they rowed towards the fort. They reached it in two boat-loads. Right around the ruined fort were heavy chains, looking like mountain pythons. The boatmen urged them to look around the fort as quickly as possible, and return swiftly. One boat left for the mainland, Tirumalai and the children having given the fort the hastiest of glances. Within the next fifteen minutes, when the rest of the party tried to climb into the other boat, the sea had become turbulent. They were only rowing boats. Beneath the surface were huge rocks. The boatmen feared to put out to sea. At first they waited and delayed, but eventually they said they could not risk it and would wait until the morning. She and Tirumalai's friends went and sat in the central part of the fort. The boatmen brought them the fish they had kept aside to take home, and Steven made a small hearth of three stones, lit a fire, and roasted the fish. Lankesh brought out a bottle that he had bought from the men. Palm-toddy. Annamalai and he poured it out into the plastic cups they had in their bags. Kaarmegam helped his Chitthappa, and handed the cups around. The fish, roasted to a turn without any masala whatsoever, melted in the mouth. The palm-toddy, which she was tasting for the first time, travelled in many directions in her head, and made her fly. Above them, the sky was a pitch-black magician, who had tied up all the stars. Lankesh took out his mouth organ. He was a fan of S.D. Burman, Manna De, and Pankaj Mallik. He began to play S.D. Burman's song:

*Sunu mere bandhu re...e sunu mere mithuva...*
*sunu mere saathi re...*

Listen, my friend, listen my beloved,
listen my companion...

A song of the boatmen. A folk song. It made them feel as if they
were sitting together, swaying in a boat. Steven and Kaarmegam began
to whistle and sing Beatles songs. The toddy, S.D. Burman, and the
Beatles went to her head, making her quite intoxicated. She lay back
on the floor and sang one of Annamalai's favourites, 'A tiny, tiny,
nose-drop; a red-stone...encrusted nose-drop...' Then, a lullaby in
Nilamabari for Kaarmegam who came and leaned against her. Her
voice, touched by the toddy, went slipping and sliding. Songs,
conversation, until daybreak.

The sea had calmed down by early morning. The boatmen came
and summoned them. On the opposite shore, Tirumalai waited
anxiously. A weariness, from having waited the whole night, was
apparent on his face. A sleepless night. His eyes were red.

'Tirumalai sir, your wife is back from the pirates' fort, safe and
sound,' Lankesh's wife said.

When they told him about the toddy and the fish and the music,
he asked his brother, 'What, Annamalai, did you actually give your
sister-in-law some toddy to drink?'

'Yes, Anna, hereafter you should give her a drink every day. It's
then that her singing voice really comes into its own.'

Tirumalai laughed with him.

After that one occasion, now once again, fish and palm-toddy.

'Yes, I'm used to it,' she said in reply to Rukminibai.

A cool breeze blew. Rukminibai filled their glasses. When she bit
into her fish and drank a mouthful of the toddy, her throat burnt.
Then, gently, gently, like a smoke-cloud, a sense of intoxication rose
in her head.

'That song that Rukminibai sang was one of Bahinibai's, wasn't
it?' she asked.

'Yes, it's always Rukminibai who will sing at any of our organized
struggles. She'll sing Bahinibai's songs, but she also knows the songs
that mock the government officials.'

Even as they talked, Rukminibai raised her voice and sang the same Bahinibai lyric, loudly. When the song was over, Minabai said, 'It is Rukminibai who sings, and Rukminibai who settles our quarrels.'

'What quarrels?'

'It's nothing,' Rukminibai hastened to explain. 'Minabai's granddaughter's husband deserted her. She was then four months pregnant. As soon as a baby boy was born, he wanted to claim him. I questioned him properly, in front of all the people.'

'What did you ask him?'

'Look here, I said, the vessel is ours and the milk is ours. Just because the man gave a drop of buttermilk to turn the milk into curd, can we be expected to hand over the whole pot of curd to him, I asked.'

'What did you say? Just because he gave a drop of buttermilk...,' Chenthiru put her glass down and began to laugh.

They laughed with her.

After that, when they had eaten the millet-flour rotis with the thuvaiyal, both her stomach and her heart felt full. When she got up to wash her hands, she hit her head on the edge of the roof, with a sharp 'ping'. At the very same moment, she heard vinai music. It is said that at the seventh stage of meditation one can hear the music of the vinai. Could there be a seventh stage of intoxication, too? Once again, the music.

'What is that, Savitabai,' she asked.

'*Biin*,' said Savitabai. On the other side of the waterfall, there was an *ashramam*. Apparently, an *ustad* lived there. People called him the Sufi Baba. He was said to be somewhat like Sai Baba of Shirdi. Sometimes, he stayed here for two or three months at a stretch. He played the instrument. Sometimes, they went to hear him.

Even after they had washed their hands and lain down to sleep, they could hear the vinai play.

On the table in the guest house, the camel-yellow notebook lay open. The pages that had already been filled were ruffling in the wind.

Rama's sister, Shanti, kept on pestering her. 'What did Ravana look like? Why can't you draw a picture and show me?' Sita's ability at drawing was well known. At last one day she agreed to her plea, took a piece of paper, and drew on it with a brush. After she had done his arms and legs, his entire body, and when she was just about to embark on his face, Rama entered the women's rooms. After an instant's confusion, she hid the picture under the long end-piece of her sari. The picture with the unfinished face was right there, under her sari. Sita was in distress, unable to move. She could not tear up the picture until Rama had gone, could she? As she was serving him his meal, Shanti mentioned the picture. 'Some people here think of Ravana the whole time,' she began, and went on and on.

The journey by chariot happened very soon after that.

Mid-day. It was the usual time for Lava and Kusa to come home for a meal, after their morning archery exercises. She laid her stylus down. The boys came in a great hurry and ate the food she served on their leaves. As she watched them, she imagined how her life would have turned out if they had both been girls. Would she have allowed them only to pick fruits and flowers, and play at home? She didn't think she would have done so. She would have brought them up, too, as women warriors. Nobody would have been able to kidnap them and carry them away.

A shadow fell over the threshold. It was Rama standing there. Lava and Kusa began telling her that they had met him in the forest; that he had asked them who they were; that they had said their mother's name was Sita, but they didn't know who their father was. They said it was possible he had followed them home. 'Good,' said Sita. 'Your father's name is Rama. He is the king of Ayodhya. He's standing in front of you now.' Without a moment's hesitation, they leapt towards their father. The kingdom was their father's, wasn't it? Had they been girls, they might have stood close to their mother. They might have looked upon a father who abandoned their mother in the forest with suspicious eyes.

Rama began to plead with her. Could Sita not understand his position? Did she think he lived happily without her? As he spoke on and on, she wondered, with a terrible pain, why the earth could not split open and draw her inside. She refused his plea with firmness.

She said her journey lay in a different direction. After that she felt as if the earth had indeed split apart and she had gone within, somewhere far, far beneath.

As soon as they opened their eyes at break of day, Savitabai made tea without milk or sugar and gave it to them, piping hot. The other two set off for their own homes.

She had not forgotten the vinai music she heard during the night. Chenthiru began to walk in a southerly direction from the waterfall. After she had gone some distance, she saw four or five small hut-like dwellings. The door of what looked like the principal hut was open. She went in, softly.

On a thick mattress, spreading from one end of a facing wall to the other, were three *rudravinai*, left uncovered. Next to them sat a man, about sixty years old, with a vinai on his lap. White bearded. He wore a chequered *lungi* about his waist. A kurta over that. He was fine-tuning the instrument, adjusting the pegs and bringing his ears close to the strings.

As soon as she went in, he spoke to her familiarly in pure Hindi, 'Come here, *beti*. Listen to this. Tell me whether it is in tune or not.'

As if she had spent her entire life listening to the pitch of a vinai every day, she went up, listened carefully, and said, 'It's just right.'

She sat down in front of him.

'Everything comes down to *sruti*, getting the pitch right, doesn't it?' he asked her. 'We speak of *sur*, being in tune. Who then is an *asur*? Not someone with crooked teeth and ten heads, but one who is ignorant of sur. A-sur. Because such a thing as sur isn't resonating within them, they run away with themselves, without subjecting their impulses or their strength or their direction to any discipline. They are not reined in by their sur.'

She nodded.

'The pitch must come right, holding everything in tune. All of us are a-sur. Seeking after the right pitch.'

'Is it such a difficult thing, then, to be in tune?'

He laughed.

'It's not a thing to be held captive, is it? It's like a wave. Even when you think you have overcome it and are riding on its crest, it can collapse beneath you. It can rise up again in a gigantic billow. It can turn into nothing but foam when it comes close to you. It will come together, and dissolve. Come and go. Drown you. Fling you right away.'

His very words sounded like the sea.

'Can you sing?' he asked.

'A little. Carnatic music.'

'Mm. Sing something. Sing in your Sankarabaranam.'

Softly she sang the opening lines, the pallavi, of the Sankarabarana varnam.

'Mm,' he said. Then taking the vinai on his lap, he pressed down on the *daivadam*, the sixth note, as if he were flicking a nerve. Then he played several cadences. Then once again that note, as if plucking at a nerve. *Dani...*

'This is the Bilaval raagam from Dhrupad,' he said. She stooped at his feet and pressed her head against the edge of the mattress. Dani...dani...dani... It ran through her body like electricity.

'What is it you want, beti,' he asked, his hand pressing upon her head.

'I don't know,' she said, without looking up. 'Even when I think I understand, I haven't really understood at all. As soon as I think I understand, I lose it all.'

'That's how it is,' he said, patting her head.

She lifted her head and sat back. 'I've left Mumbai and come away.'

'Each of us has just two choices. One is to renounce, the other is not to renounce. Why do I play this instrument? Why do you listen to it? Because we haven't yet understood what is renunciation and what is not.'

'I cannot breathe in Mumbai.'

'Mumbai can follow you here. And the forest too can go with you to Mumbai.'

She looked into his eyes.

'That's how it is,' he said. 'Bilaval was a favourite raagam of my *Mataji*'s. Whenever a dove cooed outside our window, in the narrow lane off the crowded Mohammad Ali Road, she would say it was doing *riyaaz*—practising the Bilaval. Sometimes, she would hear the dove's voice above the roaring of a bus or a train. "A perfect Bilaval," she would say. She died here last year, in this very place. She was eighty years old. It was springtime when she died. She used to struggle all night because she could not sleep. At earliest dawn, by four o'clock, she would take a chair and sit outside. Opposite her, the mango-grove. Around five o'clock, she would call out to me, "Jalaluddin! Ei, Jalaluddin! Come here. The koel is singing the Bilaval." She'd tell you exactly the notes it was singing. "A perfect Bilaval," she'd say, rejoicing. She could hear the Bilaval, wherever she went, in all places.'

He ran his fingers over the strings. A waterfall of sounds.

Some lines from a song she had learnt a long time ago, at school, came to life in her mind. In sound-shapes. In magical Sindhubhairavi.

'Like the unrestrained wind'...those low bass notes.

Outside, a sunlight which would not torment. Ustadji began the alaapanai, the preliminary free rendering of the Bilaval.

'Like the ocean that has seen the moon'...long, ascending cadences.

Ustadji's students gathered quietly inside the room. They sat down, surrounding him. Again and again, there came the plucking of the rudravinai's strings, like the plucking of one's nerves.

'Like a cascading waterfall'...the notes reached a high point and poured downwards.

Ustadji continued to play.

'Play the music on the flute of life'...the notes returned to their path after their wild wandering.

The koel which sang the Bilaval called out from the mango-grove. Dani...dani...dani...

The koel sings everywhere. The koel's song is transformed into the tune the listener wishes to hear.

She rose to her feet and began to walk towards the guest house.

Nobody was willing to accept Sita's decision. They said it was not proper to refuse to go, when the king of Ayodhya himself came to take her back. What was her goal, after all? What was she seeking?

Then there were Hanuman's long appeals. The denunciations of the rest of them. She could not recover from her sense of having gone somewhere beneath the earth, somewhere so deep that nobody could reach her.

She rose to her feet and looked around the cottage. This time it would be a total renunciation. A lone journey which left behind all those who were known to her, those who spoke lovingly, who dispensed advice. A journey that would be long, that would go very deep.

The more she walked, the more the forest seemed to extend. She crossed the river, went past a waterfall, and walked on; saw the deer drinking at a small stream, was shocked by deer-eating tigers, delighted in the sight of baby elephants running alongside the herd, encountered nights through which owls' eyes glowed, observed the shimmering of green leaves as the sun's rays fell upon them, was surprised by the leaping of monkeys from branch to branch, their young clinging to their bellies. She walked on. Eagerly. Wearily. She rested.

And again she walked.

Their meeting took place early one morning. A time when not even the sound of birds was to be heard. The sun was hidden, secretive in the skies. Far away, she saw a small hut. The dim light of a lamp flickered through it. The sound of a musical instrument came to her, tearing the darkness. As she came nearer and nearer, she recognized it as vinai music. A tune that she had surely heard at some time. As she came yet nearer, the music bound her in its melody. The door of the hut was open. She looked inside. Someone who looked like a *tapasvi*, living a life of austerity, was playing the vinai. When she asked whether she was disturbing his practice, he said no. He had been waiting for her, he said. 'Don't you know me? I am Ravana.'

Startled, she stepped back.

'I thought you died in the war...'

'This life is full of magic, is it not? When Rama demolished everyone in my palace, there was one bodyguard left. He pleaded with Rama to spare his life. And he then prayed that a friend of his should be returned to life. Rama did so, and told them both to flee before Lakshmana appeared. When they said they no longer had the strength to run, he gave them wings. They changed respectively into a kite and a parrot, and flew away. This is a story that people tell. Could I not be that parrot that has been flying about in these forests? A parrot waiting for that moment when he would meet Sita once more. A tired old parrot.'

'Even now, this infatuation? I have seen so many tragedies. My life has been like a game of dice in which I am a pawn. I am tired. I am weary. I am more than forty years old.'

'It is then that a woman needs a friend. To support her when she is distressed by her changing body. To serve her. To encourage her. To stand at a distance and give her hope.'

Sita sat down on the floor.

Ravana went on, 'I have never refused to give my friendship to anyone. Before the battle began, Rama wanted to perform a puja. There were only two people in the world who could have conducted the puja for him. One was Vali. The other, myself. Rama had killed Vali with his own hands. So I was the only one left. He sent an invitation to me. I went to him. I did the puja as he desired. I blessed him and invoked his victory.'

Sita addressed him by name for the first time. 'Ravana, words make me tired. Language leaves me crippled. I am fettered by my body.'

Ravana smiled. 'The body is a prison. The body is a means of freedom,' he said. 'Look,' he said, showing her his rudravinai. 'A musical instrument that was created by imagining what wonderful music would sound, if Parvati's breasts, as she lay on her back, turned into gourds, and their nipples attached by strings. It is an extension of Devi's body. You lifted Shiva's bow with one hand. You should be able to conquer this instrument easily. Will you try?'

'Will you teach me?'

'I did battle for you once, and lost. Would I deny you music? I will be your guru and give you lessons every day. Let the music break out of the vinai and flow everywhere in the forest. Don't think of it as an ordinary musical instrument. Think of it as your life, and play on it. Here.'

He lifted the rudravinai from his lap and stretched it out towards her.

'Leave it there on the ground,' said Sita.

'Why?'

'It is my life, isn't it? A life that many hands have tossed about, like a ball. Now, let me take hold of it; take it into my hands.' So saying, Sita lifted the rudravinai and laid it on her lap.

# A Movement, a Folder, Some Tears

Charu's message came by email.

I haven't yet got rid of my jet-lag. When others are asleep, I'm awake. When they are awake, my eyes feel heavy. Hence this letter, written while the CD plays. The usual song. Tamal's favourite, in Hindi:

Alone
in this city
    a man
seeking a living
night and day
seeking a nest…

You didn't even turn up at the airport. I waited until the last moment. Every time someone passed by with cropped hair, wearing a kurta, my heart leapt, certain it must be you. Sakina and you must have been together that day.

True, Sakina didn't say much as they travelled together on the electric train. Dark circles under her eyes. The fan where they stood wasn't working. Sakina's face was covered all over with sweat. She could never stand the heat at the best of times. In the swelter of May, she hung on to the chain in the crowded compartment, streaming with sweat. Her neck and shoulders—once burnt by fire, now swollen, twisted, scarred, changed in colour—were wet through. She didn't even notice when her face was gently blotted with her dupatta. Ten years ago, when she came home from the hospital after the event, she had said, 'Look at my neck and shoulders! It's as if some strange creature is lying upon me. You said, didn't you, that a snake tumbled about your Sivan's neck? Now, I too have a snake around mine.'

Exactly six months later she broke down. 'They're here. They've come. They are throwing torches dipped in oil into the house,' she began to scream as she ran about. A whole month passed during which she screamed and wailed and shouted. After that, gradually she quietened down. She wrote about that day for the psychiatrist, with complete lucidity.

'It was a Friday. Only Ammi and I were at home. Although it was December, the afternoon felt really warm. We had left the window open, to let in a little breeze. Ammi was asleep. I was reading a book. In the distance, I heard a cry rising to a crescendo. An outbreak of noises, screaming, roaring, clamouring. Suddenly, it had become a great deluge. Before I could get up, rolls of cloth smelling of kerosene thudded into the room. Following them came burning torches. I had a nylon dupatta about my neck. I hastened to throw it away, but it had become stuck. I prised it off and flung it. It fell on Ammi, who was hard of hearing, and still sleeping peacefully. Before she could get away, screaming, two more burning torches were on her. I fell down in a faint. When I became conscious, Ammi was beside me, a blackened corpse.'

Her voice, recorded on a tape spoke in English, without a falter.

Doctor: Sakina, do you harbour any anger in your heart?

Sakina: (Laughs.) Doctor, when I heard the shouts of those crowds, I was reading Sahir Ludhianvi's poems. The poem that begins, 'That dawn will break some day.' The next instant I was burnt by the fire. Until I broke down, I felt no anger. Only despair. Now, I have a feeling I have saved myself from drowning in my grief. Now, yes, there is anger in my heart, Doctor. That is my support. My strength. My anchor. Have you been told to remove the anger from the minds and hearts of those who have been caught in these riots, Doctor? Don't do it. I'm going to keep this anger knotted up in my dupatta. I'm not going to scatter it away. I shall go about, hereafter, wrapped in it. Listening to it. Learning from it. I need that anger to help make sure it never happens again.

'Sakina, *tabiyat theek nahiin hai, kya*? ... Don't you feel well? Did you take your blood pressure tablets?'

'Mm,' she said.

'Charu must have packed up all her luggage.'

'Mm.'

They didn't say anything more as they got off the train and made their way to Hutatma Chowk where the meeting was to take place. A small *pandal* had been put up there. There would be songs, speeches, and discussions until late evening.

At five o'clock, Sakina touched her shoulder and said, 'I'll just walk up to Nargis Khala's house, and come back. We'll go to the airport together later.'

But she hadn't come back even after the meeting was over at eight.

Nargis Khala said, when she rang her from a public telephone, 'I've just heard the news about Sakina.'

'What news?'

'Sakina fell down.'

'What? She isn't hurt or anything, is she?'

Khala's voice broke. 'She fell from above.'

'From above? Has she broken any...?'

Khala wept. 'She fell from the seventeenth floor... From the terrace of the building where Iqbal *Maamu* lives.'

She listened to all the details, and then hurried there...

Sakina's neck was broken. She had fallen on to the grass lawn. No dreadful sight of splattered blood. Her head hung down like a chicken whose neck had been wrung. Her body waited for the routine post-mortem procedure.

When she touched Sakina's arm, it felt cold. She stroked Sakina's neck. Gently she pinched her ear. Kissed her forehead. All the while, tears spurted from her eyes. A pain inside, as if she were being hit by a hammer.

At what moment did you decide to do this, Sakina? When you saw the grass far beneath you, what did you think? What came to your mind? Did you think, wretched girl, that if you fell, the grass would be soft beneath you? Did you place your foot on the hook set into the wall and climb on to the parapet? Did you stand right up there? Did you gaze at the mountainous buildings all around, reaching up to the sky? Did you see the ocean beyond the building, blue and flowing? Did you lift your arms and dive like a swimming champion? Or, did you slip and slide as you fell? Did you scream, *kannamma*? Did your voice dissolve away in the wind, *thangam*? At what instant did you die? When you touched the ground? On the way there? Or, had you died already, even when we travelled together this morning?

She continued to stroke Sakina's head.

What was it that shattered you? What defeated you? What came upon you in that instant's whirlwind and pushed you over? Was it what happened last month? Charu and you went to Ahmedabad to prepare a report. Charu's father's sister has a house there. An aunt who knew you from the moment you became Charu's friend. The same aunt who always looked forward to the vermicelli *payasam* you brought her at the time of Id. This time she refused to allow Charu and you inside her house. Her daughter and son-in-law stood at the doorway, blocking your entry. When Charu proclaimed loudly that the upstairs room belonged to her father, she was handed the key and told to use the outside stairs to go up. Charu and you stayed there for three days. There isn't a soul who has not read the report you two prepared. When Charu, you, and I were together on two different evenings, you spoke about a couple of things that happened.

First. The front door which Charu and you had to pass was sometimes ajar. When you glanced inside, once, the aunt's three-year-old grandson was playing with dolls. A small sword and shield, a few plastic dolls—these were his favourite toys. He sliced off the doll's arms and legs with his sword. He struck a blow even in that shiny place where the doll had no organ.

You called him to the door. 'Kuber!' He turned round and smiled.

'Should you cut up the doll like that? Isn't it like a little baby?'

Tiny sword in hand, he came to the door, with shining eyes.

'It's a Muchlim. I've killed it,' he said, in his childish language.

'Kuber, Sakina *Mausi* also is a Muslim.'

Still smiling, he stuck his toy-sword into your stomach.

'*Jai* Cheeram,' he said.

Second. There was a celebration in the temple at the street corner. Singing loudly and shrilly, Charu's aunt leapt up and down, calling on God's name. The devotional *bhajans* came out like hisses. At one stage, she and her bhajan companions whirled round in what appeared to be a frenzied dance, streaming with sweat, their hair loose, while the floor shook beneath their heavy tread.

When her aunt returned home, Charu called down to her, '*Bua.*' Her aunt turned her gaze towards the upstairs room.

Those were not Bua's eyes. In the fading twilight, lit by the street lamp's yellow light, they glinted like a wolf's eyes.

Now, Iqbal Maamu laid his hand on her shoulder. 'Selvi Beti,' he said, patting her, consoling her.

The whole family came to the airport. Kalavati Mausi's son sent a car and a driver. You won't believe it. Tamal's parents were there. Tamal's son, Manush, had brought them. Amala, Tamal's wife, too. She said she could understand at last, my relationship with Tamal for twenty-five years. She wished me success in my journey towards further research. Tamal's father stroked my head and blessed me. He said, 'Who knows whether we will still be here if and when you come back; go safely and return safely.' At that moment I wasn't at the airport. I was on the train to Matunga. In 1993. To us in the women's compartment, the bomb blast sounded only like Diwali celebrations. That instant when the train stopped and I peeped out with the others is still sharply etched in my mind. It goes on extending, extending, extending in my mind, like batter spreading out and out in a pan. Because of the crowds, I had joined the women, while Tamal stayed in the general compartment.

'There's been a bomb blast in one of the general compartments.' When I jumped down, went forward a little, and pushed my way through the crowds, Tamal lay on the ground. Both legs reduced to a blood-porridge below the knees. His chest covered in blood.

When I rushed to him, calling out 'Tamal,' I realized that for an instant he himself didn't know what had happened.

'What happened?' he asked. As he was carried into the ambulance, he raised himself a little and looked down towards his legs. He looked at me and folded his hands, as if to say, Save me from this. Next to him was an old Muslim man, covered in wounds. The games of History. Historical games. Nobody was with him. Some good people from the train helped me to take him and Tamal to the hospital. Tamal remained conscious until his name was registered.

'Tamal Mukherji,' he said, without faltering. Fifty years of age, he said. His religion was Humanity, he said. There was no one to introduce the old Muslim gentleman.

The police investigation came from a strange and oblique perspective. 'Did these two conspire together to place the bomb, or was it only one of them who did it?'

With the help of many people, I reclaimed Tamal's body and had it cremated in the crematorium attached to the hospital. Even when it was all over, the Muslim gentleman's family was wandering about, waiting for his body. His aged wife, who didn't have the least idea about the severity of the regulations, came to me and began, 'Beti, if an accident happens when you are travelling by train, can you claim compensation? I have two daughters. I must get them married. It was to arrange for some money that he set out this morning.'

I stood there holding her hand. You will remember. We tried to claim compensation for her. We failed. Then we set up a fund and made a collection for her.

All this came to mind, lit up as if by a lightning flash. And once again, as I write this.

Sakina put an end to herself. She was a lawyer. She was not unaware of the procedural confusions following such a death. It was not unknown to her that she should have left a letter. Surely her death could not have been predetermined. It must have been the result of an aberration, a sudden whirlwind attack, a wave of vivid emotion that overcame her. Attempting to lean over just a little, she must have tipped over completely. She suffered from blood pressure. She had received psychiatric treatment in 1992.

After Sakina's death was recorded in the police files, complete with all these explanations, in a language peculiar to government offices, her body was handed over. And buried.

Sakina had gone to collect a folder which was left in Iqbal Maamu's flat. That is what she said to him on the telephone. Soon after she arrived, she had a cup of tea, and went to the room where the books were kept.

The file was there, in an almirah. The door on the far side of the room opened on to the terrace. Fifteen minutes later, the caretaker of the building rang the doorbell and kept on ringing until the door was opened.

'A woman has jumped from the terrace of your...'

'Don't talk nonsense,' said Maamu, 'I'm alone in the flat...' Before he could finish, he remembered Sakina's presence. He ran to the library. No Sakina. The door to the terrace stood open. The door of the almirah in which the file was kept had been unlocked. The lock and key together had been left on top of the almirah. Far below, Sakina lay, a crooked line. Her black dupatta was caught at the wing-tip of the topiary bird in the garden, and was swinging in the wind.

Running downstairs, laying her in his lap, weeping aloud. The neighbours supporting Maamu...

Again and again Iqbal Maamu described it all. His beloved niece. He had supported her throughout her legal studies. He had accepted all her decisions. He spoke of them repeatedly.

The almirah was still unlocked. He opened it, took out the folder, and gave it to Selvi. The cover bore the name of their organization: Jagruti. Awareness.

When it was time for me to go in, a silence fell over all of us. Then, the goodbyes. Choking throats. Tears in *Ba*'s eyes. *Bapu* wiping his eyes with his handkerchief. As I went in, I saw my own reflection in the glass door. I was weeping. I am weeping, I told myself. I have wept before, many times. In the upper berth of a railway compartment. Waiting for a train late one night at a railway station empty of humanity, looking up at the stars. In a bullock cart, staring at the animal's tail. In the bathroom of an airport. Sitting in the corner of the upper deck of a bus. Driving at speed down the middle of a road. So many leave-takings. So many farewells. Another goodbye. Another bout of tears. In the glass door, a fifty-year-old woman holding on to her shoulder-bag and setting off for further research. Long hair, uncut. Cheeks streaked with tears. I held on to the rubbish bins for support, and let the tears flow.

'Do you need any help?' A woman, a fellow-traveller, had stopped in front of me.

'No, thank you,' I said, and walked on towards the inner door.

Even now as I write this, at this instant when everyone is asleep and I'm awake, the tears flow from my eyes. It's as if a long era of which we were part, as makers of history, has now come to an end.

I can't understand it. I sometimes wonder if it's part of the tiredness which comes with the menopause. But I think I have never felt such weariness before. When did the body control us, ever? When did it dominate us? Were we ever afraid of it? We never even thought of old age. How would it occur to us to be concerned about old age with the example of Nargis *Khala* before of us? She has never stopped working for her organization has she, even though she is eighty-seven years old now, and crippled, besides? Whenever I think of Nargis Khala, I remember the sound of her typewriter—placed on the table by the window, so that she can look out—as she taps out a statement on human rights, or writes a letter to a newspaper about freedom of speech. Last month she told me she was considering buying a computer. I said, 'Don't, Khala. I can relate you only with this typewriter.' She answered, 'Can I keep from changing, just for the sake of your illusions?'

I argued a lot with her that day. I shouted at her. 'Just be quiet, Khala. Why did people like you—people who spent the best part of your lives with Gandhi, who fought for Independence—end up later on in ashrams and small towns? Why did you decide not to enter politics? If you had given your country half the devotion you gave to Gandhi, the politics of this country might have taken a different course. Who asked you for your renunciation? In 1942, you marched through all these streets without fear, like the queens of the locality. How often have we been thrilled by the photographs of your processions, you with your banners held high. Don't provoke me. You, your *khaddar* and your spinning-wheels. You have all become mere symbols. Symbols which we hang on walls or wear as fashionable clothes and caps. Useless, marginal symbols. Cowardly symbols. Frivolous symbols. You left us no other political heritage.'

Perhaps, I spoke like that out of the emotional state in which I returned from Ahmedabad. As I spoke, I went up to her wheelchair and shook Khala. Khala didn't stop me. Then I buried my head in her lap. She laid her hands on my head, like a blessing.

The folder lay on the table. All the other books and papers from the room were in cardboard boxes. The boxes still gaped open. The schoolboy, who lived downstairs, and his two friends had offered to tie them all up. The arrangement was that they would be paid enough so that they could go watch a Hrithik Roshan film.

She asked Nandini that morning, 'We have to vacate the room, Nandu. Could you take a day off? I can't, on my own...'

Nandini answered, 'I have a lot of work at the office. Otherwise I would have helped. I have to go to Pune as well, on Saturday, for my work. Won't it do if you clear it next week?'

'The landlord insists...'

Nandini was embarrassed. She felt sorry she couldn't help. She knew Charu had gone to the United States, Sakina wasn't there any more, Selvi was on her own. Because of this, she answered without annoyance or irritation, without barking at her mother. Otherwise, she certainly would have retorted, 'Please, Amma. I work in a private company. This is not a government job from which I can take off as I please. Nor is it a women's organization where I'm allowed a day's leave if I have my periods, or my child sneezes, or my husband has a headache, if there is a feast or a fast. If we want equal employment with men, we have to be prepared to work with them on equal terms.'

Sometimes, Selvi wanted to say in return, 'It was we who laid the way so that you could find a job suited to your intelligence, earning an equal wage with men. We weeded the thorns from your path, removed the obstacles, made you aware of your rights.' But such discussions had ceased between them, long ago.

Three years ago, Charu, Sakina, and she had finished some work in Dongri and returned home past one o'clock at night. They had all decided to go straight to Selvi's place, as it would delay them even more if they stopped to eat on the way. They rang the front doorbell until their hands ached, but to no effect. No signs of anyone inside. At last they woke up their neighbours, jumped across from their balcony to Selvi's, pushed open the door which was just closed, and went in. It was a fifth-floor flat. Quite a circus feat, leaping from one balcony to the next at one o'clock at night. They were desperately hungry. Used plates and empty vessels lay strewn all over the kitchen work-surface. In an instant Charu cleaned the work-top. Sakina began to make the dough for chapatis. Selvi put the potatoes on to boil. When she took out the already boiled *dal* from the fridge, Charu seasoned it with chopped onions, ginger, garlic, and green chillies. A piping-hot meal of chapatis, dal, and potato-*sabzi* was ready at two o'clock in the night.

Ramu was alive then. When she asked him angrily, the next morning, why he had not opened the door at night, he snapped back, 'If you come home at twelve and one, I can't be expected to keep awake and open the door.'

'Why, haven't I opened the door for you when you came back at three after a night out with your friends? Haven't I fed you?'

'I was tired. I fell asleep. So must you make such a song and a dance about it?'

'We had to jump across the balcony to get in. Sakina suffers from blood pressure. You know that, don't you?'

Charu and Sakina intervened, preventing the argument from growing worse.

Later, while they were having tea, Nandini turned up and Selvi asked her, 'How could you have been so fast asleep? Didn't you hear us ringing the front doorbell?'

Nandini said, 'Amma, I could hear quite clearly the way you were fighting early this morning. That is what is known as oppression. Go on. Go and write another book.' Then, turning to Sakina and Charu, she added in English, 'Isn't that right?' When Selvi explained to her friends what Nandini had said, their faces tightened.

Even though Ramu died in an accident, the relatives spoke as if it was all owing to her lack of care. 'A good man. Half the time he made his own coffee, and drank it all alone... And for all that, it was his own choice to marry her...'

Yes. That happened twenty-five years ago. It still remained their complaint.

Nandini too had said, 'You should have looked after Appa better, Amma. You were always running off to some procession protesting against dowry or rape or whatever. People who think like that should never get married.'

At that time she had not had the strength to explain to her daughter that in their youth Ramu and she had belonged to the same group of friends, and that he had married her precisely because he admired her activism.

The landlord came and looked in.

'*Udya kali karnarna nakki*?... You'll definitely vacate the room tomorrow, won't you?'

It was an old-fashioned tiled house. As you climbed up the wooden stairs, there was a small room to the right. Their office for the past twenty years.

'Yes,' she assured him, and turned away. The sharks of the building trade had their eyes on this house. It was in an area that had become popular among actors and the newly-rich. The landlord had been muttering for the past two years about so many women coming here. When Muslim women came, he said, the house stank. As if the winds emanating from him were perfumed! Perhaps our own farts smell sweet to us. He said they stank because they ate beef. Having endured the many odours he expelled, lifting his thigh and contorting his body, they had no wish to explain to him about Vedic times.

He was concerned that they might ask for some compensation because they had rented the room for so many years. Sakina had said that before they looked for another place, they should really hold out for the money.

When she took up the folder—the folder with a purple cover— and placed it on her lap, it was as if Sakina was beside her. Snake-neck woman. She who knotted up her anger in her dupatta.

You were angry when I began to apply for research grants. You shouted at me. You charged me with being a coward. You said I was running away to hide. I accept all your accusations. But my dear friend, I am also the woman who saw her lover's legs reduced to a mess of blood. I didn't give way then. I didn't run away. I stood. I opposed. I fought. These past ten years, I gave all my breath and being to the work of Jagruti. I immersed myself in music. How many Kabir *dohas* I sang, in how many places! Do you remember the devotional song , 'Aaj sajan mohé', which begins,

> Embrace me today, my love,
> let this life reach fruition.
> Heart's pain,
> body's fire,
> let all be cool...

Rising higher and higher, the song would go

> Quench my thirst, Giridhara,
> enchanter of my heart
> I thirst from the very depths of my being,
> I have thirsted for many generations.

When I sang the words 'I thirst—I have thirsted', repeating them over and over again, didn't all three of us—you, me, Sakina—weep?

It wasn't just a thirst for human love. It was that unquenched thirst within us. We are people who continue to wander about with that thirst. Even now, when I say 'from the very depth of my being', an ache like a cold wind enters my whole self. You must believe this. If I decided, in spite of that, that I had to come away, should you not understand that I had a strong enough reason?

Selvi, Kumudben Bua is not just my aunt. She became a widow at an early age, and came to live at our house with her young son. She gave me her unflinching support in all my decisions. She accepted Tamal. Just because Tamal loved fish, she allowed it to be cooked in her house. She called our house-dog 'Arjun Beta' without any hesitation, and fed it the offering from her daily puja. After Arjun died, she gave the offering everyday to a street dog, in Arjun's name. She was never held back by the requirements of ritual. She never allowed anyone to be held back in that way. It was she who taught me about humanity.

The first shock came when she refused to allow me inside the house in Ahmedabad. The look she gave Sakina was the second blow. The third whiplash was the change in her eyes that evening. There was a further blow which felt as if it ripped my flesh away. I never told you both this. Bua used to go out with other women from time to time. Always, when she returned, there would be a kind of energy in the way she walked. Once, on her return, I came face to face with her. She lifted her hand to stop me from touching her. Selvi, the stench of kerosene came from her hand. My whole body began to shudder. We left that very day.

I didn't say anything to anyone. That evening, when I was at home, Bapu said at the dining table, 'The Muslims have learnt a good lesson.' Ba added, 'Let them all go to Pakistan.' These people are all of my blood. The food stuck in my throat. How did this lake of poison come about? How could I have been so blind? Why did we never see the growth of this horror which was capable of dividing parents and daughter, brother and sister; which could come between all relationships?

Several little incidents appeared in a new light, suddenly. No one asking after Sakina for many days. Ba's simple puja of lighting her lamp becoming more and more complex over the last two years. A sticker on Bapu's car mirror, saying, 'Say with pride, I am a Hindu'. My sticker on top of that one, 'Say with pride, we are human beings'. Ba's comment when I bought a green sari, 'Why did you go for this Muslim-green?' No longer buying bread from Mohammed *Kaka*'s shop as we have done for years. Various conversations in relatives' houses. Small incidents, whose violence was striking, when added together. Each and every one had been a drop of poison. It felt as if the kerosene I smelt on Kumudben Bua's hand had pervaded our house.

A fear that this storm of madness might never cease, caught in my mind like a hook. It's a good thing Tamal died. He could never have borne this.

There's a little story in a Paulo Coelho novel. In a distant land there lived a wizard. He poured a drug that induced madness, into the town well. The people drank it and began to go about as they pleased, in a totally crazy manner. When the king tried to bring about laws to control them, they told him to leave the throne. So the king decided to abdicate. The queen, though, counselled otherwise. 'Oh, king, don't give up your throne. Come, let us also drink from the same well.' And as soon as they drank, they became like everyone else. The problem was over.

I was afraid there was no well left that the wizard had not touched, Selvi. It was then that I decided to leave the country. I did not have the strength to live with this day after day.

Today, I write this to you alone. It will take me days to write to Sakina.

In the folder, there were notes for the Jagruti newsletters, descriptions of some of their events, details of women who had come to them for legal advice, summaries of discussions, details of arguments. Records that Sakina had collected and kept with care.

There was even a note on the occasion, in 1980, when they had cut their hair. She wrote, 'On the dais, there was a debate going on about physical beauty. A professor–poet began by saying that the beauty of an Indian woman is signalled by long hair, big breasts, tiny waist, and sword-like eyes, and went on to sing a *purana* to long hair. Selvi and I exchanged glances. Since Nandu was born, Selvi scarcely has time to comb her hair. As for me, travelling constantly, long hair is a real burden. What's more, as the professor went on and on, gushing and melting about long hair, the trail of peacock's feathers, the spread of dark clouds, etc., everyone's eyes were on us. We went straight off and had our hair cut. We felt light-headed; head-strong no longer!

Selvi remembered it well. Those were times when they faced everything with an energy that said, 'You can't define us. We will break your definitions, your commentaries, your grammars, your rules.' They felt an urgency to defy everything. She and Sakina had gone to a Chinese beauty parlour and had their hair cropped close to their heads. When she went home, Ramu only asked, making no fuss, 'Well Selvi, was it a pilgrimage to Palani or to Tirupati?' 'Neither; it was to China,' she told him. Lively times, those were.

There was a little notebook containing the songs they sang in the eighties, during their marches:

Don't surrender,
don't submit,
don't drown,
don't die.
We are the Revolution.
To all injustice
we are the reply.

Charu always led the singing. All the rest joined in the chorus.

There was a copy, in the folder, of the sticker printed with the *Mandir–Masjid* song, which they had pasted on all the railway compartments after the Babri Masjid was demolished.

Temples, mosques, and *gurudwaras*
they divided from each other.
They divided the land,
they divided the sea.
Don't divide human beings
Don't divide human beings.

Charu had written a note on the occasion when Sakina was to give a speech at a meeting in a women's college near Churchgate during the Shah Bano case. The question of maintenance was being re-examined.

'They had announced that the meeting would be at six in the evening. When Sakina and I went there, there were many *burka*-clad women outside the college, carrying placards which said things like, "Shariat alone protects women," and "We will only listen to Shariat". I looked at Sakina. "There are two sides to everything, aren't there?" she remarked. There was a huge crowd in the hall. Sakina's lawyer friend, Shahid, sat down beside me. When Sakina began to speak, the burka-clad women rose up in a wave. They moved in on Sakina, shouting, "You are not a true Muslim. You don't know the Koran. You don't say your prayers. You are an enemy of Muslim women." When they insisted again and again, "Tell us, are you a Muslim or not?," Sakina became distressed, unable to move any further back. Her voice broke as she said, "I really am a Muslim. I have read the Koran. I know my prayers. Let me speak..." Shahid tried to restrain the man next to him who was jumping up and down, and said, "Why don't we listen to her at least?" The man yelled back, "Shut up, you are not a Muslim." Shahid replied, "I am, actually." The crowds became uncontrollable, and the police arrived.

'Shahid and I brought Sakina away through the back door. She was shattered. "This is going to be a huge battle, Charu," she said. "It begins with someone else giving me an identity."'

Like a sequel to this, there was an incident in the house of Charu's relatives two years later. Selvi remembered it as soon as she read Charu's report.

The discussion had begun in an apparently lighthearted manner. 'Every Muslim has four wives.' Charu and she had interrupted to say that it wasn't true, and that in any case, many Hindus they knew had more than one wife. At this, Charu's uncle's son remarked, 'Of course, Charu, you have to say that. It concerns you, after all. You are Tamal's *rakhel*, his mistress, aren't you?'

'Very well, let me be a rakhel, Sudhir. But how many wives did your grandfather have? And do you know the story of your great-grandfather? He scattered his seed all over Gujarat very generously. Watch out, there are several of his great-grandsons walking all over Gujarat, with the same features as you.'

'All that is irrelevant. Selvi, have you read *Tulsiramayan?*'

'Why would I read *Tulsiramayan?* I've read *Kambaramayanam,* certainly. As Tamil Literature.'

'Isn't Sri Ram your god, then?

'Life is my god.'

'If I ask you whether you are a Hindu, can you answer Yes or No?'

'I can only say I was born into a Hindu family.'

'Yes or No? Tell me that.'

'Yes. No.'

They didn't hit out. They didn't kick. But that was all. They roared. They thundered. They ridiculed. They spoke with contempt. When she refused to eat, they said, 'Che, this is only a friendly discussion.'

The interview with Nargis Khala was on green paper. An interview which all three of them had held with her. She had talked of her days during the Independence struggle, and had ended by saying, 'You might ask me what I achieved in my life. I'll tell you a story in reply to that. A Zen master went away to live in a cave in a remote mountain. On his return, the king summoned him to the court and asked him to give an account of the wisdom he had attained. The master was silent for a while, and then he took out the reed-flute that was tucked in at his waist, and played a cadence on it, very softly and sweetly; then walked away. Some things can't be said. They can't be wrapped up in words. If you ask me about my achievements, I will touch you with these hands. Hoping that through my fingers, the warmth of my experience will reach you. I will touch your heads with my hands. What else can I do? What do I know except that?'

How often had Nargis Khala touched her? Stroked her cheek? When Sakina and Charu returned from Ahmedabad and poured out their distress, she put her arms around both, embracing them. At that moment she looked like Jatayu.

'Broad views about life have shrunk into religions, and we have been turned into their symbols. They regard us as empty symbols. Symbols of a religion, a nation. We mustn't be trapped by that. In this war, let that be the ground of your contest. A ground that cannot be reduced to definition and detail.'

'But what are our weapons, Khala? What, if anything, can be our weapons?'

'Only this,' she said, laying the palms of her hands, wrinkled like withered leaves, against their cheeks. She smiled.

'Aunty, may we come in?' The two young boys were strikingly tall. A girl of the same age was with them. All three worked fast. When they stopped for a rest, halfway through, they danced to '*Bole chudian*' and '*Shava shava.*' Then they returned to their work. All for the sake of Hrithik Roshan.

One of the boys said, 'Our Baba told us Amir Khan is Muslim. We mustn't go to Amir Khan films. And we mustn't drink Coca-Cola.'

'Really? Hrithik Roshan's wife is Muslim. Amir Khan's wife is Hindu. Don't drink either Coca-Cola or Pepsi. Your teeth will rot. Tell your Baba.'

'I'll tell him,' he said, hesitantly. He was afraid the money might not come into his hands.

As soon as they were paid, they fled, shouting, '*Thanda matlab* Coca-Cola.'

It's night-time here. I'm sitting in a cyber centre, writing this. I'll tell you later why I'm here.

First, there is some important news. Sakina is dead. She fell from the terrace of Iqbal Maamu's seventeenth-storey flat and died. Her neck was broken. How much violence there has been in our lives! Tamal's death in the bomb blast. Ramu's death in the car accident. Now, Sakina's ill-fated death. These are violent times. We cannot redeem our lives until we have passed through them.

Sakina's death stabs at my heart even now. She was with me that day until early evening. She seemed a little weary. I was distraught because I could not understand why she told me she would go to Nargis Khala's house, but changed her mind and went to Iqbal Maamu instead. She was my friend from our school days. I agonized over why she committed suicide when there should have been so many more years of friendship ahead of us. I couldn't accept that it was suicide. Before she went she had said, 'Let us go and say goodbye to Charu at the airport.' I thought and thought about what could have happened between five o'clock and the moment of her fall; I retraced her steps again and again. Some things became clear to me.

The night before, she returned from her second visit to Ahmedabad. When she telephoned me, her voice didn't sound right to me. I insisted, 'Come round to my flat at once. You don't sound good at all. I'm sure you haven't eaten at all properly.' She came. I made her favourite soft rotis, and a potato and bell-pepper curry. She ate. Later, as we lay down and talked, she told me about an incident that happened the previous evening. It was rather late when she reached the refugee camp. A young Muslim woman was walking in front of her, she said, one child on her hip, and another clutching her hand. She walked along, supporting both children, and managing at the same time to carry a bag in one hand. The tri-colour flag was stuck between her fingers and she was walking along, extending it in front of her. Like a protective shield. As if she were proclaiming, I too am a citizen of this country.

'I wept and wept, Selvi, when I saw this. Why has it become so necessary for just a few of us to have to do this? My Khala was a freedom fighter. My Maamu heads many charitable institutions in this city. My Ammi retired from an administrative post in a school. She died a blackened corpse. My father was a high-ranking official. Here am I, walking about with a snake-neck. That girl might have come from a similar family. Or she might have been one of India's many, many poor women. I couldn't bear to see her stumbling along with her children, her bag, and her tri-colour flag.' She wept for a long time. She repeated again and again, overwhelmed by the thought, 'The time has come when I have to establish that my Khala was this, my Ammi was that, and so on and on...'

She was devastated by the thought that the actions of her family—performed naturally and as a matter of course—had to be presented now as her credentials. She said, 'Selvi, do you remember what Charu used to say? That when certain birds decide to die, they swallow many pebbles; then when they try to fly, they cannot because of the weight inside them. So they crash down and die. My heart feels so heavy—as if I've swallowed many stones.'

'You go to sleep now,' I said, patting her. She dropped off like a child.

But there was no cheerfulness in her expression the next day. Later, we stood together in the heat in Hutatma Chowk. She was participating in the hunger strike, besides. At first, she really must have set out for Nargis Khala's flat. Then, remembering we had to vacate the Jagruti office in the next few days, it could have struck her that she might as well collect the folder from Iqbal Maamu's flat since she was in that part of town. I conjecture all this from Iqbal Maamu's memory of his conversation with Sakina over tea, that last day.

It seems that while she was waiting for a taxi to take her to Iqbal Maamu's house, she met Nandini. She asked Nandini where she was off to. Nandini said to her, 'Sakina Mausi, I have to tell you something. Keep away from Amma and me for a while. I hold a responsible position. I don't wish to be caught up in any kind of trouble...' This from the girl whom you and Sakina brought up. When she was a child, she thought of Sakina's Ammi and Khala as her grandmothers.

Already Sakina was a bird that had swallowed many pebbles. Nandini made her swallow a block of granite. It seemed Sakina just patted her on her back. Soon after she got to Iqbal Maamu's flat, she went and opened the book-almirah. I went to Maamu's flat myself, and made myself go through all her actions. The instant she opened the almirah, she would have seen the photograph of Ammi holding Nandini in her arms. Sakina must have been deeply moved. I think she didn't take her blood-pressure tablets that day. She must have felt dizzy. She must have opened the terrace door, gone outside, and taken a few deep breaths. She might have remembered the topiary bird. She might have held on to the parapet wall, raised herself a little, and peered down. Empty stomach. Seventeenth floor. Suddenly her foot might have slipped. I believe that's what happened. She fell against the topiary bird, and then crashed to the ground. And that is how our Sakina met her end.

Now, please read the attachment I have sent with this message. Finish the letter later. When the girl who worked in Sakina's house had her baby, it was the fiftieth anniversary of Independence. Sakina wrote this then. I found it in the folder. I think she must have written it for us, all that while ago.

---

Attachment: For Roshni, a morning song.

A few weeks ago your mother invited me to your home to give you a name; to whisper it in your ear. In that tiny hut, where there was scarcely enough room to sit down, your mother had hung a cradle which she had bought for a hundred rupees. She had strung flowers around the room. She had bought a new frock for you. A couple of months ago I had seen you in the hospital—within three hours of your birth. You looked like a peeled fruit then! Now your face and your features were bright, radiant. When I whispered in your ear, like a secret, 'You are Roshni, you are Light,' you swivelled your eyes round and gazed at me.

Every night, your grandmother, who gave up her share of a small piece of agricultural land and left her village to come and work in the big city and bring up four daughters in this slum colony by the seaside, will sing you to sleep with lullabies. As you grow up she will tell you stories to the sound of the waves until you fall asleep. Stories of kings and queens, stories about the devil, about valorous mothers and noble wives. At dawn, the calling of the *azaan* from the mosque will wake everyone, summoning them to prayers. I have heard that in the temples too, they sing the *tirupalli ezhucchi* to wake up the gods. Roshni, this is my azaan for you, my dawn song. To wake you up and keep you awake. This is the song of my generation. The generation that has lived through these past fifty years. A generation that wants to tell many stories, in many voices, in many forms. You will hear many tunes here. And there will be some discordant notes, too. Because it spans many years. It touches many lives. Lives which are similar, and very different. But do listen to it.

During these years, it wasn't easy to grow up, to live, to make the right choices in life, in education and work. Several of us, even now, keep changing those choices. We had to oppose the mainstream and swim against it, taking care not to be caught in the whirlpools. They told us many stories, too. They told us that for women, marriage was the most important thing in life. But we had also heard of the Sufi saint Rubaiya, and of Meera. We knew about *Bhakti*. All the same, several among us were atheists, didn't believe in rituals, didn't accept that one religion alone was true. Even now, that is so.

From our childhood, the Independence movement and its ideals had merged into our lives. The men and women who had been part of it were our role models. Many of them lived among us. They came and spoke to us in our schools. You could say there wasn't a home without a picture of

Gandhi, smiling. From our schooldays we learnt the song about Gandhi's life, which began, '*Suno, suno ae duniyavalo Bapujiki amar kahaani*'. When we were still in school, we saw the film *Jagruti* in which a teacher takes his pupils all over India and sings to them, 'Take this earth, and wear it on your forehead as an auspicious sign. This is the land of our sacrifices.' For our generation it became almost a national song. We were stirred by other Hindi songs, such as the one that went, 'We have saved the boat from the storm and brought it safely ashore. Children, safeguard this land.' We wept. There were some among us who had grown up learning the poems of the poet Bharati. Iqbal's lyric, '*Sare jehan se accha*' rang out in every school. We learnt to sing Tagore's songs, '*Ekla chalo*' and '*Amar janmabhumi*', making no discrimination against any language. In another picture *Kabuliwallah*, the hero, from Kabul, sings a song, remembering his country. 'My beloved land, I dedicate my heart to you. You are my desire. You are my honour. I greet the winds that come from your direction with a *salaam*. Your dawns are most beautiful; your evenings most splendidly-coloured.' We used to apply these words to our own country, and weep. Of course, there were other labels amongst us—as Marathi, Kannadiga, Tamil, Telugu, Punjabi, Assamese, and so on. But for us who grew up in the years following Independence, the country as a whole was the important thing.

But these were not the only songs we heard. There were other sounds and voices. Proverbs, discussions, the voices of everyday life. Listen to some of them: Rubbish and daughters grow quickly. Women and cows will go where you drag them. Women and earth become fertile with beating. A woman learns by giving birth; a man learns through trade. A daughter is like a basket of snakes on the head. A leaking roof and a nagging wife are best abandoned. A woman's virtue is like a glass vessel. If a husband batters or the rain lashes, to whom can you complain? You may sit on any ground, you may sleep with any woman.

Sometimes, the older women in our homes, or travellers we met on journeys, sang yet other songs. Work songs, dirges, lullabies. Women spoke of their tribulations in such songs. Such sounds brought us down to earth from the idealistic heights where we were floating. I found some of those songs in books, too. One remains in my memory: it's a song by a widow who says she might have served society better had she bloomed as a flower on a tree and not been born a woman. The metaphor in the song refuses to leave me.

There was also something called national culture. Motherhood was at its core. A woman like Jija Mata. A woman who suckled her child with the milk of valour. Before our time, women had already left their homes to work for the country. They had accomplished extraordinary things. But we, who came after them, had to safeguard our homes. We were instructed that our duty was to reap the benefits of the previous generation, to listen without opening our mouths, never to raise any questions. Our responsibility was to create a home, set up a good family, learn what was useful to society. The advice to us was clear: Sit still. Otherwise you will rock the boat.

Our bodies grew heavy. We carried a heavy burden of stones that we did not choose to carry. I say all this, Roshni, with the clarity of hindsight. But at that time we were both clear and confused. We were not silent, though. Do you know, there is a Bengali proverb that says, no one can control a woman's tongue? So we never stopped talking. We spoke up through poems, stories, political essays, music, drama, painting; in many different ways. Many of us aimed for higher education. If you look at many family photograph albums, there will be one photograph of a young woman in a graduation gown, clutching a rolled-up degree in her hand. Wearing an expression of fulfilment. Head held high. A keenness in the eyes. I too have such a photograph. But it was also customary, as soon as this photograph was taken, to remove the graduation gown and take another photo which would be sent to prospective bridegrooms. I told you, didn't I, there were all kinds of pressures on our lives? It wasn't easy to deal with them. A woman called Subhadra Khatre has said, 'It would be good to deposit one's femininity in a safe-deposit vault and move around freely in the outside world.' She was an engineer of that time. She writes, 'Had I been a typist, I would have picked up a job easily. As an engineer, they looked at me as if I were trying to usurp a man's place.'

Until the end of the sixties we fought only within our own homes and our narrow surroundings. It was a battle to stop others from directing our lives. In 1961, the law against dowry came into force. We debated it in schools and colleges. There were some women in politics even at that time. But it was in the seventies that a serious networking among women with divergent views began through conferences, workshops, protest marches, and dialogues. We wrote many songs for our movement. We sang them. We raised our voices against price-rise, against dowry, against rape, against domestic violence, against liquor, and against the exploitation of the environment. We worked together and independently. We gained victory. We saw defeat. Sometimes, we were divided as activists and academics. But one thing we understood clearly. Just because we had similar bodies we did not need to have similar thoughts. The political atmosphere made some of us disillusioned with the movement. Some of us opted out. Others became isolated. They retreated into their shell, refusing to communicate. We became aware of one thing. We needed to learn humility. However much we celebrated sisterhood and love, there were still many demons within us such as jealousy, competitiveness, arrogance, insolence, hatred. Some of us emerged with renewed strength.

Like so many Sitas who couldn't be banished to any forest. Like so many Rubaiyas who walked their own path, singing the stories of their own lives.

Roshni, Light, I have strung together for you fifty years of doubts, rebellions, battles, struggles. This is only a song. When I write an epic for you—and I will write it one day—I will speak of all this in detail. But don't think the song is complete. It is true that communal violence, caste-wars, and human degradation have all dispirited us greatly. But our battle continues. We still raise our voices to safeguard rivers, trees, and animals. To safeguard human beings, above all. You will hear in this song, resonances of our joy, despair, disappointments, and exhilaration.

Sleep well, Roshni. And when you wake up, let it be to the sound of our song. You and I and many others must complete it.

For we believe that a song once begun ought to be completed.

Now read on.

As soon as I realized how Sakina's death had come about, I left for home. I waited for Nandini. When she returned, the questions I put to her confirmed for me what she said to Sakina that day. At once I telephoned Susie, who manages a working women's hostel, and booked a guest room there until further notice. I told Nandini to pack whatever clothes she might need into a single case. I told her I would send on the rest of her belongings later. Then I asked her to leave my house. She was shocked. She had assumed it was I who was leaving, and I think she was preparing herself for a histrionic farewell. She became furious. 'Don't I have any rights in my father's house?' she demanded.

'The house is in my name. Your rights to it will come after me.'

As she was about to leave she said, 'Don't expect me to come to your aid when you fall ill and take to your bed.'

I said, 'I know how to live alone. And I know how to die alone. You can go.'

'How can people like you call yourselves mothers?'

'I count myself a real mother. Those others live with the illusion of motherhood,' I said, closing the door.

I sent on all her belongings, including the computer. That's why I write to you from this place.

I have put all the things from the Jagruti office in the warehouse of a factory belonging to one of Iqbal Maamu's friends. A godown without any windows. A godown which never sees any sunlight. Someone belonging to another generation, perhaps one of the little girls we educated, like Roshni, might one day open the warehouse and let the sunlight stream in. We'll wait. Until such a time, we'll take up other kinds of work; little drops falling into the great ocean.

Sing a song for me, during a quiet moment there. 'From the very depths of my being, I thirst.' I shall hear those words. I send you, with this, some tears. Take them. Let me know when they reach you. Selvi.

She clicked on 'Send,' and as soon as she got the message 'Sent,' she disconnected. She rose to her feet, and paid her fee to the manager of the cyber centre. Outside the glass door a fine rain was descending.

'The first rains of June, madam,' said the cyber centre fellow.

'Yes,' she said.

She came outside, lifted up her face to the sky, and received the cool raindrops. In that instant, time stood still.

*Kalachuvadu,* July-August 2002-

# Glossary

alaapanai: exposition of a *raagam*, as an introduction.

aalolam: an expression used to drive crows away.

aappam: a variety of steamed rice cake.

Abhimanyu: son of Arjuna by Subhadra. On the thirteenth day of the Mahabharata battle, he entered the tight formation of the Kaurava army known as the *chakravyuha*, but perished there, unable to come out.

abhinayam: the interpretation of ideas and emotions through hand gestures and facial expression in dance.

addigai: necklace, fitting tightly round the neck.

akka: older sister.

Akkamahadevi (or Mahadeviyakka): woman Saivite saint who lived in the twelfth century and wrote lyrics to Shiva in Kannada.

amavasya: night of the new moon.

amma/ammi: mother.

andaa: cauldron, usually made of brass.

anna/annacchi: elder brother, used as a term of respect.

anni: sister-in-law, elder brother's wife.

appa: father.

appalam: thin crisp rounds of black gram flour.

arakku: sealing-wax; hence a dark red.

arali: oleander.

Ashokavanam: Ravana's pleasure garden in Lanka, where Sita was held in exile.

ashrama: abode (as of a hermit or devotee).

athaan: athai's son; traditionally the cousin a girl married.

athai: aunt, father's sister.

avatar: incarnation.

Avvaiyaar: ascetic woman poet of the classical Sangam times, generally portrayed as very old.

ayanam: life-story.

'Ayiga! Tya morla bag': 'My! Look at that peacock!'

azaan: call to prayer (esp. as chanted by a muezzin from the turret of a mosque).

ba: mother (Gujarati).

baakri: Maharashtrian savoury dish.

Bahinibai: Marathi woman saint, 1628–1700. Unlike Akkamahadevi or Mirabai, she did not leave home but struggled to reconcile her duties to her husband with her devotion to God.

bairagi: ascetic.

bapu: father.

beti: daughter.

bhajan: devotional song, hymn.

bhakta: devotee; follower.

bidi: tobacco rolled in a tobacco (or other) leaf, for smoking.

bodhi tree: tree of wisdom (Buddhism), the sacred fig-tree.

brahmacharya: religious studentship, the state of a Brahman or student in the first of four stages of life; asceticism; chastity.

bua: aunt, father's sister.

champaka: the tree *Michelia campaca*, and its fragrant yellowish-white flower.

chandrama: moon.

channa dal: gram dal (a variety of lentil).

chappal: footwear; sandal.

Chitragupta: a scribe in the abode of the dead, who records the virtues and vices of men.

chitthappa: father's younger brother.

chitthi: mother's younger sister.

chombu: small brass pot for water, milk, etc.

dal: pulse, lentil.

darsanam: glimpse of a god or saint.

davani: half-sari.

Deepavali: Hindu festival of lights.

deodar: sub-species of cedar, found in the Himalayas.

devadasi: women dancers who were (formerly) attached to a temple, and dedicated to the service of the deity.

dhokla: steamed savoury dish.

doha: rhyming couplets.

dosai: thin rice pancakes, made of rice and urad dal.

dupatta: shawl-like garment used by women for covering head and upper part of the body.

gandharva: semi-divine being, living in the atmosphere or sky.

ganja: hemp, *Cannabis sativa*.

garba: Gujarati folk dance (explained in the text).

ghat: landing place or wharf; flight of steps to water.

ghatam: pot-shaped earthenware percussion instrument.

gingili oil: sesame oil.

goonda: ruffian, lumpen.

gopi/gopika: herdgirls/milkmaids of Braj (who were in love with Krishna).

Guhan: a Nishada king, a ferryman and friend to Rama.

gulmohar: tree with bright orange flowers which bloom in spring.

gurudwara: place of worship of the Sikh faith.

halva: sweet made of flour or semolina, ghee, milk, sugar, nuts.

Hanuman: monkey chief or deity who was Lord Rama's ally in his invasion of Lanka.

hundi: the collection box in a temple.

idiaappam: fine rice noodles, steamed.

idli: steamed cakes of rice and urad dal.

Jairamji ki: greeting, literally meaning 'Long live Ram'.

jamukkalam: thickly woven cotton mat.

Jatayu: son of Garuda and king of the vultures, who fought against Ravana but was overpowered by him.

javali: devotional song.

javanti: a type of flower.

jutka: two-wheeled horse-drawn carriage.

kachcheri: concert, musical performance.

kachori: a kind of puri having a filling of lentils or vegetables, and deep-fried.

kadali: a variety of small banana.

kalaripayittru: a martial art from Kerala.

kalkandu: sugar crystals, made from sugarcane juice.

kanakambaram: small golden-orange flower.

kanjira: percussion instrument, fitted with small cymbals along its frame.

kannamma: a term of endearment.

kasi-thumbai: small white flower.

khadi/khaddar: thick, coarse type of cotton cloth.

khala: maternal aunt.

khas khas: poppy seeds.

kirtanai: lyric.

koel: black cuckoo.

kolam: rice flour designs made on the floor or around the hearth.

kriti: devotional song.

kumkumam: saffron powder, worn on the forehead as a mark of auspiciousness.

kural: a verse form consisting of two lines, like a couplet.

kurta: collarless shirt.

kuzhambu: spicy sauce, eaten with rice.

lassi: drink of sweetened, diluted yoghurt.

lungi: garment worn by men, rectangular cloth wrapped round the waist and falling to the ankles.

maami: literally mother's brother's wife; used generally to mean 'aunt'.

maanam: honour.

maanatthai kaatthaan: '(He) safeguarded (our) honour' (part of a song).

Mandhara: the nurse, who was the chief instigator of Kaikeyi's jealousy of Rama.

mausi: mother's sister.

milk-ocean (paarkadal): in the Puranas, the ocean of milk, said to be the abode of Vishnu.

mittai: cheap sticky sweet.

mridangam: two-sided drum, played with both hands.

murabha: a kind of preserve.

naadaa: draw-string.

namaste: salutation; greeting.

Navaratri: period of nine days at the beginning of the light half of the month in autumn when Durga is worshipped.

navasandi kavathuvam: a ritualistic dance performed by the dancers attached to the temple at the inauguration of the annual temple festival. It is performed at different junctions (*sandhi*) where three or four roads meet, and is dedicated to nine different deities, namely, Brahma, Indra, Agni, Yama, Niruti, Varuna, Vayu, Kubera, and Isana.

neem: tree known for the medicinal and antiseptic properties of its leaves, (*Melia azadirachta*).

niravel: one stage of the *pallavi*, an imaginative item in a musical concert. Pallavi is a combination of words, rhythm, and musical variations. Niravel is the extemporization of variations, first on parts of the theme and then on the whole theme, keeping the rhythmical setting intact.

oppari: funeral dirge.

Orumaiyudana ninadu: 'Singlemindedly I...' (opening words of a song).

paal-kova: milk sweet.

paatti: grandmother; also an affectionate term for an older woman.

paavaadai: long skirt gathered at the waist, worn by young girls in south India.

pacchadi: a salad-type relish, like a north-Indian raita.

pakora: batter-fried savouries.

pallavi: opening unit of a composition, often repeated later.

pallu/pallav: side/border/edge of a garment.

pandal: canopy of coconut fronds or cloth, raised for a special function.

pandit: scholar, learned Brahman.

papal: holy fig-tree, *Ficus religiosa*.

paratha: pancake of unleavened wheat flour fried in ghee or oil on a griddle.

pattini: faithful wife.

payasam: semi-liquid sweet made of milk with rice, vermicelli, etc.

periamma: mother's elder sister.

pillau: a rice preparation, with spices, nuts and meat or vegetables.

Pillayaar: Vinayaka or Ganesha, elephant-headed son of Shiva and Parvati.

pittu/puttu: steamed rice-flour, sweet or spiced.

pongal: boiled rice, savoury or sweet.

poriyal: fried vegetable dish.

pottu: auspicious spot worn in the middle of the forehead.

prasadam: food offered to an idol; the remnants of such food.

pujari: priest.

Purana: sacred narrative.

puranpoli: pastry, filled with shredded coconut and jaggery.

pushpaka: flower.

raagam: musical mode, consisting of a pattern of musical notes.

raagamalika: series of raagams in which the successive parts of a song are sung.

rakshasa: evil spirit; demon.

Ranganatha pose: the pose of Vishnu in the Srirangam temple: stretched out and turned to the right.

Rasam: a kind of soup based on tamarind.

'Ravde bai': 'Let it be, Bai.'

Ravi Varma 1848–1906: The first Indian artist to apply the traditions of Western realism to his representations of Indian literature and mythology.

riyaaz: training, practice.

rudravina: a musical instrument.

salwar-kameez: set of pajama and shirt-like garment worn by women.

sambar: spicy lentil dish, with vegetables.

samosa: triangular-shaped savoury with spiced vegetable or meat filling, and deep-fried.

samsara: the second of the four prescribed stages of life, that of the householder.

sapplaakkattai: a pair of wooden pieces strung with tiny bells, held between the fingers and used to beat the time (by performers of religious songs).

Shastra: religious treatise; prescriptions of religious ritual and custom.

shishya: disciple, student.

shiyakai: soap-nut, used as a shampoo.

sruti: the basic note to which a musical instrument is adjusted.

Surpanaka: *rakshasi*, sister of Ravana.

swamiyaar: priest, holy man.

swaram: a note of the musical scale, seven in all.

swaraprastaaram: the imaginative expansion of musical notes in many different permutations and combinations without losing track of the particular rhythm in which they are set.

taanam: stretching out of a raga (musical mode) to bring out its full form.

taandavam: the dance of Shiva, expressing bliss or destruction.

Tadaka: *rakshasi*, mother of Maricha.

tali: a gold chain or cord worn around the neck, symbolizing marriage.

tampura: a four-stringed instrument which maintains the basic note in a musical concert; the drone.

tapasvi: a renunciant, living a life of austerities.

Tevaram: The collected devotional songs, 8000 in all, in praise of Shiva, composed in the seventh and eighth centuries by the saints Appar, Sundararamurti Nayanar, and Tirugnanasambandar.

thaatha: grandfather; a term of respect for older men.

thangam: a term of endearment; literally, 'gold'.

thayi/thaye: mother, or lady.

thinnai: raised platform at the entrance of a house.

thumri: type of song, originally sung by courtesans.

thuvaiyal: spicy relish made of ground coconut, chillies, etc.

Tirupalli ezhucchi: a song sung to wake up the deity in a temple.

Tirupugazh: 3000 poems in praise of Murugan, written in the fifteenth century by Arunagirinathar.

Tiruvalluvar: fifth-century Tamil poet; author of *Tirukkural*, a classic work which dates from Sangam times, consisting of moral aphorisms arranged under Virtue, Wealth, and Love.

Tiruvasagam: the collected poems in praise of Shiva composed by Manikkavachagar in the eighth century.

tulasi: sacred basil plant.

udukku: small drum used in exorcism rituals.

ustad: teacher; skilled craftsman.

vadagam: snacks made of flour-paste, dried and stored, and fried, before eating.

vadai: deep-fried savoury, made of urad dal.

vajram: an extremely hard glue.

vanaprastha: third out of the four prescribed stages of life; the retreat to the forest.

varnam: the first piece to be performed in a music concert or dance recital.

veshti: unstitched garment, waist to ankle, worn by men.

vibhuti: sacred ash.

vidwan: learned; scholar.

vinai: musical instrument.

Vinayakar Chaturti: festival honouring Vinayaka, or Ganesha.

yaazh: an ancient stringed musical instrument.

yoni: female genital organs.

yuga: era.